Chapter 1

A Dogwood tree, there was nothing special about this tree; it stood in the garden of an old abandoned house. Year after year it had grown and flowered. So what about the tree? It knew of so many atrocities, if only it could tell the world about the happenings it had heard over the years in the house.

The house (now dilapidated) had been a grand house back in the year, it had belonged to a young couple, and they had since both grown old and died, and once finally found it seemed from natural occurrences. They had a lovely big garden in the countryside, and now it too had suffered from years of neglect and become overgrown. Seeing as the old couple had no living relatives the house had been put to auction, but no one had bought it for more than five years. But finally a buyer was found.

It was a sunny Tuesday morning; a van had pulled up, and removed the old sign. Behind the van was a green Peugeot, inside sat a young couple looking at their new home.

Tom was 30 years of age, he had bought many a property in the past and renovated them and sold them on, in fact if he did say so himself he was skilled in most jobs.

He had been left a small fortune, and since that day had built up a reputation to buy and resell properties.

Tom was 6'3" and had an air of authority with him. Sandy haired, with stubble features; he got out the car and surveyed his newest purchase. He sighed. He had seen places almost as bad as this but never in such a state.

Mary opened her door and stood next to Tom. 'Well looks like a lovely place to settle down.' She said as she slid her arm through his.

Tom chuckled; he knew Mary would make a joke out of any bad situation.

Mary was only 5'6" and 29 years old, she had been married to Tom for five years. With her long Blonde hair and slim build she looked perfect anywhere. She had met Tom when she had been at an auction. She had spent ages trying to get a property, and Tom had outbid her. Determined to find out who he was she had followed him around for a week. Tom at first found her annoying as Mary could be highly strung and had a short fuse. But Tom had fallen for Mary's charming attributes and before long they had gotten married. Mary didn't care about having the latest gadgets or modern appliances. She had a knack of turning her hand to anything. So they both went into renovating places to sell on.

It was hard work but finally they needed to find a country place to call their own and run more of a business.

The van pulled away, and Tom and Mary opened the rickety gate. They slowly walked to the front of the house, and then around the sides, making several notes of what needed doing.

The garden was at least an acre in size according to the plans of the property. Overgrown with weeds they made their way around, while Tom took photos. The grounds also housed a rundown chicken coop, two garden sheds, an old greenhouse, an outhouse also in need of some care and several trees. The only tree to capture Mary's interest was the white Dogwood tree. She studied it amazed on how it seemed to be almost perfect whereas everything else was overgrown. They walked down the garden and finally came to an old fence, on the other side were a lazy stream bubbling past. They both stood gazing out for what seemed like an eternity before heading back up to the house.

When they got back round the front Tom unlocked the front door, it creaked open and moved so slowly as if being pushed back from someone on the inside, finally they forced the door open. They stood almost shocked by the neglect of the property. Mary pulled out the plans of the house. Ever organized, she got her pad ready. The house itself (in its day) was a decent three bedroom house, two en-suites, bathroom and a study upstairs.

Downstairs were the kitchen and dining area, lounge, games room, open hallway, and a second lounge

Mary flipped her pad over, 'I suggest we start in this lounge and work our way round.' She said. They opened the small lounge door and entered, the room looked like it was stuck in the 1900's. On the left-hand side just by the bay window was an amazing Victorian mahogany sofa. Tom pulled out his camera, he was always interested in what was left behind in these old buildings and loved to catalogue them and find out what they were, where they came from, the date and cost to have it repaired if necessary.

The sofa was covered in dust and cobwebs, but still that was never going to be a problem for either of them.

The grandfather clock against the side wall started to chime, Tom walked over to the Mahogany Grandfather clock, the pendulum swung from side to side. Tom looked at his wife 'how on earth can this clock still work?' he asked bemused.

Mary shook her head, she had stopped at an old bureau; she gently pulled the lid down and noticed some leftover paperwork.

Tom snapped away with his camera, and noticed an old bookcase with a glass frontage, it was stuffed full of old books which would all need cataloguing at a later date, but no doubt all from the same era as the clock and sofa.

Their footsteps echoed on the wooden floor as they looked around the room, they had both disturbed some dust and noticed that the walls would need both stripping and papering, or painting afterward as for the wooden floor it was perfect.

An old door was at the end of the room beckoning them both forward. This would lead to an old game's style room according to the plans.

Again this room had been neglected in time and stuck in the middle of the room was a snooker table, but in dire need of repair, one leg was broken, the baize was ripped, two cues held just in place on the side wall, broken lamps on the side walls, and the light for the snooker table hanging down and brushing against the table.

Tom sighed; this would not be worth keeping. Mary took a couple of photos. She noticed how dilapidated this room was and just scribbled totally refurnish and overhaul. She knew this room could easily be turned into a small office.

They turned to the door on their right which would lead back to the hall. Try as they might the door was stuck solid. They walked back through the lounge and back to the hallway and made their way to the kitchen which faced the overgrown garden.

The Kitchen itself was massive and housed a table for breakfast and meals.

They tried the taps and laughed as nothing happened, obviously this would take a few days to get such basics back working in a rundown house.

The table itself would easily suit a family of six, with high back chairs neatly placed around it, except for one which had been placed at an angle. Tom took the camera, taking photos, and knew just who to call to fix the kitchen up and drag it kicking and screaming into the 21st century.

Mary gazed out the windows, and guessed on a beautiful day when the garden was clear you would be able to see for miles and nothing but countryside, they turned and made their way to the second lounge which according to Mary's notes and plan was unfurnished.

This was less than furnished for sure, the walls were bare, cobwebs hung from the ceiling, the light was sitting on the floor and obviously a lot of work needed doing to this to make it homely, they walked through and back to the hall.

Both eager for some fresh air and a breather they moved to the front door. Tom turned the old door knob finding the door stuck, he looked at Mary confused before trying two or three more times. Mary tried the door knob too but the door stayed firmly closed. 'You didn't lock it did you Hun?' Tom queried. Mary shook her head, she was sure they had left the door open after they had entered the property.

Tom pulled out the old keys, the only set. He tried the key in the door and unlocked it. 'My mistake I must've locked us in.' He said, Mary looked at her husband and was sure they had left the door open.

They walked back to the car, and took out a flask and some sandwiches.

They drank and ate in silence, both pouring over the notes. Mary reached in the car for her computer, and made notes on the system, she would be working hard tonight to get all information on the property.

Tom yawned. 'Shall we finish off the nightmare tour?'

Mary smiled. They got up, packed away the picnic items into the car and made their way back in. Tom stopped by the front door. He turned to Mary 'I know I did not lock the door this time.' He tried the door knob and the door slowly creaked open and they both entered.

The grand hallway was massive, covered in dark oak, which needed cleaning, cobwebs hung like drapes from the ceiling. They walked towards the spiral staircase which also had an oak handrail, slowly they climbed. When they reached the top they looked over the Oak Balcony which spanned the top level. It was amazing, for once nothing needed doing to the staircase it seemed as sturdy as if it had been put up a week ago.

Mary pulled out the plans again and her notebook 'Bedrooms one and two on the left both with en-suite bathrooms.'

They entered the first bedroom, the door gliding open with ease. They both stood in the doorway. The room was fully furnished with a four poster bed, two wooden wardrobes, two bedside tables and a beautiful oak dressing table, with mirror surrounded with an oak finish. They walked through to the bathroom which had a toilet, basin and an old bath.

Tom pulled out the camera again, taking photos of the bedroom and bathroom, Mary scribbled everything down on her notepad. She walked to the window gazing out, she could see their green Peugeot and nothing but countryside. Smiling she turned. Tom grinned back. 'This house will be perfect for us when we finish it, and you did promise a country property.'

Tom nodded 'if you like it, we will live here.' Mary was elated; she ran and flung her arms around Tom. 'I love you.' She replied happily and kissed him.

Tom kissed her back, 'Shall we finish off?'

They moved back onto the landing and round to the second bedroom with en-suite. They opened the door, and entered. The room was empty. Mary scanned the notes and nodded. The wallpaper was hanging off, Cobwebs hung in here, and one of the windows was smashed. Tom took photos of the room and moved to the bathroom.

Inside was nothing, no bath, sink or toilet. More snapshots were taken and they moved round to the study.

Mary opened the door and gasped. Inside was an Oak Bureau with drop down lid, 3 old oak chairs and an oak bookcase, again this room had no carpet, but had a wooden floor. The view from the window was breath-taking, as you could see the countryside for miles. Mary made a note on all items in the room while Tom took the snapshots.

Slowly they moved back out and along, towards the bathroom. Entering they noticed an old bath tub, small sink and toilet. Plenty of work needed doing to the walls and ceiling. Mary noted this all down while Tom finished off photographing the property. They finally came to the last room. Opening the door they walked into an empty room, which had paper peeling from the walls. Tom photographed the room and Mary just wrote Renovate.

They moved back to the staircase and slowly walked down. Mary reached the bottom first and glanced at the plans. 'According to these plans there is a cellar.' She said. Tom's eyes lit up. 'Fancy a quick check?' He asked with a wicked gleam in his eye. Mary laughed.
They walked into the kitchen again and Tom stopped. He pulled out his camera and took another photo of the table and chairs. 'What's wrong?' Asked Mary, 'I could be wrong...' replied Tom 'but I am sure that chair was at an angle when we came in here the first time, and now it is in perfect alignment around the table.' Mary looked at Tom. 'We can check that later,'
Mary looked at an old wooden door and tried the handle. 'Door seems locked.' She said.
Tom walked over with the bunch of keys and tried every key. But none worked. 'I will ask if anyone knows of a missing key, otherwise let's get off and catalogue what we have found.'
Walking back to the front of the house Mary noticed the door was shut again. Tom turned. 'I know for sure I left this door open.' He turned the door knob and the door opened. They both left the house and Tom locked up.
They both got in the car and Tom started the engine, Mary glanced at the house 'plenty of work for that brother of yours.' Tom Laughed.

Chapter 2

Tom and Mary had spent the best part of the afternoon pouring over the notes of the house, as well as getting the photos from the camera downloaded and collated on the computer.
Mary had cross referenced all the photos with details she had written about each room. She had also taken the measurements and made secondary cross references on renovating the house to be more of a home. Out of all the photos which Tom had taken only two had not shown up, the ones from the kitchen of the old wooden table where Tom was still adamant that the chair had moved.
Mary looked at her watch. It was now half six, and she needed a break from collating and suggested they both go down to dinner before they did anything else.

The Hotel they were staying in was old almost like the house they had bought, but had a wonderful homely feel. It only had eight rooms, four of which had been taken and the elderly couple who ran it were strict on when breakfast and dinner was served.
Walking down the stairs they could hear Mrs Chambers on the phone. 'Yes my dear that is what I said, the room is very spacious, with its own bathroom and tea and coffee facilities... Yes my dear, all rooms have a country view... well as I said my dear...'
Mary stifled a laugh.
They reached the bottom of the stairs just as Mrs Chambers put the phone down. She shook her head in disbelief, and smiled at Tom and Mary 'So how are my favourite customers this evening?' she enquired.
Tom laughed. 'I bet you say that to everyone Mrs Chambers.'
'Not all of them my dear,' she replied as she led them into the dining area, 'so what is the house like you have purchased, is it the old Whippletree house down the road?'
Mary gave a quizzical look, 'the Whippletree house?'
'Oh yes my dear, the one with the Dogwood tree, the lovely one with white flowers during the spring and summer months,' replied Mrs Chambers.

'Yes that's the property, but what in heaven's name is the Whipple whatever you called it?' exclaimed Mary.

'That is what we down here call the Dogwood tree. It goes back centuries, I would be happy to give you some history of it later if you feel like a good natter.' Mrs Chambers replied with a knowing smile.

Tom looked at Mary. 'We will both be pleased to hear about it, and anything you can tell us about the village Mrs Chambers.'

'That's settled then.' She said as she led them to a table and passed them two menus.

Tom and Mary spent the best part of the evening listening as Mrs Chambers reminisced about the village, she could only go back so far, as she had only been in the village and at this hotel for fifteen years. If Tom and Mary wanted to know more they could always see Mr Peterson at the Museum, as he had archives about the village and its surroundings going back One hundred and twenty five years.

Siting by the fire they felt so relaxed, that tiredness soon was taking them over. Bidding goodnight to Mrs Chambers they made their way up to their room.

It didn't take long for them to fall into a deep sleep, but it was the sound of a creak on the landing outside their door that aroused Mary, she glanced at the bedside table 3am. She turned over and then noticed a shadow walk past the door. Sitting up, she rubbed the tiredness out of her eyes. Getting up and making sure not to disturb Tom, she sat at the dressing table and turned on the mini light. Mary grabbed her laptop and turned it on. The name... The Whippletree...?

She started with typing in 'Whippletree', if memory served her that is what Mrs Chambers had called the house. Mary found plenty of information on Horses and the like and everything in the U.S. She decided to separate 'Whipple' and 'tree' to see if that made any difference in the search. She eventually tried her faithful Wikipedia to search for answers.

She heard Tom turn over, at least one of us can sleep she thought to herself. Reading through the information on Wikipedia she found information on a Dogwood tree, where the wood of the tree is used to pull a horse-drawn cart, which links the draw pole of the cart to the harnesses of the horses in file. Mary stifled a yawn; at least she knew where the name came from and had some information on it. She would have a look at that magnificent tree tomorrow and hopefully find out some answers about the house. Shutting down the laptop, Mary got back into bed and tried to get back to sleep. Turning over and yawning Mary drifted off.

The alarm went off at 06:30am. Tom leaned over and turned it off. He got up, and made two mugs of coffee. He picked up the files and sat in one of the plush chairs reading the details of the house, seeing if he could find any links to what he thought had happened to the chairs in the kitchen. He knew he would have to contact his solicitor regarding the cellar key, otherwise the door could come off and a new one put in its place.

Tom took a sip of his coffee and picked up his Laptop, in his line of work there were few people who Tom trusted to sort out large gardens, except his brother. Tom checked his emails, after deleting the spam messages he opened a new email to his brother.

Hello Brian. Need you to come down and see the new pad, garden needs some work and will you please let us have an estimate. Have included several photos, get back to me ASAP. Tom. Ps Hope the wife and kids are well; give them a hug from their favourite uncle.

Clicking send he watched the email go off.

Tom then headed off to have a shower, Mary stifled a yawn and sat up she had a sip of her coffee and wandered over to the plush chairs and sat curled up in one. This was her time; she always made sure she had two cups of coffee before dealing with anything. Tom had learnt early in the relationship that if Mary did not have her morning coffees she would be grouchy and temperamental for the rest of the day.

Drinking the last of the coffee, Mary opened the curtains and stood gazing out at the countryside. It was another lovely sunny day. She remembered as a child spending lazy summers at her grandparent's house, the endless summer days, running around her grandparent's garden, learning to ride her first bike. She smiled. Turning round she made two more coffees. Picking up her laptop and sitting at the dressing table she turned it on and double checked all the data she had collated yesterday.

Tom stepped out from the shower and walked back in the bedroom. He placed his arms around Mary and kissed her. He took his coffee and gazed out the window.

'I will contact the solicitor to see if there are any more keys to that cellar today, and have emailed my brother about the garden.'

Mary laughed, 'He will love you.'

'Well he is the best gardener we know.' Tom replied.

Mary turned. 'I thought I might nip into the village this afternoon and see what I can dig up about the village.'

Tom smiled. 'Well I think we have more than we bargained. I am still sure that chair had moved. We both know the door was left open the second time. Let's just make sure the house isn't haunted' He raised his arms 'ooh haunted house...'

Mary looked sternly. 'It is not haunted. I think it had been a long day; the dust in the place was terrible. It was tricks of the mind.'

Tom nodded. Well I intend to get back over there this morning check it over, ring some people and get the work started on the property.

Mary got up, 'Well while you contemplate that, I intend to shower and make myself look amazing.'

Tom looked up. 'You always look amazing.'

Smiling Mary went in the bathroom.

Tom turned his attention to his laptop and sat at the dressing table. He opened his mailbox and decided to send an email to his solicitor.

Morning Sam,

Please can you contact my mobile ASAP? House is amazing but we seem to be a key missing. Let me know.

Tom.

Wiping his eyes, and running a hand through his hair, he got dressed.

When Mary emerged from the bathroom she looked more beautiful than ever. Smiling Tom took her by the hand and opened the balcony door.

They both stood for a moment and looked at the endless countryside.

Mary walked back in the room and got changed, she looked at the time and they both headed down for breakfast.

Tom followed Mary as they walked down the stairs they heard Mrs Chambers at the desk humming.

As they entered the foyer, Mrs Chambers looked up, 'Good morning my dears.'

'Morning Mrs Chambers.' They replied in unison.

'Lovely day again...' she said, as she led them into the dining area. 'Mr Chambers has nipped out, silly fool wants more plants for his garden, and as if we don't have enough.... breakfast is full English.'

They both sat down and smiled. 'You're wonderful Mrs Chambers.' Mary replied.

'Enough of the Mrs Chambers my dear please call me Doris.'

Doris bustled off to greet some people who walked into the foyer.

Tom watched as the maid brought in two full English Breakfasts, and more coffee.

'Thank you.' They both said and tucked in.

An hour later, they both were ready to go back to the house, armed with cleaning equipment. They drove off and admired the countryside.

Pulling up outside their house they surveyed it from the outside. All looked the same as when they had left yesterday.

Tom pulled out the keys and made his way to the front door.

Opening it he pushed it open and they both entered the house.

Chapter 3

Brian woke up with a start, it was 7a.m. and he knew he had another busy day ahead of him, every day was busy. His gardening business had taken off and since then Brian and his family had moved into a decent four bedroom house. Brian was 32 years of age and just like his younger brother Tom he was tall but with black hair.

Making sure not to disturb his wife he slipped out of bed and made his way downstairs. Sticking on the kettle he made himself a cup of tea. He opened the backdoor and sat in the garden drinking it. He loved his garden.

The slight chill in the air sent goose bumps up his legs and along his arms. He shivered and headed back in. Grabbing his laptop he turned it on to check the jobs he had to do today.

Jobs For Today

Name	Job	Time Limit
Mrs Walters	Grass Cutting	One Hour
	Tree Cutting	Two Hours
Mr Castleford	Lawn - Weeding	One Hour
	Lawn - Aerating	One Hour
Miss Turner	Garden Surveying	Two Hours

Yawning, he made himself another cup of tea; he sat back down and checked his emails.

Scrolling down the emails, he had four junk emails, which he binned. Two emails for surveys, and an email from his brother Tom.

He checked his two surveys first and noted them down on his computer, making sure he put the numbers in his work phone.

He read Tom's email. Another house he was doing up and a big garden. Checking his diary he knew that the family had a week off the following week. Seeing as they were not going anywhere special it would be good to see Tom and Mary, and he knew that Barbara and his two children Martin and Sarah would love to see their uncle.
He opened a new email.

Morning Tommy, (he knew his brother hated being called Tommy)
Family is off for a week from 8th May, book us in somewhere nice and I will sort the garden, although family will be with me.
Hope you are having fun, and send me directions on how to get to middle of nowhere.
Keep smiling and love to that wife of yours.
Brian.

Pressing send he watched the email close.
He made another cup of tea and took it up to his wife. 'Morning sweetheart,' he said quietly.
Barbara stirred, 'Morning Hun,' she replied sleepily, she kissed him gently. 'What time is it?'
'Time you and the kids were getting ready.' He replied.
Barbara got out of bed slipped on her dressing gown and took her cup of tea downstairs. Barbara was 29, brushing her auburn hair back she started to organise breakfast. The home was her domain.
'Martin... Sarah... time to get up, breakfast will be ready in ten minutes.' She shouted up the stairs.
'Ok mum.' The two sleepy children replied.
Ten minutes later both Sarah (aged 12 going on 17) and Martin (aged 10) were sat in the kitchen at the table tucking into bacon and eggs.
Barbara looked at her children, 'have you got your bags ready for school?' she enquired.
Martin finished his mouthful, and swallowed 'yes Mum. I've got English, Maths, Home Economics, and football today.'
Sarah yawned. 'I have got Home Economics, English, Maths, Human Biology and I am stopping after school to help set up for the dance at the weekend.'
Brian wandered in. Kissing Barbara he sat at the table as the kids repeated what they had told their mum.
'Well,' he said 'I have a surprise for you all.' They all looked at Brian. 'Seeing as we have a week off I thought that you would all like a trip.'
Barbara turned and looked at her husband, 'what have you booked,' she said with a look in her eye.
'Nothing,' he replied innocently. 'Tom and Mary have bought a new property and have invited us down. We will be stopping in a hotel and we can have a look around their new property.'
The kids screamed with delight, and Barbara looked at him still dubious. 'What is the other surprise then?'
Brian swallowed. 'Well he says there is a bit of garden that he wants me to look at.'
Barbara laughed. 'Last time Tom told you about a bit of garden it was four acres and took a week and a half to complete.'
Brian laughed. 'Mind you, it brings in the cash,' he replied.
Barbara looked at the clock. 'Right time for you two to catch that bus,' Sarah and Martin grabbed their bags, kissed their parents and headed out of the door.
Brian finished his third cup of tea and kissed his wife. 'Will be home about five tonight.'
'Have a great day.' She replied and he headed out the door.

Tom and Mary had been busy working in the house. Tom had made several phone calls. He wanted all the furniture removing and putting in storage before they started renovating the rooms. Mary had been sorting out the rooms and making plans on what colour schemes needed adding to each room. It had been about three hours before either of them took a break. Wandering in the back garden they sat down on an old bench and opened the flask of coffee. Checking each other's notes they knew that the Kitchen would need gutting and a new kitchen fitting, of which Tom had already contacted a friend.

Mary had added colour schemes to the plans she had devised and passed them to Tom to get his input.

Smiling he just passed it back. 'What?' She enquired.

'Well I know what taste you have in rooms and seeing as we will be using this as our family house and having a business area I know whatever you choose will be perfect.'

Finishing off his coffee and pouring another he glanced down the garden. Mary was already up on her feet and walking around the garden area. She stopped by the Dogwood tree. 'Tom this tree is perfect, but the rest of the garden is all overgrown, do you think someone has been tending it?'

'Unsure love, but when my brother replies and comes down hopefully he can give you all the information on it.'

Suddenly the quietness was broken by Tom's phone.

'Morning Tom how's the property and what is this about a missing key?'

'Sam, we have all the keys for all rooms in the house, except for the cellar, I was wondering if you knew of any key that had been lost, misplaced etc.

'I have been onto the auctioneers and everyone I know of and what you have is the complete set of original keys, and there are no duplicates.'

'No problem Sam, what we will do is remove the old door, it is in bad shape, and thanks for getting back to me. Will pop in at the weekend and sort out any paperwork.'

'Cheers Tom, I appreciate that and if you come across any other questions or queries let me know.'

Tom put his phone down, 'Well the cellar door will have to be removed and a new one put in, as Sam has checked and no key.'

Mary turned, 'Well the door was in bad shape and a new one will be better.'

Stretching Tom got up, 'let's finish off, as I need to get into the village, and you wanted to visit the museum for any information.'

Walking inside and ensuring everything was in a safe area they made their way to the hallway.

Mary noticed that someone had put post through the letterbox. Picking up the letters she glanced through them. Water, Dual Fuel and Phone, all of which were addressed to Tom, as he sorted out the bills and had made arrangements for the companies to come out and have a look around and get the house essentials.

Mary got to the last letter, which had been hand delivered. It was addressed to the new occupants, inside she found a note, Mary read it, and then re-read it. Sitting on the stairs Mary felt slightly faint.

Tom took the letter off Mary. 'Are you feeling alright Hun?'

Mary didn't answer and just looked still almost shocked.

Tom sat on the stairs next to her and read the note.

I thought it was about time that someone actually told you something about the property you have purchased. The house is evil; it has housed the worst kind of atrocities you can even imagine. I refuse to step over the threshold. I suggest that you cut your losses and get rid of the house. Did it not occur strange that it had been on the market for over five years?

Tom turned the note over, no name no address. Tom started to laugh.

Mary glanced at him 'Who would send someone a letter like that.'

Tom took her hand 'whoever it is they are probably just jealous,' he gave her hand a squeeze 'anyway,' he said smiling 'we need to get into town.'

Mary got up and they left the house. Locking the door they made their way to their car. Mary got in the passenger seat and looked at the house. Yes it looked dilapidated and after it had been spruced up, renovated it would be perfect. The top balcony window caught her eye, she shook her head... not possible... she looked straight ahead and then back to the top balcony window, she closed her eyes momentarily, she could swear she had seen a shadow go past.

As Tom started the car and they drove off she chastised herself. Stop letting that note get to you, there is no such thing as ghosts or ghouls.

Sam had spent the morning going through the paperwork. He had been a solicitor for 25 years and worked up through the ranks so he was a partner in the solicitor firm he worked for. Sam was 50 almost bald and certainly overweight (according to the doctor.) He had a strict regime on his dinner hour; he always went out for a walk so he got away from the building. He walked to the florists and ordered 10 Calla Lilies for his wife as it would be their thirtieth wedding anniversary on Friday.

He then went to the park and watched the world go by for twenty minutes before taking the five minute walk back to the office. He walked through the door and into the staff room and had his dinner which his wife had packed him up with.

After his dinner he walked back to his office. He looked at the diary knowing he had two people coming in at half three and half four about house sales.

As he sat at his desk he noticed a hand delivered letter had been placed on his desk.

On the front of the envelope printed was his name.

No other distinguished markings on the envelope. He pressed his intercom. 'Margaret.'

Margaret his secretary knocked on his door and entered.

Margaret was the best secretary he had ever had. She was 40 years old, and very efficient, with that air of authority, in fact from time to time he did wonder if she was a silent partner in the firm as she did believe she owned the building.

He held the envelope up. Margaret looked at him. 'It was dropped in while you were at lunch and seeing as it had no postmark etc. I placed it on your desk,' she paused 'Why is there anything wrong?'

Sam looked at her 'Well do you know who dropped it in?'

Margaret shook her head. 'I have never seen the person before; he just said make sure you get the letter,' pausing for a second she then turned and then stopped. 'He freaked me out, but I have checked the database about all your open and recently closed cases and he has not matched any description. It could be from someone else and he was asked to drop it in.' Turning on her heel she reached the door grabbed the doorknob and stopped. She turned facing Sam. 'I do have one idea though.'

Sam sighed. 'And that would be...'

Margaret opened the door turned her head 'I suggest you open it,' and with her cutting words she left the office.

Sam went red in the face, pressing the intercom he said 'Thank you Margaret, and yes a cup of Tea would be lovely.'

He was determined not to let her win all the conversations.

Opening the letter he pulled out a slip of paper.

I am sorry to contact you, but I thought it was time you knew what sort of property one of your clients has just purchased.
If you would like to meet in person we can discuss this in further details but I am sending this friendly letter to inform you that the house is evil and they need to get out.

My email address is Darklingwood@gmail.com

I look forward to hearing from you.

Sam read the note three or four times. He was used to letters like this and they had certain protocols to follow in similar incidents.
Sam had to admit he was slightly intrigued, he pressed the intercom 'Margaret.'
Margaret knocked and entered the room. Before she could speak Sam held out the note to her.
'Please email this note to the other partners and ask them that we need to hold a meeting this afternoon at five with their thoughts and what action is to take place as per the protocol.'
Margaret took the note and glanced down. Reading it and nodding in agreement 'This will be sent immediately and I will ensure that your appointment at 4:30 does not run over even if I have to finish late with the paperwork.'
Closing the door she walked back to her desk and emailed the note to all the partners and with a request of a meeting at 5pm.

With this done Margaret had to admit she had been privy to some similar letters and the action they had took was mainly Police and she could see this being no different.

Chapter 4

It had ben five days since Tom and Mary had received the note, and since then more work had been carried out on the house. Tom had organised for all the furniture to be placed in storage. They had contacted a kitchen fitter (friend of Tom's) to come down plan and price the kitchen up.
Mary had an appointment booked to look at all the archives in the village, especially about the house.   Tom had booked rooms at the hotel for his brother and family and they would be down in two days.

It was a dreary Saturday morning, as Tom woke up just before the alarm went off, yawning he made his coffee and gazed out of the window.
He picked up his mobile and checked for any messages. Restless he wandered around the room as quietly as possible. Finally settling in the chair he checked what needed doing today.
The schedule was just to visit Sam.
Mary yawned and got up. Tom quickly made her a coffee and sat back down in the comfy chair.
'Morning Hun, sorry did I wake you?'
Mary wandered over with her coffee and kissed him. 'Morning darling, sorry looks like we both could do with more sleep.'
Mary looked at her reflection in the mirror.
Tom smiled, getting up he wandered in the bathroom and had a shower and then got ready for his trip.
'Hopefully I shouldn't be too long at Sam's, but I am taking the train so you can zip around the village in the car.'
'Since when did you want to travel anywhere by train?' Mary enquired.
'Since I intend to get to the bottom of this note business and have a word with some friends.'

Kissing Mary he headed out of the room and greeted Mr Chambers.

'Ah young man, I have sorted you a lunch pack for your trip,' Mr Chambers held the wrapped package 'the wife said you were going on a trip, but she says don't worry when you return as a meal can easily be rustled up.'

Tom thanked Mr Chambers and climbed into the waiting taxi.

Mary watched Tom get in the taxi from the balcony and sat back down.

That note, it was almost etched in her mind, in fact both Mr and Mrs Chambers had both been disgusted that they had insisted they had their meal in their room that night.

Mary stretched and wandered into the bathroom, after a nice long shower she got dressed, she knew she had to go to town so decided to go for the country look, and if time permitted she would make some more arrangements for when Tom's brother's family visited.

Looking almost human, Mary made her second coffee. She gazed outside from the balcony.

Tom had been just as bothered by the letter and when he had spoken to Sam, Sam had been more eager for him to visit him. No doubt Mary would find out more tonight.

Mary left the room and wandered down the creaking stairway down to the lobby, Mrs Chambers bustled out the kitchen greeted Mary and bustled outside. Mary was quite shocked that they both had so much energy to run such a hotel, regardless that it was small.

After a delicious breakfast Mary climbed in the car and drove into the village.

The village was small; Robertson's the Butchers, a small convenience store with post office, a Church and small churchyard, a village hall, two banks and several shops selling anything and everything.

Mary parked up, buttoned up the top button on her coat and made her way down the high street, through the churchyard and down a lane where the small museum was. The Museum hardly looked like a museum, it certainly was old and needed some work doing to it, but in these small towns it would take the whole town several years to raise funds to restore these buildings.

Mary pushed open the door and walked in.

'Hello... Mr Peterson?'

Mary looked around the corner.

Suddenly Mr Peterson strode out of the store room. 'Good Morning.' He said.

Mary turned, and noticed several papers in his arms.

Giving him a hand Mary took them out of his arms and placed them on the counter.

'Thank you, sorry been all fingers and thumbs this morning.'

He held out his hand, and Mary shook it.

'So you bought the old property on the outskirts of the village did you?' He enquired.

'Well yes we needed a country home, and the village is delightful but...' Mary looked at him confused 'how do you know?' She asked.

'Well according to that Doris at the hotel' he raised his eyebrows 'you want some information on the house and the village,' turning he ventured back in the store room whilst still in full flow 'well she has been ringing me constantly that I have dug up as much information as I could,' taking a breath he placed some more files on the counter. 'This is everything you wanted to know.'

Marys draw dropped 'but...'

Mr Peterson laughed 'it may be a small village but our information goes back centuries, I even found information on the land that the house stands on.'

'You have been busy then,' she said but Mr Peterson had vanished back in the store room.

He finally emerged. 'So anyway I knew you would want to have a look at some details,' he pushed his glasses back up from the bridge of his nose. 'I have collated as much data as I could from certain information we have stored on archive slides.' He turned, looked around, stopped. 'I have also copied so much information and as we are in the 21st century have disked it for you.'

He passed Mary the disc.

'But for the time being you can have a look through these files which are not only year order but give as much information on the village as you require.'

Mary thanked him and sat down.

She had never expected so much information on the village, but she would have a look through the information but she still didn't have much idea of what she was actually looking for.

Making herself comfy Mary started with the first file.

Obviously the work took Mary several hours to go through, and she had had the smart way of starting with the most recent and working back through the years.

Mr Peterson had delivered coffee to keep Mary going as Mary made several important notes on her laptop.

It had been four hours and Mary stretched. Wandering outside into the fresh air she strolled around, taking in the ambience of the village.

After about half an hour Mary wandered back in. Mr Peterson smiled. 'I gather you weren't expecting as much information.'

Mary laughed. 'It has taken me by surprise and I have been through these four folders, and will need to come back another time to check more archives.'

Mr Peterson held up his hands 'not a problem,' he picked up the files and stacked them in the store room. Mary helped him stack the other folders and then she packed up her laptop and bade him farewell.

The clouds had broken and rain started to fall. It looked like one of those wonderful English days.

A short drive later she pulled up outside the hotel.

Mrs Chambers was at the main desk as Mary entered.

'How did you get on my dear?' enquired Doris.

'So many details are archived in that museum Doris and I have a disc to go through too.'

'I will happily bring you a coffee my dear, and if you want to use the bar/lounge area it is very quiet today.'

Mary glanced back and smiled. 'Thank you Doris.'

'Oh by the way Mary,' Doris bustled forward. 'I have made up the rooms you required and have booked everyone in for two weeks to be on the safe side as I know we are not fully booked.'

Mary thanked Doris and walked into the bar/lounge.

Plugging in her laptop, she collated the information on the house, making a hard copy of the information.

Mary had made some notes on the village in case anything was linked to the house or the previous owners.

Year	Details	Questions/Information	Notes
			Current
2011	Property Purchased	Mr and Mrs Plant	Owners
2006	Property On Market	5 Years? No Buyers?	
2006	Mr and Mrs Farley Found	Old age?	
			Previous
1969	Property Purchased	Mr and Mrs Farley	Owners
1963	Property Unwanted	Why unwanted?	

1960	House Renovated	Finished or started?	Finished
1959	House Damaged	Severe Storm	
1953	Property Owned	Mr and Mrs Hamilton	Previous Owners

Rubbing her eyes she drank the coffee Doris had put on her table. Needing a break she got up and wandered outside, the rain was falling harder.

'Not exactly summer my dear,' said Doris from behind. 'I have had a phone call from your husband; he has just left the station and will be home in an hour.'

'Thank you Doris,' Mary turned to go back inside.

'I will bring you a fresh cuppa my dear,' replied Doris.

Mary smiled. She wandered back into the bar/lounge area and packed her laptop away. Grabbing her notes she noticed a handwritten envelope had been placed on top of her notes. When Doris returned with her coffee she showed her the envelope.

Doris glanced down. 'I have no idea where it came from; it wasn't in the post which was delivered this morning.'

Mary placed the envelope in with the notes. Whatever was going on was getting stranger by the day, and she would show it to Tom before opening it.

Two hours later at six o'clock Tom arrived back. He walked into the room and Mary flung her arms around her and kissed him.

'What's happened?' asked Tom after the kiss.

Mary wandered over to her notes and showed Tom the envelope. Tom turned it over in his hands 'Well,' he said 'I have so much more to tell you and I think these notes should go somewhere safe.'

As he talked he pulled out another note. It was Sam's.

Mary glanced at it.

'Ok I have to say whatever is happening is starting to freak me out Tom,' turning she put the kettle on 'I think the best course of action is to leave this place and find somewhere new.'

Tom looked at Mary. 'Let's get through next week.'

Mary nodded 'Okay.'

Mary mentioned all reservations were set for Tom's Brother and family, and that they would be arriving tomorrow. In all fairness, especially to Tom's Brother and family they should shelve the problems till after the visit.

Looking at his Watch Tom noticed it was now quarter to seven.

They got ready and were in the dining room by seven.

Mr Chambers served them a delicious meal, and they decided to sit in the bar/lounge area all evening, Mrs Chambers kept them company by reminiscing about how they had got a small hotel up and running.

By eleven they were both yawning. Bidding good night to Mr and Mrs Chambers they made the short journey to their room. It took them only a few minutes and they were both fast asleep.

The footsteps on the landing could only just be heard. Two a.m. in the morning. He paused outside Tom and Mary's room. Pulling out an envelope he slid it under the door.

He made his way back down the stairs and slipped out the back way, past the kitchen and outside. He walked slowly round to the front of the hotel. He looked up to the second floor. He hoped they would forgive him in time.

Chapter 5

Tom woke up first at 6:45am. He rubbed his eyes and made his way to the bathroom, glancing in the mirror he smiled. At least today he would see his brother and his family again.

He wandered back into the bedsit area, turned on the kettle and then noticed the envelope on the floor. He hastily picked it up and stored it with the others, making a quick note of time and date. Mary yawned. He made the coffees and turned on his phone.

'Morning love,' he whispered to Mary 'here's your coffee. I'm just going to ring Brian to see when they are arriving.'

Tom slipped out the door. Mary got up, opened the curtains and glanced outside. The sun was just coming over the hillside. It looked another lovely day.

Mary drank her coffee and then got changed, she would spend time gossiping with Barbara while Tom went through everything in the garden with Brian. As for the kids, well they would have a wonderful time exploring the garden area, and no doubt looking round the old house. Mary stuck the kettle on for a second cup as Tom came back in the room, he passed her the phone, and she heard a chorus of 'Hello Mary/We love you,' from Brian's children.

Mary put the phone down, wrapped her arms around Toms' waist. 'So what time do they arrive?' she asked.

Tom grinned 'they left an hour ago, Brian has the directions and has put the house's postcode in his sat nav. and they will be here by half nine. I also met Doris who says the rooms are ready.'

Mary laughed, 'I hope Doris likes children.'

After a lovely breakfast they made their way to reception and out the door, the sunshine had gone and the sky had turned grey, 'Looks like rain today...' startled they turned round and Mr Chambers stood behind them. 'Sorry to make you folks jump, you ok? It's... well... Doris said you have been having strange letters and whatnot.'

Mary turned 'Well Doris is keeping an eye out for anything arriving for us and, to be honest...' Mary paused. '... I think Doris considers herself to be the next Miss Marple,' and with a laugh from all three they wandered back in.

As they stood by the desk, Tom pulled out his wallet. 'Mr Chambers as you know my brother and family are arriving today, can you make sure that all their bills are paid for.'

Mary nudged him. 'Well it is not often we get to spoil the kids and no doubt you women will be in town one day to spoil them rotten.'

Tom and Mary drove to the property, and parked up. The sky had turned darker still and it certainly looked like rain was imminent, they entered the house, and picked up the mail, just checking for any disturbing notes, but none. Mary for once was relieved.

Tom made his way to the kitchen and checked the mail. Kitchen fitters would be out on Monday from 9am. The Gas and Electricity would be checked at 2pm today, and Water would be sorted by Monday.

Mary wandered from room to room, she was determined to check everything out, but the shadow had been playing on her mind for a while. She pushed herself to go upstairs and check the bedrooms out.

Wandering in each room she found no sign of anything, the dust was still undisturbed. Sighing she made her way back down the spiral staircase.

Tom was in the hall and looked as Mary glided down the last few steps.

'My Lady,' he bowed.

'My Lord,' she curtseyed. Laughing they wandered back out the front.

Tom and Mary had never believed in fate or destiny, but true to his word the car drew up at half nine.

Brian got out first, followed by Barbara and then the two kids, who ran and flung their arms around Mary.

'Wow what a house!' exclaimed Sarah

'Mega garden uncle Tom,' Martin cried.

Mary and Tom laughed as they made their way and greeted Barbara and Brian.

'Adorable,' said Barbara as she kissed Tom on the cheek

'Me? Or the house,' he laughed.

'Mary you look more wonderful than when we saw you at Christmas,' spoke Brian as he kissed Mary.

Mary blushed. 'I now know where Tom gets his charm from.'

They all laughed.

Tom led them all back in the house, to give them the grand tour and to mention what would happen in each room.

Starting on the ground floor the roamed around with lots of gasps and 'wow,' from the children.

As they entered the kitchen, Barbara laughed. Tom stopped. 'What' he enquired.

Barbara smiled 'I heard you were no good in the kitchen Tom but Mary does deserve a place to cook.'

They all laughed. 'Kitchen gets gutted and dealt with on Monday onwards.'

As they got back to the grand hall, Mary noticed an envelope on the floor. Rushing over she picked it up. Hand written, she pulled out her pen and dated it and glanced for the time. Mary re-joined Tom, Brian and the family as they made their way up the grand staircase to finish the tour.

Half an hour later they were all standing by the cars. Mary had flasks of coffee and tea and squash for the children.

The kids were running about in the overgrown garden as the adults had a drink.

Brian had his planner out; he had seen the best view of the garden from the upstairs study and had made a rough drawing of the area.

Mary and Barbara were catching up on all the gossip as Tom and Brian made their way round the back to the overgrown area.

Brian had seen areas worse than this and made notes of everything as they moved around. Brian walked the length of the garden with his measuring wheel. He scribbled down dimensions and then they both walked round to the front as Brian took more measurements and sat on an old wall.

'Well Bro, it is a big job, and it will take a while but you knew I would do it before I arrived,' Brian laughed.

Tom grinned.

'Martin... Sarah come on were going to a hotel to get settled in.' Shouted Brian

Two breathless kids came running from the side of the house.

The two cars made their way to the hotel.

Mary had chance to mention the envelope she had discovered when all six of them had been in the house. Tom looked. He then opened up about the previous envelope pushed under their door.

Mary sighed. 'Ok Tom I know I am spooked enough but come on,' Tom nodded 'you better ring her then.'

Mary pulled out her mobile and scanned through the numbers.

'Yes hello, I need to speak to Marie. Tell her it's her sister,' Mary listened to the line 'I am sorry she is busy in a meeting at the moment, shall I get her to ring you back?'

'Just tell her she needs a break from working like a damn fool. She will ring me back.' and with that Mary ended the call.

Tom laughed. 'Your evil to your sister you know that.'

'How else does she ever contact us?' Mary laughed and they drove the rest of the way in silence.

By the time they got back to the hotel the rain had started to fall, and it was a quick run into the foyer. Doris greeted them all and booked Brian and family into their rooms. After they were settled in they all had dinner, with Doris insisting that they all sit with them for their first meal. Doris loved the children and told them that while the adults were talking she would let them hunt through the hotel, and no doubt she had some games they could play while the adults talked shop.

While Doris and the children were away, Tom and Mary explained the strange goings on about the house; they had decided that Brian and Barbara had to know. They explained about the letters and that they had contacted Mary's Sister.

After dinner and drinks, they moved to the bar/lounge area and joined Doris and the children.

'Right you two time to let Mrs Chambers get on, while we go back and you two can explore the garden.'

The children looked round. 'Thanks Uncle Tom.' they both said in unison.

'We will be back by 6pm Doris.' said Mary as they ushered the children out.

When they got back to the house, the children automatically went running round the back, determined to see what was about.

Mary had given them a pad and pencils each and asked them to make a note of what they could find. Mary knew they would enjoy getting muddy before attempting anything.

Mary watched them from the kitchen window. She gazed out along the fields and just hoped that someday everything would be explained.

It was just before two o'clock when the doorbell went off. Tom answered the door and let the man from British Gas inside the property. The man whistled as he gazed around.

'Right guvnor where's the mains?'

Tom showed him into the kitchen and the man set to work.

Martin and Sarah were having the time of their lives as they made miniature plans of each part of the garden. They had plenty of experience learning from a young age all the names of the plants, and decided that it was easiest to do half a garden each. Martin had taken the left hand side and Sarah the right.

Martin had started down the bottom of the garden by the fence, where he noticed weeds which his dad would deal with, moving up slowly he wandered into the overgrown bushes, scraping his arms and slowly discovering if anything was behind the bushes, and found nothing. Sighing he made his way back out. He wrote on his pad about the bushes and that he could squeeze his way through.

He made a little tick on his pad and moved up where he found the downtrodden and dilapidated chicken coop. He poked his head in and fell back when a crow squawked and flew out. Apart from the Crow there was nothing much inside but he liked the old design and would have to ask his uncle and aunt if they were keeping it.

He wandered up the garden where he came to the trees. He made a note of which trees he had, Birch, Elm, Ash, and the list went on. He turned to see how well Sarah was getting on.

Sarah was having a great time, she had made a note of new greenhouse, new garden shed and would have to ask her dad about the tree she had found. She was sure she had seen it somewhere before but for the life of her she couldn't think where.
She was making her way down the garden when she heard a crow squawk past.
'Martin... Sarah... do you fancy a drink?' Barbara asked from the top of the garden.
Both children made their way round, breathless but happy.
Uncle Tom and Aunty Mary were standing at the back door drinking coffee, while their dad and mum had chairs to sit on.

Mary took Martins pad and looked at it. She laughed when she got to the part of chicken coop keep? 'Do you really see your uncle waking up at 5am to feed and harvest chickens?'
Tom nudged her 'More to the point can you see the chickens coping with this one and her tempers.'
Mary laughed.
'I'm sorry, but no chickens in the future, unless they come freshly cooked from the supermarket.'
A tap at the kitchen window made the kids take a step back, Tom turned saw the electrician/gas fitter and wandered in.

Martin and Sarah both finished their drinks and went back off to have a scout around the garden. Together they showed what each other had found, but as they neared the greenhouse Martin noticed a gap in the hedge. He moved cautiously through and called for Sarah. Slowly they walked past the hedge and along where they found an old brick wall. They seemed to be moving back up the garden and could hear their parents talking. Martin took another step and came to a halt, with the lack of light behind the hedge and against the wall they had to feel forward. Martins boot kicked a brick wall in front of him; he reached out but nothing in front of him. Sarah came up behind him and stopped. 'Why you stop?' She asked slightly irritated. 'Some kind of small wall...' he replied. Sarah felt around Martin and slowly leaned forward. Slowly moving round she found a post, and pushed at it. 'Come on round found a post.' Martin made his way round and felt the post and then a chain. Pulling on the chain he heard creaking underneath. He tugged again and he suddenly got a decent pull on the chain. He pulled and pulled and Sarah reached out, she felt what was like wet wood. Feeling inside she touched the ice cold water. 'This is a well!' she exclaimed, She pushed her hand into the bucket and felt something at the bottom, grasping it she pulled out a chunk of metal. 'Come on we better go back and show this to Uncle Tom.' They felt their way back through the undergrowth and back towards the greenhouse. Once back in the light Sarah looked at her hand and discovered an old metal key, covered in rust. They ran back to the adults.

All the adults except Tom were still chatting. Sarah walked up to Aunt Mary. 'Look what we found behind the greenhouse,' Mary looked at the old key, at first she thought it was nothing more than a remnant from an old age. Then remembering the cellar she took the key from Sarah 'Where exactly did you find it, it's all wet.'
Sarah and Martin beamed 'You have a well which leads from the undergrowth behind the greenhouse and you follow the wall up.'
Barbara looked at the kid's clothes, 'Looks like showers and new clothes before you go anywhere else.' She shook her head.

Brian looked at them both. 'I knew you two would cause trouble getting all dirty, less gardeners more treasure hunters.'

They all laughed.

Tom returned ten minutes later with all the information and they would have all the electrics for the house sorted by the end of next week.

Mary picked up the key and passed it to Tom 'They found it in an old well behind the greenhouse.'

Tom looked at the key and then smiled.

'Come on you lot,' and he ran in the house he rushed through into the kitchen eager as a schoolboy almost breathless as he pushed the key in the lock and turned. The door unlocked and slowly creaked open.

Grabbing a flashlight from his bag he shone the light down in the dank dark cellar.

He slowly moved down the steps keeping an eye on the steps. Slowly one by one the others followed him down. Mary had passed more lights round and they slowly reached the bottom step and walked into a massive cellar. The cold clung to them almost sapping heat from their bodies as beams of light shone from roof to floor left and right across the cobbled stone walls and all around.

Tom was the first to speak 'I suggest we get more lights and then explore this tomorrow.'

With this they made their way back up. Tom reached the door and pushed it open and they all stepped back into the kitchen.

They packed away and made their way to the cars, and back to the hotel. No doubt Doris would ask the children what they had been up to and want to know if they had found anything interesting.

Chapter 6

Tom, Mary, Brian and Barbara sat in the hotels comfy bar/lounge, they had had a busy evening explaining the findings to Doris, and the kids were dead excited after finding the elusive cellar key.

Tom had sent an email to Sam explaining where the key had been found.

Dinner had been a spirited event, mainly from the children but they had been sent to bed at 8pm. With Sunday nearly upon them Tom decided that they could have a rest. Brian would spend the day working how much and how long it would take to fix up the garden.

Mary and Barbara would visit the town on Sunday and have a great day with the children.

At 11pm they went to bed, Brian and Barbara checked on the children who were both fast asleep.

Tom and Mary went to bed and it did not take long for them to be fast asleep.

At 7am they woke up both feeling refreshed. It was not till Mary checked her mobile did she find a text from her sister.

She read it out allowed to Tom. 'Evening Sis, what's happening? What's the problem and what help you needing? Ring me.'

Tom laughed; Mary sat down and sent a reply regarding the letters. After they got dressed they met Brian and family already seated for breakfast.

Doris Scowled as Tom and Mary entered slightly late. 'I really do not understand you two, your brother and his family have been down for half an hour already,' shaking her head she wandered in the kitchen and returned momentarily with two plates of full English. 'Get these down you, your both looking peaky.' Doris wandered off chuckling.

Tom watched her walk off and shook his head. 'Typical. You've been here less than a day and we get pushed into second best.' Mary nodded in agreement while the children laughed.

When they had finished Tom and Brian waved the children and ladies off. Wandering back in they went into the bar/lounge and Brian worked his magic with figures.

'To be honest Bro, it is going to be a long job and working on the information it will take at least three weeks to get it all sorted. We are going to need a skip to get rid of the old shed and greenhouse. What do you intend to do about the chicken coop?'

Brian rambled on while Tom made notes regarding what needed doing and quickly.

Restoring the house to be habitable was one thing but the garden would be good to relax in too.

After lots of head scratching Tom decided that the chicken coop was going.

Brian pulled out his pad from his bag, he never felt happy unless he had it with him where ever he went.

Drawing another rough sketch he marked areas where the most work needed doing.

Tom watched Brian work and added bits and pieces to the map.

After Brian had finished He gave Tom his Estimation. Tom whistled but knew what Brian meant and agreed to the fee of £1500.

'I will get as much done as possible this coming week and then I know the family have to go back and I will book you in for the rest of the job.'

'Excellent.' Tom said as he relaxed back in the chair.

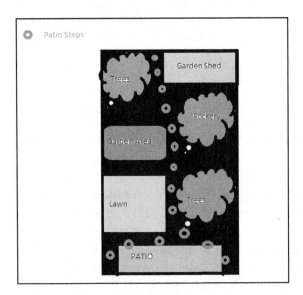

The rest of Sunday was spent lounging around reminiscing about their childhood days and talking about the family.

It was about three hours later before Mary and Barbara returned with bags galore and two smiling children.

Tom looked 'I do believe you were not going to spend much.'

Mary shrugged 'They twisted my arm.'

Barbara laughed as did the children.

The rest of Sunday was spent relaxing and Doris had found more games to entertain the children. The children explored the hotel from top to bottom and the surrounding area.

By the time they had had their meal in the evening the children had run themselves ragged and had gone to bed.

Tom and Mary had a quiet night relaxing in the bar/lounge. Doris was busy in reception.

It wasn't long before they also headed up and had an early night.

Monday Morning soon came round. Barbara took the children into town so that Tom, Mary and Brian could get on with the house.

Brian set to work in the garden, getting the worst of the weeds up while Tom dealt with the people who were fitting kitchen units.

Mary was busy upstairs sorting out what needed dealing with next. She pulled out her ever handy notebook.

Room	Action	Job Required	Completed
Kitchen	New Kitchen	Fitters In	Not Completed
Lounge	Requires Painting		Not Completed
Lounge 2	Requires Painting		Not Completed
Games Room	Requires Painting		Not Completed
Open Hallway	Requires Cleaning		Not Completed
Bedroom 1	Requires Painting		Not Completed
Bedroom 2	Requires Painting		Not Completed
Bathroom 1 and 2	New Bathroom Suite	Organise	Not Completed
Study	Recall Items	Storage	Not Completed

She set her notebook down and gazed out the window. Even though it was a cloudy day, the view was spectacular. At the end of the garden she could see the slow stream and the small clump of trees both side, and then nothing but fields.

She sighed. A creak behind her made her whirl round. Tom stood in the doorway. Grinning that grin when something actually was working. 'We have water.'

Mary followed Tom back down the spiral staircase. The fitters had half of the kitchen in place and Tom turned the tap on and crisp clean running water poured into the sink. 'One of the workmen used to be a plumber. He checked the pipes which are sound and managed to connect them all up, saves the water board coming out.'

Mary laughed 'So when will I be able to stop relying on meals from Doris then?'

Tom shook his head and drew breath in through his teeth. 'Two three days tops they reckon.'

'Not bad,' replied Mary.

She strolled from the kitchen and to the car where she pulled out 4 flasks of coffee and two flasks of tea.

'Come and get it,' she shouted

She poured the drinks and they sat in the kitchen. Brian wandered in looking dishevelled 'That garden is in very bad shape but I have three wheel barrow loads of waste.'

He sat down and grabbed a cup of tea and took a sip. 'Ah, just what I need.'

Brian spent the afternoon in the garden bagging up the waste and then making sure everything he had done was safe and secure.

He made a list of what items he needed for the big jobs and wandered back in the house where Mary and Tom were in the kitchen, it too had been transformed and no longer looked like a shell. The sink was plumbed in and so were the lower cupboards. Two walls still need repainting but Mary was adamant that she could do that job herself.

As they prepared to leave the house, Mary stopped. 'Brian can you have a look at one tree for me please.'
Bemused he followed Mary round the side to the back. Mary stood gazing at the Whippletree, which still looked perfect.
'I know it is called a Dogwood tree or a Whippletree for its wood but it looks... well... '
'Very well kept...' Brian questioned.
'Well yes,' Mary felt relieved that Brian had noticed too.
'I would say it has been looked after but it surprises me why someone would care for one tree and not the whole garden.' Brian paused for a second whilst looking round 'Did the previous owners have a gardener?' he questioned.
Mary was unsure but she would ask around.
They made their way back round to the front of the house where Tom was waiting in his car.
'Come on you two, we haven't got all day,' he laughed.

Time spent with Brian and his family had made Tom and Mary feel so glad that they had family who were so helpful that by the end of the week the Kitchen was decorated and the open hallway was cleaned.
The garden which looked all full of weeds now looked quite bare without them. Brian and the children spent each day removing and clearing what they could. Barbara was a godsend in the cleaning and painting area and after a long hard week Brian made a discovery in the front garden. They had weeded and trimmed back several of the bushes, making it look more fresh and inviting and less like an overgrown forest. It was when he was trimming the hedge did he come across a metal pole with a metal sign above it.
On the sign in rustic style was the name of the house. "The Whippletree", Barbara had spent the last day cleaning it all up so it stood out; it shone like a beacon for everyone to see when they passed.
Doris was upset to see Barbara and the children go and made sure they had a picnic for the drive home. Tom and Mary watched from the porch as Brian drove his family home and he would return in a week or so when he knew had some free time to finish it off completely.

Once they were out of sight Mary and Tom sat relaxing, it was wonderful sitting in silence, but it wasn't to stay that way.
Brrrr Brrr ... Brrrr Brrr ... Mary glanced at her mobile.
Picking it up she looked it was her sister.
'WHERE THE HELL HAVE YOU BEEN SIS?' screamed the voice on the phone.
Holding the phone from her ear she let her sister rant and rave.
'Finished yet?' she enquired.
'Well you ring me for help, I finally get round to making sure I had nothing extra to deal with, then the text and then nothing for days.' Her sister ranted.
'I am not at your beck and call 24/7 you know I have stuff to sort out here. When are you going to send these damn letters or do I have to drive up and see them for myself?'
Mary grinned. 'Come on up, Tom is looking forward to seeing you so visit and see the property, it has most amenities now.' With that Mary hung up and sent the postcode and house address to her sister via text.
Laughing she then switched her phone off.

Looking at Tom she calmly said 'My sister will be visiting for a few days.'

Tom's face dropped. It looked cloudy outside now; by the time Mary's sister arrived he could expect thunder storms and hell on earth.

'Oh joy,' he replied.

The rest of the day was spent at the hotel; they walked around the grounds of the garden, noticing several plants which they thought would look good in their garden.

At the end of the evening they said goodnight to Mr and Mrs Chambers and walked up to their room. Both yawning they soon fell asleep.

Her footsteps echoed on the old stone steps which led down the cellar. Wearing a headlight which shone a dusty beam through the air, she made her way down slowly, taking her time, her breathing getting heavier as she descended.

Once she reached the bottom she turned on her trusty torch, the light shone across the room as she surveyed the damp looking stone walls. Moving slowly across the room she turned to her right instinctively as if knowing what she had to do. Turning the corner she studied the walls around her. Her hands reached out to the sides to steady herself against the uneven stone floor. She moved forward slowly, breathing heavier, if only she could find it. She looked left and right through the dark dusty air, the dust bit at her throat as she coughed and choked slightly. 'Nearly there,' she said out loud as she crept forward. She came to a stone wall ahead of her and felt her path now blocked. 'No... no... no...' she screamed.

Mary sat bolt upright in bed drenched in sweat. She was breathing heavily as she looked around she was in the hotel in their room. She looked at her hands. Still shaking she got out of bed and splashed water on her face.

Just a bad dream nothing more nothing less she told herself.

Climbing back in bed she soon fell back to sleep.

Chapter 7

It had been a week since Mary had had her dream, she had been dwelling on it for so long that even Tom had noticed her change in attitude. She could only hope that when she saw her sister in two days everything would be sorted.

The house was coming along nicely; the kitchen was finished except for the cellar door which would be sorted by the weekend. Brian had visited and with a contractor had got the garden sheds, greenhouse and chicken coop removed. New grass had been laid in places and it started to look like a decent garden again.

The trees had been cut back and when you looked out the kitchen window you could see right to the bottom of the garden.

Paving stones would be arriving within the week and lighting would be rigged so you could walk down.

Mary had stocked up the kitchen with essentials. Busy making teas and coffees for painters (living room one and bedroom one) and Tom working on paperwork she had time to think of nothing but the nightmare. She still remembered how her hands had shaken; she was adamant that it had been a dream but the feeling inside her. Had it been more than that?

She turned and looked at the imposing door. She grabbed the keys from the table and unlocked the door, grabbing her torch she opened the door and stepped into the dank cold cellar. She made her way down the stairs; once she reached the bottom she turned on her torch and made her way round, just like in her dream. She felt the damp cold stone walls, could feel the cold clinging to her. She shivered but turned the corner. She pushed forward shining the light left and then right, she also looked at the ceiling. Moving slowly she edged deeper into the cellar the footing underneath her became less stable as she felt the ground dip. Pushing forward breathing heavily she inched her way round feeling nothing but cold stone walls. She looked up and around her. Frustrated she made her way back.

When she emerged from the cellar she closed and locked the door. What purpose did that prove? She chastised herself for letting a dream or nightmare distract her. She finished the drinks and took them into the living room.

Paul and Chris were painting the ceilings white, both wearing as much paint as the ceiling as Mary entered. 'Cheers love,' they said as they took their drinks and downed tools for a well-earned break.

'I really think more paint on the walls instead of your overalls.' Laughed Mary

Paul smirked. Paul and Chris had been painters and decorators for ten years, had done excellent work for Tom and Mary and were always the first called when a new house needed doing up.

It had become a full time business and with two more staff taken on they ensured that a decent job was done.

Mary picked up the tray and made her way to the first bedroom. Martin and Carole were doing a wonderful job. They had nearly finished the ceiling and were contemplating the walls next.

Mary put their drinks down smiling. Carole (the only woman working for Paul) was a godsend keeping the smut as she called it to a minimum; she also gave them a hard time.

Walking on she entered the study. Tom was sat at the bureau checking figures ensuring all budgets were met.

Placing his drink on the side she placed her arms around him and kissed him. Tom stopped and kissed her back.

Determined to put the dream behind her, she sat down on a spare seat and they both went through the books.

'When does your sister arrive again?' enquired Tom.

'Two days and I think by then we should be living here; as half of the work is done especially as we have bathroom fitters arriving tomorrow.'

Nodding in agreement Tom checked the paperwork. The bathrooms would both be completed in two days.

The bedrooms could be sorted hopefully by then.

Doris would be sad to see them go, but they promised to pop in for meals on occasions.

Mary glanced out the window as drops of rain started to splash on the window, another perfect summer day. She sighed.

'I am going back down, want to get started on a few jobs. Make sure it is perfect for sis when she arrives.'

Tom laughed. 'She will have to lump it if she don't like it.'

Mary made her way down the stairs and back into the kitchen. Sitting at the table she finished her cup of coffee.

Two days to go. Then this will be finished.

She got up and stopped in her tracks. The cellar door was open ajar. Mary moved towards it and opened the door. She grabbed her torch and shone it down the staircase.

Two days she said to herself just two more days.

It was Saturday; two days had passed without incident, no more letters since the one pushed under their door at the hotel. The house was almost complete. The open hallway was a sight when you walked in, the chandelier hung majestically from the ceiling with side lights giving the room plenty of light. The lounge to the left was painted and all the furniture had been recalled from storage. Everything looked amazing in that room. The room which housed the broken pool table would be decorated from Monday onwards. Kitchen was complete with water, gas and electricity. Lounge two would be started also on Monday.

Upstairs Bedroom one was painted to perfection and the room fully furnished. The en-suite was done out in a vibrant old style of black and white. As much as Tom had almost disagreed he knew Mary had perfection in her mind.

Bathroom two was decorated in white and light blue. Everything was coming along; the furniture for that room had arrived early.

Tom had finished the paperwork for all the bills and once the main lounge was decorated and furnished the house would be perfect.

Brian would be back in two weeks to finish off what he could do in the garden. A new greenhouse, shed and garden furniture would arrive when he returned.

Mary was lounging on the Victorian Mahogany Sofa which had been restored. Coffee on table she knew that her sister would be arriving today. Happy yet apprehensive she tried her best to relax. She had last seen her sister at their parent's funeral three years ago. Marie had had hardly spoken to Mary, but She could sense that she blamed her for not visiting them on a regular basis. Marie had spent a year looking after her parents while Mary had gone ahead with Tom and his career.

Mary got up and paced the room. It was no good, whatever happened the past would no doubt rear its ugly head and they would have to cross that bridge and hopefully bury the hatchet. The letters had been placed on the table. Tom and Mary had spent an hour reading them all.

Tom half smiled as he entered the lounge. 'Blue BMW just pulled up.'
Mary got up and looked out the window.
Marie got out of the car and ran a hand through her dark brown hair. She was 27, feisty and as Tom always considered 'the devil incarnate'. She opened the boot of her BMW and removed a holdall, after closing the boot and locking the car she made her way towards the gate. She walked with an air of authority; she had been working in security for two years, and worked her way up the ladder. She considered her job to be her life.

Mary quickly answered the door and Marie stepped through into the hallway. She glanced around obviously impressed.

Mary took her holdall and Tom took it to the second bedroom.

They looked at each other and then hugged. 'Well sis. I have to admit it is a great house.'

Mary led her into the lounge 'well everything would be perfect except for these damn letters sis. I needed help and I hoped you would be able to get to the bottom of this mess.'

Marie sat down 'Oh not yet sis. I am visiting first. I need a drink, then a tour and...' pausing she let the sentence hang.

Tom entered the room sensing the atmosphere. He walked over 'So lovely to see you again Marie,' he said trying to remain calm as he kissed her on the cheek.

'Likewise Tom and nice place, my darling sister was about to give me a grand tour and I am gasping for an iced tea.'

Tom wandered off to make iced tea; he rolled his eyes as he passed Mary. Smirking slightly Mary led Marie around the house.

It took a good hour to go through the ins and outs of the house and the garden which she also insisted on seeing. Tom kept himself busy in the kitchen preparing the evening meal.

Once they both came back in they were both smiling which worried Tom slightly.

'Okay... what? 'He looked at them both.

After dinner of roast beef, Roast potatoes and three veg they all adjourned into the lounge.
Marie sat down and looked at them both. 'Before I dare look at these letters...'
Mary looked up 'I know you still blame me for not visiting our parents.'
Marie closed her eyes and shook her head. 'I never blamed you sis. If anything I was jealous.'
Mary looked shocked while Tom looked at them both. 'But...'Tom started to say.
Marie stopped him. 'Right let me explain. I loved you sis and I loved our parents but having to
watch you two follow your dreams meant I was stuck. Mum and Dad were great comfort but
when they both became too ill to look after I resented the fact that I had wasted MY time.
I could've got help with them and I thought it was my duty that one of us looked after them.
So at the funeral seeing you both so successful and happy brought back feeling of how I had
wasted my life. That is the reason I never phoned. Why I never kept in contact my stupid
jealousy.'
Mary got up and sat by her sister, without words she hugged Marie and they both started to
cry. Tom got up, 'I think drinks are in order.'
Taking a tissue each from the box on the sideboard they hugged. 'I am so sorry sis, and when
you...' Marie sniffed 'rang I knew I wanted to get this out in the open.'

It took another hour of childhood memories, old photographs that Marie had brought with her
and lots of tears and laughter that it was too late to start on the letters.
Tom yawned and they called it night.
Marie glanced at the letters. 'I will look at them all tomorrow morning, oh and do you have
somewhere I can plug my laptop in.'
Mary laughed as she led her sister to her bedroom and wished her goodnight.
Closing the door to their rooms Mary glanced out the window. Tom wandered up behind her and
kissed her. 'So all is well that ends well eh?'
Mary turned. 'Morning will tell, and I know if anyone can explain the letters Marie can.'
Tom got into bed setting his alarm for 6am.

Mary wandered down the stone steps of the cellar. The light from the torch dancing around the
walls as she slowly reached the bottom step. Feeling the cold stone against her hand she edged
round to the left, her breathing heavy as she wandered deeper into the cellar.
Each footstep echoed on the stone flooring as she moved along. She paused for a moment as
something brushed against her left hand. Shining the torch she knocked the spider to the floor
and watched it scuttle into the darkness.
Steadying herself she carried on deeper into the cellar. Nearly there she kept saying over and
over.
She could almost feel what she desired; she just had to reach it. Feeling in her pocket she
pulled out the cellar key. She bent down shining the light to floor, the gold padlock held a
trapdoor in place. She placed the key into the lock and felt it slowly turn. Removing the padlock
after all these years she placed it on the stone floor. She felt the trapdoor handle and pulled.
Nothing happened, she kept tugging and pulling but without any luck.
No... no... no... no. She tried once more. 'It won't open for you yet Mary...'
Mary turned startled as the voice penetrated the shadows of the cellar and she screamed.
Mary sat bolt upright bathed in sweat, her breathing heavy as she looked around. She was in
the bedroom. She got out of bed careful not to disturb Tom and his snoring and splashed water
on her face. She looked in the mirror. She splashed more water on her face and looked again. A
shadow caught her eye from the far corner of the room, she whirled round but no one was
there.
Climbing back in bed she looked up at the ceiling. What the hell is going on?
With that Mary rolled over and fell back to sleep.

If only Mary had looked out the window she might have seen him. He made his way to the door. He shivered. Why hadn't they listened to his pleas and warnings and who was this person staying with them. He needed answers. He pushed the letter through the door, making his way back to the waiting car. Please not again I do not think this town would survive if it happens again. The car drove off heading into town.

Chapter 8

Mary was first up in the morning; she saw the letter on the floor and placed it on the table with the others, she glanced outside. The rain had set in and the sky was a dark menacing colour. Shivering she turned towards the cellar. What was actually down there? Making herself a coffee she moved to the lounge and curled up on the sofa. She glanced at her laptop and turned it on running an internet search on dreams and nightmares. She knew better than to let things like this get to her, but there had been many strange things happening.
She put her laptop down with disgust. I am not going to let this affect me, especially now my sister is here and she will get to the bottom of this stupidity.
With this in mind she made her second coffee.
By 9am the rain had set in and this lowered Mary's mood. Tom was busy trying to sort out paperwork, and would be leaving on Monday for two days to sort out everything with his solicitor.
Wandering in the kitchen he placed his arms around Mary. 'You ok sweetie? You've been quiet today.'
Mary turned. 'You trust me don't you?'
Tom looked at her. 'You know I do. What is bothering you, you have been quiet for a while and I am concerned.'
Mary turned away, looking out the window. Deep in thought she finally turned. 'I have been having nightmares... about this house. It has happened twice now and it takes place in that cellar.'
Tom looked at the cellar. 'Ok, let's go down then and you can talk me through what you see.'
He unlocked the door and they both grabbed torches and descended the stairs.
Mary felt stifled this was the last place she wanted to go with or without Tom.
When they reached the bottom Mary walked round moving slowly forward explaining what she felt in her dream or nightmare.
Moving round deeper they finally came to a stone wall which blocked their path.
Mary turned to Tom. 'I got this far the first time, but in the next dream I get to move further on and there is a trap door on the floor. I unopened the lock with this key and then struggle but cannot open it. When I try a voice is behind me warning me not yet.'

Mary and Tom surveyed the walls and floors and found nothing. They made their way back up to the kitchen and Tom locked the door.
'Listen Hun if you want to you can seek some help, there are several people who can interpret dreams... and maybe... 'The sentence hung.
Mary looked at him. 'I know for sure no one in my family had dreams like this but maybe I should tell...'
'Morning' Marie said as she wandered in. She looked at Tom and Mary, 'what happened you both look dreadful.'
Mary smiled. 'I suggest we talk sis, because what is happening is driving me mad and I think this house has questions that I want answers to, and I think this ties in with the notes.'

Marie smiled, 'Looks like you need my services and for which Tom I need some items, firstly a cuppa as I am gasping.' Marie made a list for Tom and with a wicked smile ushered him away. 'Right sis what problems are you having.' Moving outside in the garden Mary explained it all.

It took a good hour and more drinks made to get all the information down and in note form for Marie to check through at a later date. Also they poured through the notes and date stamped it all.
Collating the information for when they bought the property, to when the notes arrived and when the dreams or nightmares started.

Tom finally arrived back with shopping bags and Marie's items he put the bags down and made his way into the kitchen. 'Have either of you been in the cellar?' He questioned.
Mary and Marie both made their way in. 'No,' they both said but the door was open ajar.
Marie grabbed her camera and took a photo and made a note, knowing that they had had a drink less than twenty minutes earlier and the door had been locked then.
Mary ran out of the house followed by Marie and Tom, 'What is wrong with this house!' she climbed in her car and sped off heading towards town, Marie and Tom stood watching as the car vanished from view.

Slowly walking into the house they sat in the lounge. Tom looked at Marie. 'Ok let's go through the information you have collated and let's start getting to the bottom of this ever growing problem.'
Marie pulled out her mobile phone and turned it on. 'I just need to make a phone call.'
After a long ten minute conversation Marie put the phone down. 'Right you want to know what is going on. I have photocopied the letters via my mobile and emailed them to my friend who analyses writing, I am also sending the letters for analysis as I want to check for prints. Maybe we will get lucky.'
Tom smiled 'such a wonderful house, full of stuff when we arrived.'
He suddenly got to his feet and moved to the bookcase.
He pulled open the doors and looked at the books pulling them all out one by one. Marie stood behind checking the books as he put them on the floor.
'You say these were all left?'
'Yes along with the bureau which had paperwork in it.'
Marie opened the bureau and pulled out all the documents. Reading through them they tried to find anything to link this to the house.

Marie wandered in the kitchen and made the drinks. Where could her sister be now, and what was going on? She was determined to get to the bottom of this problem.
Putting on her gloves she picked up the letters and placed them in an envelope, and decided she would drive them to her friend to get them analysed.

Tom looked through some loose pages that had fallen from one of the books. Letters to the owners and a couple of photographs in black and white, dog-eared from time.
'Marie can you have a look at these please.'
He passed her the letters and she glanced at them. 'Nice find Tom I will have these looked at too,' she placed them in the envelope and walked towards the door. 'I will get these sorted as soon as I can and be back later on today.'
She got in her car and sped off.

Tom watched her go and sat on the sofa. Picking up his mobile he turned it on. He checked for messages and was close to ringing Mary but stopped.

No she needed some time and that is what he was going to give her.

With that he picked up the key to the cellar and made his way down the cold stairs.

He flashed the torch down the stairs and felt the cold stone against his hand.

Whatever was happening, this had some answers.

Moving down the stairs slowly he flashed the light from side to side glancing around as he made his way down the steps.

As he reached the bottom he flashed the torch from left to right, his breathing ragged. He moved to the left as Mary had done during her nightmares.

He turned the corner and felt the stone cold wall.

The skin on the back of his neck tingled as he shivered.

He slowly moved forward his footsteps echoing, he flashed the torch from side to side.

He carried on deeper, knowing that any minute now he would feel a brick wall.

Slow footsteps echoed as he flashed the torch forwards and then side to side. Where was the wall? He scrambled around what was going on, it wasn't this far back surely.

He edged around and finally came across the corner, shining the torch up and around, he came across the stair rail.

He moved his way up the stairs, his breathing ragged, He was determined he was going to fit lights in here and get the details for this place it was driving him mad.

He climbed up the stairs and found the door shut. He reached out, but..... What in God's name Was going on..... Where was the handle?

He pushed at the door then remembered the door opened inwards when opened from the kitchen and with no handle on this side how was he going to get out. He pushed at the door, without avail. Sitting on the top step he pulled out his mobile phone and called Mary. He listened as it rang and rang and then went onto voicemail. Tom ended the call. Please just let Marie or Mary return soon.

He turned off the light, no good wasting the battery he didn't know how long he was going to be stuck down here.

Chapter 9

It was June 1969, Tony and Maureen Farley had been living in the Whippletree property for 3 months. Tony was 32 years of age, tall with dark hair. He loved to garden and worked hard at the offices on the outskirts of the village; Maureen was 30 years of age with dark brown hair, she considered her job was to keep the house spic and span.

Maureen was cooking Bacon and Eggs on her white Rangette gas cooker. Tony wandered into the kitchen, kissed Maureen and sat down at the table. Dressed in his suit he was ready for the office. Maureen placed the coffee pot on the table and finished off cooking breakfast.

Maureen gazed out of the window. It had been a cold June so far and with the anticyclone still travelling across Britain the weather was hardly likely to pick up. She sighed. Serving up breakfast she passed Tony his plate and sat down opposite. Tony was already engrossed in the paper.

'Soak the driver!' Princess Margaret scatters crowd. Maureen glanced at the front page and shook her head. Why did people want to be in the public eye? Royals... she rolled her eyes and carried on eating her breakfast.

'What time do you think you will be home tonight?' enquired Maureen.

'Will be home by 7ish, got to finish some paperwork and then weekend to ourselves.' replied Tony. He folded the newspaper and tucked into his breakfast.

'If this weather ever picks up we can tackle the garden again.' he said as he swallowed. Maureen laughed. 'Well at least we can sort out the rest of this house I think I will deal with those pile of books which we were given, put them in that lovely cabinet your dear mother gave us when we moved in.'

Tony finished his breakfast and got up. Kissing Maureen goodbye he headed out.

Maureen started washing up and tidied the kitchen. Making herself another cup of tea she headed into the small lounge and put the radio on.

Classical music blasted out of the speakers.

She loved her classical music.

She busied herself with the housework and with such a massive house it was a chore and a half, but Tony brought in enough wage for them to live in comfort.

Maureen fetched 5 heavy boxes full of books from the upstairs study, down into the lounge, sitting down she started taking them out of the boxes. Sorting them out she placed them in alphabetical order before starting to put them in the cabinet. She made sure she looked in each book, as some she had borrowed from time to time and she wanted to make a note of certain chapters of certain books.

It was midday and she was sitting in the back garden with her cup of tea, this was her time, she was determined to make the best of this house and she loved it. She loved her garden as did her husband but he worked long hours and did not get that many weekends free.

'Hello… Hello…' The voice startled her at first until she saw Samuel come round the corner. Samuel Henshaw was 25 years old and one of the first people they had met when they had come to the village; he had given them information on the local town and was always a welcome visitor.

'Samuel, come on round, fancy a cup of tea?'

'Never been one to turn down a cuppa.' He said as he tilted his hat.

They moved inside into the kitchen and they caught up on the town's news. After they had finished their drinks, Samuel looked out in the garden.

'If you need help with such a garden I would be willing…' he let the sentence hang for a second.

Maureen smiled 'Well we were going to attempt it this weekend, assuming that the weather clears.'

'Be more than happy to drop by and give you both a hand.'

Maureen nodded and agreed. 'Come round about 9 and I will fix us all a picnic style dinner.'

'No need to go to so much trouble.' He replied.

'It will be a pleasure,' Maureen glanced at the cellar door. 'Be nice if we could open the cellar. It has been stuck fast since we moved in, and I'd love to know what secrets lay behind that door.'

Samuel scratched his ear 'Well I will bring my tools with me and see if we can get it open on Saturday.'

Maureen led Samuel to the front door and bade him goodbye.

The rest of the afternoon was spent tidying and preparing Tony's' meal.

As promised he was home just after 7 and looking very pleased with himself.

As they sat down to dinner he discussed what had happened at work. 'Been a productive day, all that paperwork sorted and a new project starts a week Monday, Looks like another chance of a pay rise.'

Maureen beamed with delight.

Maureen then mentioned that Samuel would be popping over and offering a hand with the garden.

Tony smiled 'good man that Samuel, always willing to help others. If this new project takes off I would hire him to keep the garden in shape.'

Maureen laughed, 'I am sure he would appreciate that. He also said he will bring his tools and have a look at that cellar door.'

They both turned, looking at the door with its paint flaking off.

It had been an eyesore when they first walked round, but no one had a key for it.

'If Samuel can get it off, I will let him fetch a new door.'

Smiling Maureen tidied the plates away and washed up.

Nothing gave her more pleasure than making a home look tidy.

In the evening they both sat with a glass of wine, relaxing in the lounge. The radio was on in the background; Maureen snuggled up next to Tony and smiled.

'I think this is the best move we have ever made.'

Tony agreed, 'I am glad too,' he kissed her on the forehead, 'let's get to bed, if we are tackling the garden in the morning.'

Climbing the stairs they made their way to their bedroom.

Maureen stopped at the top of the stairs and glanced at the open study door.

'That is strange?'

Tony looked at her 'What is?'

'Well I fetched some books from the study room earlier today and I instinctively remember closing the door.'

Tony walked in the study.

Nothing looked out of place.

'Maybe you thought you did. You mentioned you had Samuel pop round.'

Maureen shook her head. 'No, Samuel popped round when I was having a drink in the garden, after I had finished the books.'

She peered in the room, 'You're probably right it has been a long day, let alone a long week.'

They closed the door to the study and entered their bedroom.

As they turned off the light they soon fell blissfully asleep.

The chill of the night fell upon the house, it was 2am and an owl sat in the tree outside, watching the night, using its senses searching for mice, its head turned, as the study door opened.

The owl stared its eyes intense, the hunger and the flight of the chase, its desire for food. It hooted and ruffled its feathers. Then movement caught its eye from inside the house, it flew off the branch landing on the bushes, hooting indignantly.

Slowly and silently something moved down the stairs of the house, gliding through to the kitchen. The shadow paused at the cellar door. The door slowly creaked open. The shadow descended the steps and the door closed slowly on its own.

Chapter 10

Beep... Beep... Beep... it was 6:30 on a sunny Saturday morning; Tony yawned and slowly got up.

Maureen stirred, 'Is it that time already?' she asked.

'You can have longer if need be,' he leant over kissing her on the forehead.

Maureen sat up, 'No, think today is going to be a long day.'

She walked over to the window and saw the bright sunshine; she shivered and wandered into the bathroom.

By 7:30 they were both dressed and eating a full breakfast.

Maureen had already sorted some food out for dinner which she would prepare later on.

Tony sat reading his newspaper, 'Should be sunny all weekend.'

He got up and wandered outside, it was chilly but at least they could get some work done in the garden. As he wandered in he looked at the cellar door. It needed to go, it looked dilapidated, but never been removed.

By the time Samuel had arrived, Tony had started in the garden; he had done the mowing and raked the grass up.

Samuel had bought his clippers for the trees and bushes.

As noon arrived they downed tools and had a picnic prepared by Maureen on the patio.

The garden looked much better, more neat and tidy.

'To be honest Samuel with me working all the hours I have to, it makes sense for someone to keep this garden in check.' Tony remarked.

'Well if I can help you know I will.' Samuel said as he put his knife and fork down and picked up his glass.

Tony raised his glass 'Well we will pay you, we never expect anything to be done for free.'

'It will give us much pleasure to sit out her on a summers evening, bathing in the sunlight as it sets.' Maureen replied.

Samuel laughed 'Well if you are both happy, I will come once a week.'

With that settled they packed away the picnic and finished off what they could.

'What surprises me is that this house has so much potential and ground and yet it went so cheaply.'

Samuel turned away.

'Well I am not sure... You see...' he stammered.

Tony looked 'What is it?'

Samuel took a long drink from his wine. Closing his eyes he exhaled.

'It is said that the previous owners....' he paused collecting his thoughts. '...Well some say they went mad, others say ghosts haunt this house.'

You must be joking,' Tony laughed.

Maureen looked at Samuel. 'Well I am not sure what to make of that Samuel but I must tell you.'

She looked at Tony.

'Last night!' she exclaimed 'the study door!'

Tony looked at her.

'Come, come, we put that down to you over working in the house and the long week.'

'You did!' she exclaimed.

Samuel watched them both.

'Well this place has a history, and I am not sure what is available in town at the record office, but....' he trailed off again 'I could always look up previous happening in the village and let you both know.'

Maureen jumped at the chance, 'That sounds like a wonderful idea.'

With that they finished their drinks and moved inside.

'I never did have a good look round the house myself, I almost considered buying it for...' his sentence hung.

'Well I remember you saying the cellar door.'

'Tony stood up, 'Ah... yes this door.'

They all moved over to it.

Samuel examined the door. It was old, the paint peeling off. 'No key you said?'

'Never found one, if it can be removed and a new one fitted?' enquired Tony.

Samuel chuckled. 'Well I know Mr Barston in town has doors, maybe pop in and see him?'

Tony clapped Samuel on his back, 'We'll pop in tomorrow.'

With that sorted they spent the remainder of the evening in the lounge chatting about the village.

They left the house early on Sunday morning, they drove into town in their prized Yellow Mini, and first stop was the church. Sunday service was something they always did; it had been instilled in them since childhood.
After a wonderful sermon and service they took the short walk into town.
They walked along the cobbled streets, occasionally stopping to speak to people, their coats buttoned up, as the weather was still cold.
Finally they reached the Hardware store. They peered through the window glancing around.
Maureen went to the door but it was closed.
'Well cannot see much through these old windows but we can pop in tomorrow and have a look around.'
They made their way back to the church and drove home.
They spent the rest of the day relaxing, listening to music and sorting some more books out for the cabinet.

Monday morning. The sky was grey and menacing.
Tony and Maureen got dressed early and drove to town. Once again they parked at the church and took the short walk to the hardware store. Mr Barton was an elderly gentleman in his sixties; he opened promptly at 9am. Glancing through the dirty windows he noticed Tony and Maureen heading towards his shop. As they entered, Mr Barton busied himself. 'Let me know if I may be of any assistance.'
Maureen and Tony smiled 'Well were after a door.' replied Tony.
'Ah... Hmm doors.' Mr Barton motioned them forward. 'This way please.'
He walked off around the corner. Tony and Maureen followed him.
'I have a selection here, is it for front of houses, back of houses....'
'Cellar type door,' replied Tony.
'Oh' his eyes brightened 'Yes cellar doors.' Moving father back he came to a selection of sleek wooden doors. 'This would be better suited.'
Tony looked at them all. 'This one,' he said pointing to a plain wooden door.
'Good choice, fine detail... a nice choice of door.'
Tony smiled at Maureen.
'I can have it ready for you by tomorrow, and do you need it delivering or will you be picking it up?'
'Please deliver it,' Tony said casually.
'Very well Sir,' came Mr Barton's reply.
They moved to the front of the shop, and paid for the new door.
Mr Barton looked at them both 'Delivery address?'
'Ahh yes we bought the house out the village,'
Mr Barton looked up. 'The house just outside the village, with that tree growing by the side?'
'Yes....' replied Tony.
'I know the place. I will deliver it Tuesday morning.'
With that all sorted they left the store.
Tony laughed when they got outside. 'Well he is one of those characters, think he was around when this town was conceived?'
Maureen slapped him 'Don't be cruel, but he looked shocked when we mentioned the house.'
'Towns and stories my dear, towns and stories.'
They walked slowly back through the town.

Mr Barton watched them from the window. He had heard of the house. Walking away he shook his head.

Tony dropped Maureen off at the house and headed off to work. Maureen busied herself in the kitchen, radio on classical music filling the room.
After the kitchen was tidy, she tidied around in the lounge. Suddenly there was a knock on the door. Maureen walked out into the hall and opened the door to find Samuel.
'I am so sorry to call on you this early Maureen, but... well...'
'Come in, come in Samuel.' Maureen ushered him in and led him to the kitchen.
While Maureen filled the old kettle Samuel sat at the table.
Maureen filled two cups and she sat down. 'Now tell me what has got you so agitated this morning.'
'I... it seems so silly...' he clasped and unclasped his hands. Shaking his head he stood up.
'I was speaking to some neighbours this morning and we got on about stories of the village.' He said finally. 'To be honest,' he stopped 'I have never taken any notice of stories, but after what you mentioned yesterday.'
Maureen looked at him 'Start at the beginning.'
Sitting down he took a sip of his tea.
He closed his eyes and then looked directly at Maureen.
'Right,' he said 'This morning when I walking through the village to fetch my newspaper I bumped into Miss Horncastle, you may not know her, but she has been in this village for years.'
'She remembers the previous owners, a lovely couple they were,' Samuel stood up and paced the room. 'The house, she claims, is evil.'
Maureen stood up 'Oh nonsense.'
Samuel sat 'let me finish.'
He reached in his pocket and pulled out a dog eared newspaper clipping.
He passed it to Maureen.

Strange Goings On: Couple Never Found.

Today an inquest into the disappearance of Cecil and Edna Hamilton was finally ended and the property will go to the estate of Cecil's Brother Reginald.
Cecil and Edna hadn't contacted their brother in over a month and Reginald decided to pay them a visit.
After arriving at the house he found the house in perfect order, but with no sign of his brother or sister in law.
Concerned he contacted the local police.
After a thorough investigation and with nothing missing the police were baffled.
It is only guessed upon that they visited the lake at the end of the garden and vanished.
The lake was drained and no bodies found, the well was also checked.
The whereabouts of Cecil and Edna Hamilton remains a mystery to this day.
The house on the outskirts of town will, according to Reginald, be sold.

Maureen looked at Samuel. 'When did...' She paused.
'There is more.' said Samuel as he pulled out a second clipping.

Fire Destroys House.

On Thursday last a terrible storm broke out. Lightning struck the top most part of the Whippletree property and started a fire of such intenseness that the property was severely damaged.

The owner one Reginald Hamilton was informed.

The property had belonged to his Brother and Sister in law who both vanished.

Mr Hamilton claimed that this house is to be restored to its former state and sold.

Asked upon whether he had heard from his Brother or sister in law, he commented that neither had been seen since he heard the tragic news.

Maureen shook. 'Oh this is dreadful...'

Samuel took her hands, 'I didn't want to...' he trailed off 'but I thought you better know of these things.'

Maureen stood up, 'Right, well since you have bought these to my attention, you better stop.'

Samuel stood up and looked. 'Miss Horncastle was the historian of the village before she retired. She lives just before the church.'

Maureen turned and smiled. 'I will show these to my husband tonight.'

Samuel gave a weak smile. 'I am so sorry, I was in two minds weather to visit and inform you.'

Maureen smiled 'I think for the time being, I am glad you did, but I think I would like a chat with Miss Horncastle. Do you think you can arrange that for me?'

Samuel nodded.

'Well since you're here. The new door will be arriving tomorrow for the cellar, so I would like you to pop round tomorrow and sort the door out.'

Samuel smiled.

Maureen walked him to the door and bade him goodbye.

She walked back in the kitchen and busied herself with the evening meal.

Tony knew something was wrong as soon as he got home, the atmosphere in the house felt cold, but Maureen refused to tell him what was going on until after their evening meal.

As they sat in the lounge Maureen went through all the happenings and showed her husband the two newspaper cuttings.

Tony read them in silence. 'Well...' he finally said 'If you want to find out if any of this is true, I will not stand in your way.' He smiled.

Maureen kissed him. 'I just need the truth.'

Little did they know this was only the beginning...

Chapter 11

(2011)

Mary drove into town, her tears nearly dry, but she wanted answers and she knew where to go.

Pulling up in the town she walked to the Museum.

Mr Peterson was reading the local newspaper when Mary rushed in.

'Sorry to bother you, but I want all the files again on the house.' she asked slightly breathless.

Mr Peterson got up 'Are you alright?' he enquired.

Mary shook her head 'Let's just say I've had betters days.'

Mr Peterson passed her a tissue and then wandered into the old store room 'I thought that the information on that disc would give you most of the information you required.'

Mary turned 'The disc of course!' with her mind clearing for the first time she remembered the disc, which was at the house.

Mr Peterson cleared some room for Mary to work. She put the first four files to one side and opened the next file.

'Would you like a cup of tea?' enquired Mr Peterson. 'If there's one thing I do know, Tea clears the mind.'

Mary glanced up and smiled, 'Thank you, most kind.'

She watched him vanish and then started going through the papers.

She worked feverishly skim reading the information on the town, and looking for information connected the house, scribbling down notes every so often on.

Mr Peterson busied himself in the museum. He paused for a moment. 'Mary can I suggest something?'

Mary looked up from what she was reading 'What do you suggest?'

'Well this is a museum and maybe, just maybe something of importance might be in on show.'

Mary got up. I am in a museum surrounded by paperwork she thought 'Right give me the tour, I want to see everything.'

Mr Peterson beamed.

The tour took a good hour, with them studying all the artefacts of the town, old town maps and nostalgia that had been donated through the years.

Mary made some notes and could think more clearly after the tour.

'Well the woman who used to know everything about this town died many years ago, half of her books on the town were sent here.'

Mary stopped. 'I wouldn't be able to have a look at those too would I?' she enquired

Mr Peterson looked at her 'Well that is a good question, I know they will be somewhere in the archives. Let me go and check.' with that he walked off.

Mary sat down and pulled out her mobile phone, calling up her phonebook she dialled Tom's number.

'Hello darling it's me.' She said.

'I am so glad you rang, but you need to get back to the house right away.' Tom replied quickly.

'What's happened?' she asked.

'I am stuck in the cellar.'

Mary dropped her phone, running she found Mr Peterson surrounded by boxes.

'I have to go!' she exclaimed

Mr Peterson turned round 'What's up my dear?'

'Can I just leave the files here, I will...' she shook her head 'We will be back in short while.'

With that she ran out the door and through the town, through the churchyard and to her car. She sped off tyres squealing.

She needed to do this; she was nothing without Tom, urging the car faster she drove through the countryside.

She pulled up outside the house and ran to the front door. She turned the handle. Nothing, it was locked.

She pulled out her keys and unlocked the door, scrambling in the house and through to the kitchen. She stood before the cellar door. 'Tom... Tom can you hear me?'

She grabbed the handle and turned it, the door refused to open. She removed the cellar key and reinserted it, she pulled at the handle 'You will open...' she screamed, she pulled several more times before the door finally opened.

Mary flung her arms around Tom. Weeping on his shoulder 'I was scared I ...'

Tom hugged her, kissing her 'I am alright.'

Mary grabbed her laptop and the disc 'You're coming with me.'

She grabbed his hand and he stopped.

'Where are we going?'

Mary looked at him, determination in her eyes.

'Were going back to the museum, but we have one last place to visit first.'
With that they left the house, ensuring it was locked up.

Mrs Chambers was at reception when Tom and Mary walked in. 'Hello my dears how are you both?' she enquired.
Mary smiled 'I need a favour.'
'Oh is it a meal for two?'
'A meal would be lovely, but we also need two rooms for a week.'
Mrs Chambers looked at them both 'Two rooms?'
'I... we don't have much time to explain Doris but please if you can have the rooms ready and a meal for three for when we return.'
Mrs Chambers smiled 'I will see to it. Dinner will be about half six.'
They thanked Doris and ran back to the car.
Pulling out her mobile Mary rang her sister.
'Marie... listen not much time to explain, do not go back to the house. Go to the small hotel just as you enter the village. Say Mary sent you.'
Putting her phone away she drove back into the village and parked by the church.
They both got out and walked quickly to the museum.

Mr Peterson was relieved when Mary returned, she looked different, determined. 'This is my husband Tom,' she said as she walked to the files. 'Nice to meet you,' replied Mr Peterson as they shook hands. 'Likewise,' replied Tom.
'I am not sure what is going on but I bet you would both love a cup of tea.'
Mary smiled. 'That will be perfect, now do you mind if I show my husband around the museum?'
'Go right ahead. It's not like we get many visitors in here.'
Mary put her laptop and disc on the table and led Tom around the Museum.
Tom stopped. 'I am a little unsure what is going on,' he said 'but I think we need to sit down and talk about what is happening.'
Mary glanced at Tom. 'I will explain tonight.'

Mrs Chambers was behind a counter when Marie arrived at the hotel 'Hello...' Marie said as she approached the desk.
Mrs Chambers looked round. 'How can I help you dear?'
'Tom and Mary sent me. I just hope this is the right hotel.'
Mrs Chambers chuckled. 'Yes my dear you're at the right hotel.'
Marie smiled 'Yes, but do you know why I am here and not back at the house?'
'I have no idea why you're here, but they are stopping here too for a week.'
'Right,' said Marie confused.
Mrs Chambers smiled 'Let me show you your room, I have made sure that you are next door to Tom and Mary.'
'That is very kind of you.' replied Marie.
Mrs Chambers led her upstairs. 'I have to ask my dear. No luggage with you?'
Marie chuckled, 'That's at the house.'
Mrs Chambers opened the door to her room 'Dinner will be about half six.'
Marie thanked her and sat on the bed. Well this is fun she thought. She checked the room over and then wandered downstairs. Pulling the paperwork and information from the car she ran in to find Mrs Chambers.
'I am so sorry to ask but where can I get a cup of tea?'

Mrs Chambers smiled, 'go sit yourself down dear in the bar/lounge and I will bring one through to you.'

Thanking Mrs Chambers she wandered into the empty bar/lounge and set her paperwork on the table.

She read all the information she had received from the letters she had borrowed. Running her fingers through her dark brown hair she sighed.

Mrs Chambers walked in with a cup of tea, and bustled off.

Marie picked up her mobile.

Tom and Mary had spent a good two hours going around the museum and then looking at all the paperwork and files.

Tom looked through older files while Mary carried on where she had left off.

Every so often Tom would make a note regarding the village, but everything so far seemed normal for a village.

He still felt slightly shaken from being locked in the cellar. He was just lucky Mary had rung him.

Mary was reading some newspaper clippings when Mr Peterson wandered in. 'Sorry to say but I need to lock up soon.' Mary looked up, 'Sorry Mr Peterson you have been wonderful, let me give you a hand with this paperwork.' Mary picked up her files and handed them over. She then took Toms and placed them next to hers.

Mr Peterson thanked them both, and stopped. 'You remember those books I mentioned, the lady who curated before I did.' Mary stopped 'have you found them?' she asked eagerly.

Mr Peterson fetched them over. He handed over 6 small books. 'Don't let anyone know that I let you take these away with you.'

Mary kissed him on the cheek. Placing the books in her bag they left the museum.

No sooner had they reached the car after walking through the churchyard, Mary's phone rang. 'Sis its Marie, I am at the hotel now.'

'Ok sis we're on our way.' Sliding her phone back in the bag she turned to Tom.

'Marie is at the hotel. Let's see what she found.'

Tom climbed in the driving seat and they drove back to the hotel.

Chapter 12

Mary and Tom rushed into the hotel, and Doris gave them their key explaining that they had a room next to the young lady who arrived earlier.

Mary smiled and explained it was her sister Marie who had arrived.

They made their way up the stairs and stopped at Marie's door. Marie was glad to see them both and they all sat down.

Marie put the kettle on and made them all a drink. They all sat in silence drinking, each knowing they had a story to tell.

Marie put her cup down. 'Right I am not sure how we will sort this out, but I have news regarding the letters.'

Tom looked up. 'When you left,' he looked at Marie 'I got trapped in the cellar.'

Mary looked at them both. 'I went to the museum and think I have some more information.' She pulled the notepads out of her bag 'Hopefully these will also shed more light.'

Marie closed her eyes. 'I suggest we go in chronological order here. We know Mary left and went to the museum, so we will leave you for a little while,' she carried on with an air of authority. 'I went to get the letters checked over, which then leaves Tom going first.'

Tom looked at them both. 'Not really much to tell, Mary had gone in the car, you had gone to sort the letters, and I decided I would go down the cellar,' He paused and closed his eyes trying to bring it to the forefront of his mind. 'I unlocked the cellar, and wandered down, but...' he turned to Mary 'you mentioned in your second dream that you got farther than in your first dream,' Mary Nodded 'well so did I. It disorientated me and when I got back up the door was locked.' He closed his eyes again. 'I heard no one and saw nothing.' He rubbed his hands across his face and through his hair.

Marie made notes of what had happened. 'How did you escape the cellar?' enquired Marie.

'Mary rang me I told her where I was and she came back and unlocked the door.'

Marie turned to Mary 'and where was the key?'

Mary looked at her sister 'The key was still in the lock.'

'Are you sure?' asked Marie.

Mary closed her eyes the event still fresh in her mind, 'I rushed in the house, through to the kitchen, shouting Toms name. I ... must've turned the key.'

Marie stopped her. 'Okay.'

Marie made notes trying to prise as much information as possible out of them both.

She turned to Mary 'What happened after you left us at the house?'

Mary looked at her sister. 'I drove to town, I wanted answers, and ... I went to the museum I couldn't think of where else to go.'

Marie pressed on 'you stopped no-where else?'

Mary looked at her sister. 'I went straight to the museum and saw Mr Peterson who gave me the files. He made me a cup of tea, I worked through more files and I checked my phone, rang Tom then drove back and unlocked the door. We then drove here to book rooms and then back to the museum and went through the files and walked round the museum before coming back here.'

Marie wrote it all down.

Pausing she pulled the letters from her bag.

'Well Tom is aware that I went to get these letters copied and checked for fingerprints and got one of my office workers to do a check on the handwriting. I knew that by going to the local Police and informing them of who I was I could get the information quicker. Luckily once they checked my name and rang my superiors they couldn't help me enough,' she paused 'I then got your message to come here, and here we all are.'

Tom looked at them both. 'So what have we actually learnt?'

'The letters you received here and at the house, including your solicitor belong to a Mr Samuel Henshaw. He has lived in the village for over fifty years. He has no criminal background, but he knew the previous owners.'

Mary looked at Marie. This was the first breakthrough they had had since it had all started.

'So is he connected to anything that has happened?'

Marie laughed. 'Not in the slightest, but he has information we can use. I have his email address and I have his home address.'

Tom was deep in thought. 'Sorry Marie but I do not understand how you can know that he knew the previous owners.'

Marie smiled. 'When I was doing the background checks I also checked on the previous owners. What I do know is that whatever is happening, I believe it has happened before.'

She pulled out a file. 'This is the obituary of Tony and Maureen Farley who owned the property before you.'

Mary and Tom took a copy each. They read in silence. Mary put hers down first. Tom read his and slowly lowered his copy.

Marie looked at them both. 'So as you can see, he read at their funeral. He knew them both well. He even states clearly he worked for them.' They both looked at Marie.

Marie carried on 'I suggest we look him up and invite him round here, because from those letters he sent, your house has him spooked.'

Mary looked at her watch. 'We better freshen up I am hungry and think we could all do with some food.'

Marie agreed. Tom and Mary went to their room and quickly showered. Knocking on Marie's door they all went down to eat.

Mrs Chambers greeted them all, 'I have reserved you a table in the corner tonight.'

After a delicious dinner they sat in the bar/lounge. Tom was first to speak. 'Tomorrow we go back all of us. We need clothes and I left my laptop. We get what we need and we leave.'

Mary nodded. Marie agreed.

The day had been long, everyone was tired. They bade goodnight to Mr and Mrs Chambers and retired for the night.

Mary and Tom entered their room and undressed. It wasn't long before they both drifted off to sleep.

Marie sat up in her room. She looked at her watch ten p.m. She felt restless. She made herself a cup of tea and sat in one of the comfy chairs. She re-read what she had written and put it in order.

Adding the letters to a timeline she looked for a pattern. Placing the paperwork on the table she drank her cup of tea. She climbed into bed and sleep soon took hold.

Marie's alarm went off at six a.m., yawning she got out and made herself a cup of tea. She opened her curtains and glanced outside. The sky was full of dark menacing clouds. Marie sighed. She sat down and relaxed, clearing her mind, whilst drinking her tea.

She showered and dressed knowing that she needed to go back to the house for her holdall. Picking up her papers she checked what she had gone through the night before, surely there had to be a link? She made herself a second cup and checked her mobile. Even though she was visiting she never gave up on her job. She went through her messages and sent a text to her secretary.

Once done she went downstairs.

Mrs Chambers was bustling around. 'Morning my dear, breakfast will not be long.'

Tom and Mary soon came down, both looked more refreshed than the day before, and they all need a change of clothing.

Mary hugged her sister, and Tom smiled. 'We need to go back to the house this morning and get some clothes' he said.

Mary laughed 'Well looking at the state of you.'

Marie laughed also.

Mrs Chambers wandered through 'Look at the state of you three this morning.'

Marie laughed, 'so sorry but we will get some clothing today and look better later on.'

Mrs Chambers smiled. 'I have no idea what has happened, I thought the house was almost finished.'

Tom looked at her. Then turned to Mary, 'the painters were coming again today.'

Mary pulled out her mobile. The low battery symbol flashed up. She turned it off.

'Doris I need to borrow your phone' Doris smiled. 'Use the one in reception dear.'

Mary ran to reception and rang the painters telling them not to turn up for the rest of the week.

Mrs Chambers bustled passed them, 'Breakfast is ready.'

After a full English breakfast they made their way to Marie's car. They drove to the house. They sat outside looking at it.

Marie broke the silence. 'Let's go in and stick together.'

Marie knew she wanted her laptop and holdall. Slowly they got out the car. Tom unlocked the door and they walked in. The grand hall was silent. They made their way upstairs to Marie's room. She packed all her stuff away and sealed her holdall.

Moving across the hallway they entered Tom and Mary's room, grabbing a suitcase they filled half of it with clothes.

Together they ventured back down the stairs. Mary knew her charger was in the kitchen.

Together they walked into the kitchen, Mary grabbed her charger. They looked at the cellar door; Tom moved slowly towards it and tried the handle. It was locked. Checking the lounge they picked up a few extra items and walked back to the front of the house.

Tom grabbed the handle of the door, and turned it. It opened and they walked outside.

They climbed in Marie's car and Mary looked at the house. We will get to the bottom of you; I promise she thought to herself.

Marie drove off back to the hotel.

Chapter 13

(1969)

Three weeks had passed since Samuel had shown Maureen the letters, the cellar door had been removed and a new one was standing in its place.

Samuel came round weekly tending to the garden, trimming the trees and making sure everything ran smoothly.

The garden shed housed all the gardening tools, and a second shed was for extra items they needed to house.

Maureen loved the garden, and spent time in the greenhouse potting plants.

It was a sunny Monday morning; Maureen was cooking eggs when she suddenly turned to Tony.

'Do you realise how much these eggs cost a week?' Tony looked at her over his newspaper, 'When has eggs ever been an issue?' he queried.

'Since Mrs Bromley in the village has several chickens she needs rehoused and if we had a coop...'

Tony put his paper down. 'If we get a coop are you going to learn how to look after them?'

Maureen swatted him with the tea towel 'I can easily do that.'

Tony laughed. 'I don't doubt your ability.'

Maureen finished in the kitchen and gazed outside. 'I think I'll move the empty boxes we have stored into the cellar today.'

Tony put his paper down. 'Right, I better get to work.'

He kissed Maureen and headed out.

Maureen cleaned the kitchen, finished her chores in the rest of the house and sat down with a cup of tea.

Glancing at the clock she decided that she would sort out the boxes next.

She unlocked the cellar door and slowly descended.

Once the new door had been fitted, Tony and Maureen had checked the space out. Although it was dank it still was dry enough for boxes to be stored.

Maureen turned on the light, the cellar lit up shining a dusty light around the cellar.

She spent the next thirty minutes storing boxes in the cellar. She shivered. She slowly climbed the steps and switched off the light, and locked the door behind her.

Maureen glanced at the clock it was one o'clock, she knew she was seeing Miss Horncastle at two o'clock, and that Samuel was picking her up at quarter to two.

Maureen freshened herself up, at quarter to Samuel knocked on the door.

Maureen had the two newspaper clippings in her bag. After a short drive through town they reached Miss Horncastle's cottage.

Miss Horncastle sat in her chair, she was a thin lady and her glasses seemed to balance on the end of her nose, at the age of 57 she still kept herself active on what happened in and around the village.

KNOCK... KNOCK... KNOCK... she looked up at her clock on the mantle and smiled. She got out of her chair and walked to the door. She greeted Samuel and Maureen and ushered them into her living room. She walked into the kitchen and made the drinks and brought a tray with tea and biscuits into the living room.

'My dear, I believe that young Samuel has shown you the two newspaper clippings, I also hear you would like to know more.'

Maureen looked at Miss Horncastle and then Samuel. 'Well... the thing is... I am not sure where to start Miss Horncastle.'

Miss Horncastle laughed. 'You start at the beginning and you call me Naomi.'

Maureen smiled. 'Right Naomi... Samuel showed me the two newspaper clippings regarding the previous owners. I want to know if any of the gossip is true.'

Naomi rose out her chair and wandered to her book cabinet. Reaching up she removed two folders.

'These dear,' she paused as she wandered slowly back to her seat 'are the archives I have made on this town.'

Naomi passed then to Samuel who passed them onto Maureen.

Maureen opened the first file and flicked through, the folder was full of newspaper clippings from the town.

Maureen looked at Naomi. 'Is there anything about my house?'

Naomi looked up. 'The Whippletree property has stood on that ground for as long as I have known,' Naomi took a sip of her tea. 'I have lived in this village all my life and in all that time I have noticed two things. Your house lost its residents in a frightful way, and then that destructive fire.'

Maureen looked at Naomi 'Well did anyone find out what happened to the previous owners?'

Naomi got up again. 'The occupants were never found.' Naomi wandered back over to her book cabinet. She opened a drawer and removed three small notebooks.

Settling herself back in her chair she opened the books. 'These books are my own journals. I started them when I was historian of the village,' she chuckled 'no doubt young Samuel here has mentioned I am historian of the village.'

Maureen smiled 'He did mention.'

Naomi closed her eyes. 'Let me tell you a story. About twelve years ago I was fortunate to visit the owners of the Whippletree house. I knocked on that large door and Mr Hamilton answered the door. He was a gentle man, kind hearted and had time for everyone. I was a regular church goer and was trying to organise a sale at the church. Mr Hamilton invited me in and I had a long chat with both Mr and Mrs Hamilton. Mrs Hamilton was more than happy to help out, and Mr Hamilton said he would do what he could. I will never forget their generosity.'

Maureen watched Naomi.

'I spent the next two weeks organising the stalls around the village and was a frequent visitor to the house. Mrs Hamilton was good willed and helped with baking. Mr Hamilton helped in the churchyard.' Naomi paused. 'As the sale date got closer I had little time to visit, but on the off chance I would visit them, to keep them informed. I would sit in that big kitchen, but their demeanour changed slowly. I would catch them glancing at the cellar. Or... they would seem to be different.'

Maureen watched Naomi. Naomi's face dropped. 'I do not know what possessed me to travel to them one frightful night. The rain was lashing down, the wind howling. But...' she paused 'when I knocked on the door and Mrs Hamilton finally opened it, I noticed a change. Mrs Hamilton was shaking. I remember asking if everything was alright, but Mrs Hamilton stood rigid on the doorstep, neither moving nor speaking. I helped her into the kitchen and sat her down, made her a cup of tea. Mr Hamilton came up from the cellar locked the door and sat down. Neither spoke. Well naturally I made my goodbyes and left the house. People in town would see them over the coming weeks neither of them spoke or stopped. They seemed different.'

Naomi looked at Maureen. 'Now I do not know what happened to them, I refuse to speculate or make rash judgements against kind folk but... they were not the same people I had first met.'

Maureen put her cup down. 'So what happened afterwards Naomi?'

Naomi smiled 'I visited them, if I could help I would. Sometimes I used to sit with Mrs Hamilton, but her eyes seemed fixed on the cellar, and then she would look at me. I asked if she needed anything from down the cellar, she never spoke.'

It didn't take long for people to notice how they had changed, some say they became recluses, others considered them both mad. They only left the house once a week for groceries. Mrs Hamilton was found one night wandering along the road in her nightgown; Mr Hamilton would sit in the churchyard talking to the grave stones.'

Naomi stopped. 'You see rumours started,' Maureen nodded. 'I do not know where they went or where they vanished to, but I do know they spent time in that cellar.'

Maureen looked at Samuel. 'Do you remember me saying I had no key for the cellar?'

Samuel nodded.

Maureen looked at Samuel, and then to Naomi. 'The cellar door never opened since we moved in, we got a new door and Samuel kindly fitted it. I have put boxes down the cellar and well...'

Maureen paused briefly 'it is a small cellar with nothing else to talk about.'

Samuel sat quietly; he had fitted the door, and remembered all of them going down the steps to the cellar. It was cold but just a cellar. They had looked around but apart from walls had nothing else to see.

Pouring another cup of tea Naomi looked at them both. 'I can give you no more information about what I saw and what the neighbours said. After they vanished... people said they had gone mad and in a small town like this... gossip rules. After the disappearance I had the fortune of meeting the Hamilton's only living relative, Mr Hamilton's brother. He kept in contact for a few months. He couldn't quite get over the fact his brother and sister in law had just vanished. Not to mention the fire the house suffered from the storm. He was distraught when he visited, he was a wealthy man but the house was the only remnant of his family. He wanted it rebuilding. It took several years but I tell you, I know it is like the original house. He used to visit monthly to check on the progress and spent some time in the town. He used to pop into the museum and have a chat. He was like his brother kind hearted but hated to talk about his missing family. Once that house was completed he put it on the market, it sat empty for years until you and your husband purchased it.'

Maureen looked at Naomi. It had been a story and a half but the information left her none the wiser to understanding anything. 'Well thank you for your time Naomi and please feel free to pop in for tea one afternoon.'

Maureen and Samuel left the cottage and drove back to the house. Samuel could sense that Maureen felt frustrated that she had no more information about the previous couple.

Once they arrived back at the house Maureen asked Samuel in for a cup of tea. They entered the kitchen and sat, going over all the information they had gathered.

Maureen got up and unlocked the cellar door. 'Let us check for anything out of the normal.'

Samuel grabbed a spare torch and they slowly descended the steps.

Maureen reached the bottom first and shone the light from floor to ceiling looking for anything. Samuel walked round the corner 'How far does this go back?' he enquired. Maureen walked round and followed Samuel. 'Samuel I do not remember walking back this far last time we came down.' Samuel carried on walking till he reached the wall. He then started to walk back towards Maureen when he shone his torch to the ground.

'Maureen over here.' he shouted eagerly.

Maureen followed his voice and found Samuel kneeling on the floor, beneath him was a rusted doorway and a lock.

Samuel shone his torch on the lock; he tried to pull on the lock hoping to break it but with no avail.

Maureen shone her torch at the walls and ceilings. 'I suggest you stay for tea Samuel and then you and I can show Tony this.'

They made their way back up to the kitchen and into the light.

They closed and locked the cellar door.

In the darkness of the cellar a shadow glided silently towards where the trapdoor was. 'Soon you will be free' it whispered.

Chapter 14

Tony arrived home about seven o'clock. Maureen had been eager to tell him everything that had happened down the cellar but refrained till after they had had their tea. Samuel had been working in the garden for the remainder of the afternoon.

Maureen was an excellent cook, and after they had eaten, washed and packed away she ushered Tony into the lounge.

She explained what they had learnt from Miss Horncastle showing him the files and the booklets.

Tony flicked through them reading bits and pieces. Maureen glanced through one of the books, as Samuel read through another.

Once Tony had put the first file down Maureen broke the news of the trapdoor in the cellar.

Tony glanced 'We have both been down that cellar and neither of us found a trapdoor.'

Maureen smiled. 'I am fully aware of that,' she snapped. 'Samuel found it this afternoon.'

Tony stood up, 'Right let's have a look.'

Maureen unlocked the cellar door and armed with flashlights they walked down the cold dark steps of the cellar.

Once they reached the bottom Tony turned and walked towards where he had found the trapdoor. Tony and Maureen both followed in earnest.

Tony kneeled on the cold stone floor and shone his torch at the trapdoor and the padlock.

He shook his head; he had been down here yesterday, but he had to admit the wall seemed to go back father than the day before. Where on earth had this trapdoor appeared from?

He studied the padlock, it was golden in colour with no visible signs of rust, and in fact it seemed perfect. The padlock had no dust and as he shone the torch on it he saw no visible marks what-so-ever.

He looked at the end of the padlock and noticed that a key would open it. Maureen glanced down watching him all excited yet apprehensive at the same time. When they had first bought the property no one had mentioned how deep the cellar was, and it never showed up on any of the plans they had seen.

Maureen knelt beside her husband. 'What do you think is underneath?'

Tony scratched his head 'I only wish I knew.'

Samuel knelt down looking at the inert padlock. 'Well I did notice it needed a key, but I suppose it will need to be sawn off.'

Tony looked up. 'I am more concerned of how we have more wall space back here.'

Maureen looked at the trapdoor, shining her light around it.

"You will be but be unseen,
The past is here but in a dream,
Touch me once and you'll see all,
Treasures of the mind now hear my call"

Maureen looked from Tony to Samuel. 'I wonder what that all means?'

Tony shook his head in bewilderment.

Maureen looked at the padlock; she took the cellar key from her pocket and inserted it. Tony looked at her 'How on earth is that ever going to fit.'

Maureen turned the key and the padlock sprang open.

Tony took the padlock and the key. He made his way back through the cellar and into the kitchen. He looked at the padlock with the key inside. 'Maureen... Samuel... you better take a look...'

Maureen and Samuel came up the steps of the cellar and glanced at the padlock and key.

The key once a dull lifeless silvery grey colour had turned golden like the padlock. Tony took the key out. It slowly turned back to silvery grey.

Maureen gasped. 'What on earth!'

Samuel picked them both up and re-inserted the key. Slowly the key changed back to a golden hue. 'I have never seen anything like that in my life.'

Tony shook his head. 'This is preposterous, impossible.'

Grabbing the padlock and key he walked through to the lounge and grabbed a pen and sheet of paper. 'Let us look at that inscription again.'

They slowly made their way back down the cellar and looked at the trapdoor. Maureen shone her torch on the trapdoor and re read the inscription.

"You will be but be unseen,
The past is here but in a dream,
Touch me once and you'll see all,
Treasures of the mind now hear my call"

Tony scribbled it down on the paper.

He shone his torch at the ground looking at the trapdoor itself. The inscription was on the outside with a silver plating cover. He looked at the handle and pulled, nothing happened. Samuel bent beside him and slowly they managed to release the trapdoor.

They peered down into the darkness, their torches shining. Tony knelt on the ground and could see steps leading down father underneath the house.

He stood up, and slowly descended. The disturbed dust slowly bit at his throat 'there are steps but I cannot see how far down they go...' he shouted up.

Maureen slowly entered next with Samuel bringing up the rear. The steps went deep underneath, a wall either side of the steps guided them farther into the darkness.

Tony shone his light as they all made their way down, each step echoing on the cold stone ground. Tony saw a wall coming up as he reached the last step. He turned to the left and followed the steps down until he entered an atrium he could see a light emanating from an opening. Maureen soon joined him as did Samuel. They stood in silence, shining their torches across the walls.

Tony looked at Maureen. 'Well this is a shock!'

Maureen glanced around. Samuel stood behind them both and whistled. 'What is this place?'

They slowly edged towards the entrance where the light emanated.

Tony walked forward and entered the cavern, shining his torch at the floor and around. 'What in God's name is that?' Maureen and Samuel followed him as they made their way into the cavern. They moved cautiously the light beckoning them forward.

Tony glanced at the Silver orb. The orb floated above the pedestal, around the side of the pedestal was the same inscription that was on the trapdoor itself. Tony shone his torch at the inscription as he walked around the pedestal. The pedestal was golden in colour like the padlock; he touched the pedestal feeling its coolness.

Maureen broke the silence first. 'I do not know what is happening, but that...' she pointed at the pedestal and orb 'is not right.'

Tony put his arm around Maureen. 'Shall we go?'

Maureen nodded. Samuel shivered. They walked back across the cavern back to the steps. They climbed the steps and slowly entered the cellar. Tony lowered the trapdoor back down and locked it up. They climbed the steps to the kitchen and locked the door.

As the door locked the shadow drifted back towards the trapdoor. 'Now is the time master.' it whispered.

Chapter 15

(2011)

Tom, Mary and Marie were sat in the hotels bar/lounge, pouring over all the information. Mary sighed exasperated. 'Well I suppose one of us should make the call.'

She picked up the phone and dialled the number. She waited, hearing nothing but the ringing tone. Finally the phone was answered.

'Hello?' they answered.

Mary paused. 'Oh hello... I am Mary, am I speaking to Mr Henshaw?'

'Yes.' he replied. His voice sounded old.

'My husband and I bought the Whippletree property.'

Mary strained to listen. What seemed like minutes was only seconds but Samuel finally answered. 'Get out of that property.' with that he hung up.

Mary put the phone down and looked at Tom and then Marie.

'Well short and sweet, but told us to get out of the property and then hung up.'

Tom stood up. 'I suggest we visit him, we need answers, we have questions, and he knows something.'

Marie put her files together and put them in her laptop bag. 'I'll drive.' She said grinning

Tom pulled Mary to one side. 'Is it me, or is your sister enjoying this a little too much?'

Mary smiled 'Does a dog with a bone mean anything to you.'

'Come on you two.' shouted Marie.

They wandered outside and climbed in the car. Marie sped out of the car park. 'According to the information he lives not more than five minutes from where you live'. Marie said as she turned left into the village 'So should be easy to spot'.

They pulled up outside Samuel's house and looked around. Opening the creaky gate they paused at the front door. Tom knocked.

They heard shuffling as an elderly man opened the door. 'I'm sorry I am not buying.'

Mary smiled. 'That's good because were not selling. I'm Mary.'

Samuel's face dropped, 'I take it you have received my letters but failed to take heed of my warnings.'

He ushered them into the lounge.

Marie spoke 'Please Sir, we need information, we have questions and we think you're the only one who can help.'

Samuel sat down, he was 67 years old now and feeling it, 'I have helped you already. I told you to get out. No one listens to me.'

Marie pressed on regardless 'We know that something strange is happening inside the house. The cellar door, opens ajar on its own accord, which, and believe me I do not believe in ghosts.'

Samuel looked at Marie. 'I... cannot recall.' He stood up, 'but I do have dreams.'

They all sat intent, eager to learn more.

Samuel stood up; I keep the book by my bedside table. They heard Samuel shuffle up the stairs.

Tom looked at Marie, 'Pushy much, he looks like he is about to have a heart attack as it is.'

Marie smiled one of her annoying smiles. 'We need answers, he has them. For all we know he may have murdered them both. You also need to know about the tree.'

Tom nodded.

Samuel shuffled back in the living room. 'I keep this book by my bedside table. When I wake up I write as much down as I can remember. When the house was bought I asked around. The villagers told me where you were staying. It was only after my dreams that I was able to write information. That is why you got letters. I keep copies of all the letters I send.'

Marie took the notebook from Samuel and flicked through it. His writing may be slightly scrawled, but still legible. Marie noticed images. 'Do you mind if I borrow this?'

Samuel shook his head. 'I keep two books in my room.'

Marie smiled. 'I have just one more question for you, the tree outside the property.' She asked.

Samuel smiled 'OH the Whippletree or Dogwood tree as it is now called. I think I can guess your question. Yes I do remember the tree and I have always maintained it,' he paused as if remembering something, 'they would've wanted that.'

Marie looked at Samuel 'who would want that... the previous owners?'

Samuel just looked at them as if the question had never been asked.

Tom looked at Samuel. 'Did you also send a letter to my solicitor?'

Samuel looked at Tom 'I did young man,'

Tom nodded.

Marie thanked Samuel for the book and they all made their goodbyes.

Climbing into Marie's car, they glanced back at the house. 'Poor man,' said Mary, 'do you think he cannot remember due to age?'

Marie drove off back to the hotel. 'Not sure sis, but whatever has been happening, hopefully an answer will be in this notebook.'

After another wonderful meal at the hotel, they retired to Marie's room to pour over the book, to see what sense could be made from it all.

Marie read out extracts as Mary typed them on the laptop.

Tom got his camera out so they could photograph the images that Samuel had drawn. It was a long process, but by 11:30pm they had all the information down.

Marie placed the notebook back in her bag. 'I will drop this back to Samuel in the morning, but for now, I want sleep.'

They bade Marie good night and went next door to their room.

Mary popped the kettle on, she wanted to go through the notes again, and add the images from the camera.

Tom made the coffees, as Mary uploaded the images. After they had drunk their drinks, they decided enough was enough.

Tom put the letters he had in a safe place and Mary shut the laptop down. Turning off the light they soon fell asleep.

Tom moved down the steps of the cellar, he knew what he wanted and what he desired. His steadied himself against the damp cold wall. His torch shone a beam of light down to the bottom step.

He rounded the corner and edged further into the darkness. His torch shone a dim dusty beam of light on the floor as he approached the trapdoor.

Kneeling on the ground he pulled out the cellar key. He grabbed the padlock and inserted the key, the key rusty with age, slowly turned in the lock and turned a golden hue. Tom Smiled.

He removed the padlock and left it to one side. He looked at the inscription around the trapdoor. Slowly he managed to lift the lid of the trapdoor and slowly followed the steps leading under the trapdoor. His torch flickered and he steadied himself against the wall as he descended.

He finally reached the bottom step and shone the torch around as he entered the atrium.

He could see a faint light from an opening and walked forward, the cavern came into view. He entered the cavern and gazed around before his eyes settled on the pedestal and orb.

The silver orb, shone brightly, oblivious to time. The golden pedestal still looked magnificent as he edged closer to the orb itself.

He reached out with his hand.

'Touch it and join me Tom.'

Tom sat up in bed, bathed in sweat, breathing heavily. He rubbed his face and glanced at the clock. Five A.M.

He looked at Mary, she was sleeping soundly.

He slowly got out of bed and crept into the bathroom. He splashed water on his face. He looked at himself in the mirror. Turning off the light he climbed back in bed. Closing his eyes he drifted back to sleep.

Chapter 16

Mary yawned and looked at the clock it was 06:30am. She got out of bed and put the kettle on. She set two cups and looked at Tom. He slowly stirred and looked at Mary.

'Morning, want a brew?' she asked.

Tom smiled 'Love one.' He got out of bed and wandered into the bathroom. As he closed the door he glanced in the mirror. What was that dream all about last night? He grabbed a towel off the rack and decided to have a shower.

Mary poured over her notes on the laptop, looking for something, a lead to take them to the next step of this puzzle.

She finished her coffee and put the kettle on for her second. She looked at Tom's cup.

He shouldn't be that long having a shower surely?

She opened the bathroom door and heard the water running. 'Tom… Tom you ok in there?'

The water kept running but Tom never answered. She grabbed the shower curtain and turned off the shower. She screamed. She ran from the bathroom and out into the corridor, rushing to her sister's room she banged on the door. Marie wiped her eyes as she opened the door.

'Ring for an ambulance,' she cried.

Leaving her sister all confused Mary rushed back into the bathroom.

Tom laid in the bath. She grabbed his wrist feeling for a pulse. The pulse was there but weak.

She pressed her ear near to his mouth testing for breath. She sat up glad to know he was still breathing.

Marie rushed in the room. 'Ambulance is coming.'

Mary hugged her sister. Should we drag him out, get him dressed?'

Marie shook her head. 'Let the ambulance personnel deal with him.'

Marie got dressed quickly and rushed downstairs to inform Doris and her husband.

Doris sent her husband outside to wait for the ambulance.

'Now do not go worrying my dear, He is young and overworked with the house and everything. He probably slipped. Once they have him in the ambulance you come down, and have breakfast with your sister in the bar/lounge.'

Doris bustled off, and Mary rushed back upstairs.

Marie watched as Mary just stared at her husband. 'What happened?'

Mary turned. 'I have no idea, but whatever it is, it is connected to that damn house.'

Doris bustled upstairs. 'The ambulance men have arrived.'

Mary thanked Doris and rushed downstairs.

Fifteen minutes later the ambulance personnel had Tom out the bath and in the back of the ambulance.

Mary watched as they drove away. She slowly walked back in.

Doris ushered her into the bar/lounge. 'What did they say?'

Mary looked at her hands. 'They believe he must've slipped in the shower or just blacked out. They tried stimuli tests but none worked. They have taken him to the hospital and they can run some tests.'

Doris walked round and rubbed her shoulders, looking up Doris saw Marie. 'Here's your sister.'

After eating a slice of toast and having a cup of coffee, Mary felt a little better. Marie had tucked into her breakfast as if she hadn't eaten for a month.

Marie went back up to her room and fetched her jacket and car key. She walked into the bar/lounge. 'Let's get to the hospital.' She said softly.

Mary followed her sister outside and Marie drove to the hospital. Marie got out and walked with Mary towards the Hospital entrance.

The receptionist looked up at them both as they entered. 'Good Morning, how can I help?'

Mary smiled. 'Good Morning my husband was rushed here this morning.'

'What's his name?' the receptionist asked.

'Tom... Tom Plant.' Mary replied.

The receptionist typed feverishly at her keyboard.

'Ah yes,' she looked at Mary and Marie. 'He is on ward three. Go to the end of this corridor, up two flights of stairs and turn right.' The sister on the ward is Diane Kilpatrick.'

Mary and Marie thanked her and made their way up to ward three.

They entered ward three and walked to the desk.

One of the nurses looked up from the nurse's station. 'Good Morning, can I help?'

'My husband was brought in earlier. Tom Plant.'

The nurse checked her register. She stood up. 'Please follow me.'

Mary and Marie followed her into a small room. 'I will just fetch the sister.'

With that she closed the door and Mary and Marie sat. The door suddenly opened and Sister Diane Kilpatrick entered the room, a middle-aged lady with red hair, she sat down and looked from Mary to Marie.

'My name is Sister Kilpatrick,' she spoke with a strong Irish accent. 'May I ask which one of you is married to the young man?'

'I am,' replied Mary.

'I am Mary's sister.' spoke Marie.

'Well we have run some tests on your husband, and he has regained consciousness. He does not remember much of what happened. Can you fill in some of the blanks for us?'

Mary looked up. 'I was having my coffee and Tom had gone for a shower. I drank my coffee and noticed that Tom hadn't returned so I decided to check to see if he was okay. That is when I found him in the bath, with the shower running. I checked his pulse and felt his breath against my cheek, but he just didn't respond to anything else.' She said as she wiped a tear from her eye.

Diane looked at Mary. 'Well he doesn't even remember going for a shower, so at least we have more information to go on. He does remember his name and he has a lovely bump on his head. We will keep him in for observations for tonight.

'Can we go and see him?' enquired Mary.

'I suggest only one visitor for the moment, he is in bed 6.' replied Diane.

'I will wait here.' smiled Marie. Mary got up and left the room.

'Sister, can I ask. Any idea of why he collapsed in the first place?' asked Marie.

'Diane smiled. 'I wish I knew more, but I cannot divulge such information, patient confidentiality.'

Marie nodded and thanked Diane.

'If you'll excuse me,' Diane got up and left Marie in the room alone.

Mary entered the ward and found Tom sitting up in bed. He had a bandage round his head, but he smiled when he saw Mary.

'Thank Christ you're here,' he said with a smile 'they keep prodding and poking me.'

Mary laughed. 'Well I am just glad you are well, you gave me a fright.'

Tom touched her hand 'Apparently, Nurse Hitler says I have to stay in for observations. Any chance your sis can pull strings to get me out early?'

Mary kissed him on the cheek 'Do as the nurses say, and I will be back later.'

'Hopefully with a big steak and chips?' he enquired.

'Yeah good luck with that order,' Mary kissed him and left the ward. She found Marie in the corridor. 'How was he?' Marie asked

'He hasn't lost his humour, so I think he will be fine.' replied Mary.

They left the ward and walked back to reception, Marie felt relieved as they left and she drove back to the hotel.

Doris was at reception as Mary and Marie entered. 'How is Tom? Doris ushered them into the bar/lounge and sat down opposite.

'He is conscious but he doesn't remember too much of what happens, he doesn't even remember having a shower. So they are keeping him in for observations.'

'Well if you need anything my dears, just ask. I will go and fetch two cups of coffee for you both.'

Doris left the bar/lounge. Marie looked at Mary 'Well at least he is ok.'

'That is true, but I want to go back to the house. I have a niggling feeling that I just cannot explain.'

Marie looked at Mary. 'Well if you're going, so am I.'

Mary smiled 'I am so glad you are here.'

Doris walked in with two cups. 'If you need anything else, just ask.'

Mary thanked Doris and smiled. As soon as Doris had left the room she turned to Marie. 'After this drink, I want to go to the Library, and then onto the house.'

Marie smiled. 'What about Tom or letting Doris know?'

Mary shook her head. I want to look in the cellar and find out what is going on.'

Chapter 17

After stopping off at the library they then made a quick visit to the town hall. Mary wanted the plans of the house dating back to before the fire destroyed most of the property.
The clerk at the town hall wasn't very helpful, but, Marie used her position to get the plans drawn up quickly.
Mary and Marie left the town hall and drove back to the house. Still slightly daunted by the houses mysteriousness they knew that they needed to go in and find out what was happening.
Leaving the comfort of the car, they walked up the garden path to the door. Mary pulled out the keys and unlocked the door, pushing it open. She picked up the mail off the floor, and they both walked through into the kitchen.
Everything was still. Mary looked at the cellar door. She opened one of the draws and pulled out a door stop and two torches. They both checked the torches worked.
Unlocking the door Mary wedged the door stop under it tight.
They both slowly descended the steps, the cold biting at them as they reached the bottom. Mary shivered.
They turned and followed the wall along, Tom was right it did seem to go further than when they first visited. Mary stopped, her torch shining on a rusty looking padlock.
'I remember this from one of my dreams Marie, but I had no key.'
Marie shone her torch around the trapdoor. She brushed at the floor with her hand. 'Can you see some sort of inscription?'
Mary looked closer. 'We need a brush.'
Together they went back to the kitchen. Mary pulled open one of the cupboard doors and removed a dustpan and brush.
They both descended down again.
Mary swept around the trapdoor. Marie pulled out her mobile phone and turned on her camera. She took several photos of the trapdoor and the inscription.
Mary tugged at the padlock. She pulled out the set of keys and tried them all but none fit. Disgruntled she turned to Marie. 'Any plans?'
Marie looked at her sister. 'Well we never removed the cellar key from the door. It is the only key left, but otherwise we will need to break the lock.'
For the second time they both went back to the kitchen. Mary put the brush away and Marie removed the cellar door key.
They both descended. Mary took the key from Marie and inserted it into the padlock and turned the key.
They both watched in awe as the key and padlock both turned a golden hue and the padlock unlocked.
They both removed the padlock and key.
'I have no idea what is happening, but that...'
Marie looked at her sister. 'I have never seen anything like that either.'
Putting the padlock to one side they tried to lift the trapdoor. Mary tugged and heaved at it. Marie helped her. It was stuck solid.
Mary looked at Marie. 'Okay, what do you suggest?'
Marie smiled. 'I have one suggestion Sis. Let's go back up and take the padlock and key with us.'
Mary looked bemused.
'I think Tom would like to see what just happened.'
Taking the padlock and key they both left the cellar.
Marie locked the cellar door and they both left the house. Locking the front door they drove back to the hotel in silence.

Pulling up outside the hotel Mary looked at her clothes. 'Not too sure how we can explain our clothes, so I suggest we go and change and then look at that inscription on the phone.'
Marie concurred.

After a quick shower and change Mary knocked on Marie's door.
Marie opened the door and ushered Mary in.
'Okay, I suggest we also document everything that just happened,' suggested Marie.
Mary nodded in agreement.
After an hour of Marie documenting everything they both went down for dinner.
Doris bustled around them eager to find out if they had any more news about Tom. Mary was slightly ashamed that they had to lie to Doris and said he was making a fine recovery but was unable to know fully when he would be let out.
After another fabulous dinner the sisters adjourned to the bar/lounge and had a cup of tea in a relaxed atmosphere.
Mary knew that they should go back and see Tom and also knew that he would be angry yet excited at their find.
Sitting back in the chair she looked at Marie.
'I am not sure Tom seeing the padlock tonight would be a good idea, I do think he needs to get better before we show him.'
Marie laughed. 'Sis, he will be peeved with the pair of us for what we have done today.'
They were both laughing as Doris entered the bar/lounge. 'Nice to see you laughing my dear,'
Doris wandered behind the bar/lounge and collected a bucket of ice. 'Always someone...' she left the bar/lounge shaking her head.
Marie glanced at her watch. 'Well if you want to go to the hospital tonight, I can drive you in.'
Mary got up and stretched.
'Better not keep him waiting, he will be going crazy.' They both laughed and left the bar/lounge.

After a short drive they arrived at the hospital, making their way up to the ward. The nurse's station was empty when they arrived, but Mary showed Marie where Tom was.
Mary walked ahead and into the main ward. Tom sat in his bed and smiled when Mary came through. 'Get me out of here.' he pleaded.
Mary kissed him, 'Sorry but it is for your own good. So have they figured out what happened?'
Tom shook his head and then looked past Mary. Marie strolled in, smiling she pulled up a seat next to Mary and sat. 'Lovely to see you clothed.' she chuckled.
Tom blushed. 'Well I have had doctors and nurses, prodding me, poking me and taking blood.'
Mary glanced at his patient record sheet. 'Well your Blood Pressure is fine as is everything else as far as I can understand from this information.'
Tom glanced at them both. 'I have no idea what is happening but they seem to visit me more often than anyone else in this room.'
Marie looked at Tom 'Sounds odd...'
Mary looked around the ward, apart from Tom there were only two other patients.
'Well I am going to find a nurse, as I would like to know when I can take you home again.'
She kissed Tom on the forehead, and wandered out.
She wandered down the corridor without finding one nurse. She knocked on Sister Kilpatrick's door but there was no answer and the door was locked.
Mary continued her search checking the side wards yet still no sign of a nurse. Slightly annoyed she wandered back to the ward.
'Well no nurse's anywhere.' she said as she sat down in her seat.
Tom looked at his wife. 'Not to sound all psychic but, a nurse will be in here at this bed at 8p.m exactly.'

Mary and Marie both looked at Tom.

'I am serious. Check that form, it is every hour on the hour.'

Marie picked up the patient sheet and checked the details.

'Tom sometimes they put it at the hour, but they are sometimes a few minutes late.'

Tom shook his head as a nurse entered the room. She made a beeline for Tom's bed.

'Good evening Mr Plant just going to do your observations.'

Mary watched as she took Tom's blood pressure, and checked his pulse. She wrote the details on the patient record sheet.

'Excuse me Nurse.' Slightly shocked the nurse smiled at Mary 'When will my husband be allowed home?'

The nurse continued smiling. 'You will have to ask Sister Kilpatrick in the morning.' with that the nurse left the bed and the ward.

Tom looked at them both 'See I told you, and she never checks on any of the other patients in here.'

Mary looked at the clock. Ok listen we will go now, but we will be back at 9a.m to see Sister Kilpatrick.'

She gave Tom a kiss, and Marie smiled at Tom. 'Hang on in there,' and she winked.

Tom watched them both leave.

Mary and Marie left the ward. 'Sis, something odd is happening, and I intend to show you something else that is strange. Follow me.'

Marie followed Mary around the other wards, the side wards, and behind the nurse's station. Yet there was no nurse to be found.

They made their way outside and back to the car.

'I am not sure what is happening, but no nurses?'

Marie nodded in agreement. She suddenly stopped. 'You don't think it has anything to do with removing the padlock?'

Mary shook her head. 'I have no idea.'

Chapter 18

(1969)

It was a typical Monday morning, Maureen had done the washing made the bed, cleaned the house and was relaxing on the patio with a cup of tea.

Samuel was trimming the hedges and had made the garden look amazing. It had taken Maureen a week to convince Tony to let her have a chicken run, which now housed six Dorking Chickens. Since their arrival Maureen had collected several eggs. She also had all the feed she needed for the coming winter in a second shed.

Maureen closed her eyes. She had felt uneasy since they had discovered the trapdoor and the cavern, but none of them had talked about that day since.

The Dogwood tree was in full bloom, and Samuel had trimmed it to perfection.

'Samuel dear, I am sure that you could do with a cup of tea, I'll stick the kettle back on.'

Samuel waved his hand in acknowledgement, he grabbed the rake and started getting all the leaves up. Bagging it all up he made his way to the patio, removing his cap, he sat down.

Maureen wandered out with a tray and set it down.

'It is finally nice to have some sort of summer and lovely to have a wonderful view,' she said smiling 'and you have got that garden to perfection.'

Samuel chuckled. 'It has been a pleasure making this garden look perfect, and it is nice to see you got your way with those chickens.'

'Tony claims he can hear them day and night, I think it is all in his head, he has not been the same since I got them, slightly more irritable.' Maureen replied.

'He needs a holiday!' exclaimed Samuel. 'Why do you think I work part time gardening, and part time at the local library?'

Maureen nodded, I will have to drop some hints to him.'

After having their drinks Maureen went in, she need to plan the meal for tonight. Every time she entered the kitchen she glanced at the cellar door and shivered.

Tony had put the key somewhere safe and no one was allowed to enter. Maureen knew Tony had been short tempered since that fateful night, if only she could get him to talk about it.

Her line of thought was disrupted by a knock on the door. Wiping her hands on her apron she walked through to answer the door.

She opened the door to find Naomi Horncastle outside, smiling she invited her in.

Naomi looked around as she entered. 'Oh this does look how I remember it,' she followed Maureen into the kitchen. 'How can I help you Naomi?'

Naomi smiled, 'I only popped round to mention the fete that is happening in town this weekend, I was telling Mrs Castlethorpe who is running the event, said she hadn't invited you. Well. I was shocked, that needed to be rectified, so here I am to tell you.'

'That sounds like what we need. Tony has been working far too much lately; he will probably enjoy getting out and about.' Maureen said.

Naomi glanced at the cellar. 'I take it everything else is well, have you learnt anything more from my books?'

Maureen laughed, 'You don't beat around the bush, I have looked through them, made some notes, not that my husband is aware of this, Tony thinks it is all stuff and nonsense.' She said rolling her eyes upwards.

Naomi laughed and then pointed outside. 'Oh the garden looks wonderful, no need to guess whose handiwork that is. I recognise Samuels gardening skills anywhere.' Naomi waved to Samuel who waved back.

'Anyway Saturday, 2pm, Village Square, be wonderful to see you.'

Naomi stood up, and they walked to the door.

Samuel came in through the kitchen 'How was Naomi?' He asked. 'As sprightly as ever and mentioned a Village Fete...' Samuel put his hand across his mouth 'I apologise, I totally forgot about the fete on Saturday.'

Maureen touched his arm 'not a problem.'

The rest of the afternoon was spent cooking, Tony arrived home at six and Maureen had his meal ready.

Kissing Maureen on the cheek he sat down. 'More orders this week, been trying to get them all organised.'

Maureen looked at him. 'Naomi visited earlier she mentioned a fete at the weekend, we have both been invited.'

Tony looked across the table 'Sounds like fun.'

'I hope you're not working Saturday.'

Tony smiled, 'I am sure we can both go.'

Maureen smiled back.

The rest of the week passed without incident, Tony seemed to back to his old self, and Maureen had donated several eggs for the fete.

On Saturday morning they made their way to the town, Maureen and Tom always did the shopping together on a Saturday, and if anything else was needed then Maureen would fetch it during the week.

After visiting Mr Cawsthorpe at the Bakery, and Mr and Mrs Decker at the Butchers, they then brought the vegetables and other sundries from the grocers before driving past the village green.

Everything was being set up, the marquee was erected, and banners flew high. 'No idea what they're celebrating.' voiced Tony.

Maureen glanced at him 'It is the village fete, I did tell you about it at the beginning of the week,' she paused momentarily 'anyway, it is a time to get together and have fun.'

Tony snorted and they drove back to the house in silence.

After they packed away, Maureen set out the clothes that they would wear for the fete. She then rushed around in the kitchen organising a few sandwiches as she knew food and drink would be part of the festivities.

Just before two they locked up and drove the short distance into town. Parking the car in the church yard they crossed the road and walked the short distance to the village green.

Samuel was sat in the marquee eating sandwiches when Tony and Maureen entered. He was off his feet and quickly guided them out again. Tony looked aghast 'Samuel what is blazes is going on?' Samuel ushered them round the side. 'Everyone who is anyone is here today, just to forewarn you, they love meeting everyone in the village.'

'Samuel you know by now that they will gossip about us later,' said Maureen as Samuel blushed. 'We promise to be on our best behaviour.'

With that they all walked back into the marquee.

The fete was a complete success and the money raised was going towards the church which desperately needed a new roof. Tony and Maureen had met several of the locals who were interested in where they had come from, what they did for a living, and several invitations to lunches and coffee mornings.

By the time they left it had gone seven. Maureen yawned as they drove home. 'Not a bad turn out,' Tony nodded. 'How many coffee mornings did you get invited to? They only want the gossip.' Maureen laughed, 'I think they do these coffee mornings and visit each other on a regular basis, therefore at some point it will be my turn.' Tony groaned.

They eventually pulled up outside the Whippletree. Maureen unlocked the door and wandered in through to the kitchen. 'I'll make us a cuppa.'

Tony wandered into the big lounge and flopped down on the sofa. What a day he thought.

Maureen wandered in with the drinks and sat down. 'Well I don't know about you, but I am not even hungry,' Tony shook his head 'me neither.'

They had a lovely quiet night relaxing, but tiredness soon caught them up. It wasn't long before tiredness took over.

Slowly they made their way to bed and drifted off to sleep.

A cool breeze blew across the village, it was 3am and Tony couldn't sleep. He got out of bed quietly and wandered down the stairs. Opening the bureau draw he removed the cellar key and walked through into the kitchen, opening the door he descended into the dark abyss of the cellar. He knew his way so well. He almost smiled with joy. Reaching the trapdoor he removed the padlock and lifted the lid. He followed the steps down into the atrium almost eager to reach his destination. He finally entered the cavern and looked at the golden pedestal. The orb hung effortless in the air, just above the pedestal. His fingers edged closer towards the orb, he could almost feel it.

His fingers finally touched the orb and he stood frozen in time. He watched unable to talk, unable to move unable to do anything.

Cecil and Edna Hamilton were before him, he could see them so clearly as if he was in the cavern with them, he watched as they looked at the pedestal, pointing at the orb.

He opened his mouth to speak, but no words came out, Tony wasn't surprised by this, this wasn't his first visit to the cavern since its discovery.

Cecil and Edna walked around the cavern, Tony felt like he was walking with them, they looked at the walls, he saw some pictographs, he must remember what they were, it obviously was important. He closed his eyes and Edna and Cecil were back at the pedestal. Tony knew it would show him what he had already seen. He closed his eyes again and found himself in the cavern. He blinked his eyes. What am I doing down here he thought? He found the staircase and climbed up, back through the trapdoor and back into the cellar. Locking the trapdoor he returned to the kitchen and put the key back in the bureau which he then locked.

He rubbed his face. Tired he made his way back to bed, Maureen was still asleep. He climbed back in bed and fell fast asleep.

Down in the cellar the shadow glided towards the trapdoor. 'He is ours.' The shadow whispered. The shadow silently glided to the trapdoor and vanished deep inside.

Chapter 19

Maureen yawned and got out of bed, after a quick wash, she walked downstairs and made herself a cup of tea, cradling her cup she walked through to the lounge. She felt so relaxed especially after such a fun afternoon at the fete the day before. She heard creaks upstairs realising that Tony was awake she wandered back in the kitchen to make his breakfast.

Tony yawned and rubbed his eyes, he felt awful, all that tossing and turning, images in his head. He washed and walked down the stairs and into the kitchen. Maureen kissed him and poured his cup of tea.

'How did you sleep?' Maureen enquired.

Tony looked at her... he felt so tired... the images in his head... he couldn't concentrate fully. He stood up... blood rushing through his body, causing his anger to rise. He looked at Maureen. 'I slept well,' he slowly got up, watching... waiting. Maureen started to fry the eggs. Tony saw the bread knife and grabbed it, dropping his table knife in the process. Maureen turned and screamed. 'What... what are you...?' Tony lunged forward with the knife, the blade missing her, she turned and ran. Grabbing the knife Tony went after her.

Maureen rushed into the lounge pushing the sofa and other items against the door. Her breathing ragged. What on earth was wrong with him today? She pushed as she tried to move a dressing table. Tears running down her face, she pushed again at the dresser but it was no good.

Tony stood the other side of the door and tried the handle, the door opened an inch. He pushed at the door putting his weight behind it. The bitch he thought, she has pushed some furniture against it, he banged his fist on the door and stepped away. He wandered to the staircase and slowly climbed the stairs, he waited out of sight. The smile on his face said it all. I can wait.

Maureen waited, she needed to escape, the windows in this lounge had never opened, yet she knew that she had to leave by the main door. What had happened to Tony? What was making him act like this, had it been something she had done? It was no good she had to get out and get help. She started to move furniture as quietly as possible, it took a good ten minutes and she could smell burning, she knew she had left the eggs on and they were ruined. Too many thoughts running through her head, should she go for help or should she go to the kitchen? She slowly opened the door ajar, the smoke slowly drifted into the room, Maureen stepped out and ran into the kitchen, her heart pounding, she saw the burnt eggs in the pan and threw a cloth over it and turned off the gas. Grabbing another pan she slowly made her way towards the front door.

Tony had seen Maureen dash into the kitchen, he slowly walked back down the stairs and stood behind a wall. He smiled he could almost taste the joy of finally completing a job. He stood still. His heart racing, pounding, it felt like it was echoing around the house. He slowly brought his arm up holding the knife high. The footsteps were getting closer. Surely she would head for the main door, in an attempt to escape. He wanted to laugh, he knew she would go for the door, she was so predictable.

Maureen reached the edge of the hall. She could see her goal she needed to reach the door, holding the pan tight she edged forward. She had her keys in her pocket and wanted to run to the door.

She slowly stepped forward, her heart thumping, she was sure it would give her away. Her hand reached the wall. She put her hand round and took another step. Tony brought the knife down hard and fast. He could see the blood gushing as Maureen toppled to the ground the hot sticky blood on his hand as he dropped the knife. No... no... no... he screamed.

Tony sat up in bed drenched in sweat. He rubbed his face and looked at Maureen's side of the bed. She wasn't there.

He wandered into the bathroom splashing water on his face; he could still see Maureen's body on the floor in his mind. He rushed down the stairs and entered the kitchen.

Maureen was at the stove frying eggs, she smiled as Tony entered he rushed over to her and kissed her. He had never been so glad to see his wife. What was going on? Why had he dreamt of killing her?

He sat down and drank his tea, and then took a piece of toast. Maureen broke the silence by asking tony how many eggs he would like. Tony glanced at her 'Better make it two today.'

Maureen smiled and carried on frying the eggs. Reaching in the oven she pulled out a plate of bacon and placed it on the side. She finished Tony's eggs and then fried another egg for herself.

After a delicious breakfast Tony got up 'Suppose I better get ready for work.' he yawned and stretched. Maureen looked at him. 'You're not going anywhere,' replied Maureen 'it's Sunday.' Tony looked at his wife. Smiling he kissed her again. 'How about we go out for the day?'

'That sounds lovely.' Maureen replied.

It took neither of them long to get ready for a drive in the country, both laughing and joking, both of them having the time of their lives.

Back at the house the cellar door slowly creaked open.

Chapter 20

(2011)

The next morning Mary and Marie were in the hotels bar/lounge and were looking at all the photographs and collating the information from when they opened the cellar. Marie had placed the padlock and key in her room.

Mary yawned. 'I still think we should go back and put this padlock back on that trapdoor.'

Marie shook her head. 'This is significant I want to find out how a door key and an ancient padlock go together.'

Marie nodded in agreement. Let's go see Mr Patterson then.'

After a short drive into the village they parked in the churchyard. Mary got up looking at the magnificent church, the ivy climbing up the walls and the gravestones.

Mary and Marie walked through into town and down to the Library they entered and called out for Mr Patterson.

Mr Patterson came down the stairs and smiled when he saw Mary. 'What can I do for you today ladies?' he enquired.

'Well we need to go through some of the books again if possible.' She replied sheepishly.

Mr Patterson led them both into the archives and pulled down the folders. 'I'll stick the kettle on,' with that he walked out of the archives and out of sight.

They split the piles in two and decided to look for anything regarding the old town layout, and anything else that would be useful to them.

After an exhausting two hours they both wandered outside for a breather. They had found old plans of the town and even spent time looking around the library. Nothing had jumped out to either of them.

Mary just wanted one clue of where to look next. She opened the Library door and went to find Mr Patterson. 'Mr Patterson, can you tell us of any old shops that were around many years ago in the village but are no longer around now?

Mr Patterson scratched his head taking off his glasses he cleaned them. 'We used to have a hardware store, but that was taken over, and we had a haberdashery store where the Post Office is now.'

Marie looked at him. 'Did the Hardware store sell doors?'

Mr Patterson thought for a second 'Yes, it did, we had one for this library when the last door was damaged.'

Mary looked at him 'By any chance can we see the key?'

Mr Patterson looked at them both. 'I'll just go and fetch it.'

He returned with his set of keys and handed them his Library door key. Marie rummaged in her bag and pulled out the photo of the padlock and key. She placed the Library key against the photo and studied it.

'I am not saying it matches, but it looks identical,' she passed the key and the photo to Mary who also had a look. Mr Patterson also took a look. Taking off his glasses he went behind the counter and fetched a phonebook. 'I am no expert on keys but old Charlie in the village has been making keys in this area for years. He might be able to help I'll just give him a ring for you.'

Mr Patterson returned from his lengthy conversation with a piece of paper 'This is Charlie's address.'

Mary took the piece of paper 'Thank you.' She said.

Mr Patterson looked at the both. 'Now I suppose you will be rushing off to see old Charlie and leaving me with this to tidy up.'

Marie rushed around closing files and placing them in piles.

Mary's phone suddenly rang 'Hello Tom?' she paused and listened. 'Yes we can pick you up,' she listened some more. 'Were on our way.' she closed her mobile shut and looked at Marie 'Let's fetch Tom and get him back to the hotel.'

They bade Mr Patterson farewell and headed out of town towards the hospital. Mary looked agitated. 'You okay sis, it's... your looking worried...'

Mary lowered her head. 'Tom sounded distressed.'

Marie put her foot down on the accelerator 'Well let's go and get him out of that place.'

Mary held on tight as Marie swerved round corners, to get to the hospital.

She pulled up fast just before the front doors of the hospital. Mary got out and rushed inside, she ran past the clerk at the front desk up two flights of stairs and past the nurse's station to where Tom was lying. She stopped Tom wasn't in his bed.

She briskly walked to the nurse's station. She waited for over a minute for a nurse to appear exasperated she walked to Sister Kilpatrick's door and knocked on it.

Sister Kilpatrick opened the door and ushered Mary inside. Mary rounded on her 'Where is my husband?'

Sister Kilpatrick sat down and looked at Mary. 'Today your husband took a turn for the worse. I am sorry to say, he was ranting and raving, we have had to sedate him. He was talking about people who were not there, he was shouting at them not to touch it. He was frightening the other patients.'

Mary looked at her. 'I had a phone call from him not more than twenty minutes ago. He sounded agitated and distressed. Now take me to him.'

Sister Kilpatrick stood up and led Mary out the room. Marie rushed along the corridor and looked from Mary to Sister Kilpatrick.

Marie could see the anger in her sisters' face and followed Mary and Sister Kilpatrick. They walked down two corridors, up a flight of stairs and into another ward. Sister Kilpatrick spoke to the sister in charge of that ward and then motioned Mary and Marie forward.

'This is Sister Charlotte she will take you to your husband.'

Sister Charlotte was a short lady, and gently motioned Marie and Mary into a side room. 'I am sorry but they brought you husband up no more than ten minutes ago. He has been sedated and we are running tests.'

'What sort of tests?' asked Marie.

Sister Charlotte looked at Marie 'I suggest I let his wife see him first and then we can answer any questions.'

Mary looked up, tears welling in her eyes 'I... I want my sister with me.'

Marie stood up with Mary.

Sister Charlotte looked at Mary, she felt the pain she had known this sort of pain and anguish. 'I will let you both go in.' Marie smiled and thanked her.

Sister Charlotte led them out the side room and down the corridor. They reached another side room and Mary saw Tom lying in bed, he had monitors surrounding his bed and nurses checking his vitals.

The nurses looked up when Sister Charlotte entered the room. 'Sister?' she enquired.

Sister Charlotte smiled at the nurse. 'I am letting them both see him, we won't be long.'

The nurse finished taking her observations and left the room. Sister Charlotte moved to the door. 'I will be at the nurse's station when you are ready.'

Mary leant over Tom's body, tears dripping on his face as she wept 'You have got to come back to me, I need you,' Marie put her hand on Mary's shoulder she looked intently at the machines working around him. 'Sis, whatever has happened we will sort it out.'

Mary looked at her sister and then back at Tom, she squeezed his hand.

They both left his bed and walked to the Nurse's station. Sister Charlotte motioned them both to her office.

She motioned them to sit and explained what had happened to Tom. 'I believe he made a phone call to you, how did he sound?'

Mary looked up her eyes puffy and red. 'He sounded distressed which is why we rushed over here as fast as we could.'

Sister Charlotte nodded 'has anything like this happened in the past?'

Mary shook her head 'No.'

'What is actually wrong with him?' Marie asked

Sister Charlotte looked at Marie 'we think he may be suffering from delusions, has he been working hard lately, pushing himself?'

Marie shook her head 'I have known that man for a good five years, and in all that time he has never shown any sign of breaking up or going mad or whatever in hell you want to call it. I know Tom is not a mental case.'

Sister Charlotte looked at them both. 'The tests we are running will give us more information in the morning.'

Mary looked up at her 'Well I am not sure if this will be of any relevance in your tests, but when we visited him last, he was saying that one nurse would check his vitals every hour on the hour, but no one else's then we looked for a nurse before we left and couldn't find any.'

Sister Charlotte made a note in her book. 'Which night was this?'

Marie looked at Mary 'It was two nights ago.'

Mary nodded. Sister Charlotte looked at them both 'Did you see this nurse?

Mary closed her eyes thinking. 'We did, she did his vital at'... she paused biting her lip, struggling to remember at what time, 'roughly seven or eight.'

Sister Charlotte made this note. 'I will let you know if there is any change. You are staying with Mr and Mrs Chambers correct?

Mary nodded.

Sister Charlotte smiled. 'I will ring you in the morning.'

They all stood up, and Mary and Marie thanked Sister Charlotte. Slowly they walked the corridors and down the stairs.

Mary paused 'Let's visit Sister Kilpatrick, she can tell us what happened before he was taken to that ward.' Marie followed her sister to Sister Kilpatrick's office. Mary Knocked and waited.

Sister Kilpatrick opened the door and asked them to enter. She sat down behind her desk.

Mary closed her eyes a second gathering her thoughts and calming herself down. 'Sister can you tell us what Tom was saying again.'

Sister Kilpatrick looked at them both. 'I had taken his vitals, he has been quite the patient, and I had told him that he could be released.' Mary and Marie listened intently. 'I told him to ring you, so he could be picked up.' Sister Kilpatrick paused for a second 'I then checked my rounds and suddenly I could hear screams. I ran back in the ward and he was screaming and shouting.'

Marie stopped her 'What exactly was he screaming?'

Sister Kilpatrick looked at Marie 'He screamed "Don't touch it, keep away from the orb", he kept shouting at two people, but I know no one was in ward except the other patients, who are all bedridden.'

Marie made notes and they both thanked her. Mary lowered her head, 'I apologise I shouldn't have started on you earlier.'

Sister Kilpatrick smiled, 'Water under the bridge.'

Mary and Marie made their way back across the car park, and to the car. Mary looked at her sister 'Whatever has happened to Tom I am sure it is because he was trapped in that damn cellar.'

She opened the passenger door and slammed it shut. Marie got in the car, she started the engine. 'We will go back to the hotel and tell Doris what has happened, we will then see Charlie and then we will visit Samuel.'

Chapter 21

Marie drove back to the hotel where Mr Chambers was behind his desk filling out booking forms, he smiled as they entered the lobby.

'How's your husband? He enquired

Mary feigned a smile 'He has taken a turn for the worse Mr Chambers.'

Mr Chambers lowered his head 'I am so sorry to hear that news let me find my wife,' with that he wandered off towards the kitchen.

Mrs Chambers bustled into the lobby, slightly out of breath. 'My husband... he just told me...' the sentence hung in mid-air as she looked from Mary to Marie.

'He's in...' Mary finally broke down in tears, Marie led her into the bar/lounge and Mrs Chambers followed.

Marie sat Mary down 'Tom is going to get better.'

Mary stifled a laugh 'It's my fault,' wiping her eyes she glanced at her sister, Marie took her hand. 'What is that supposed to mean?'

Mary took a deep breath 'I am the one who saw the property advertised in the first place. I am the one who talked Tom round into buying it. If I hadn't talked him round he would be with me right now.'

Marie turned 'What happened to that steadfast sister I once had, who had no fear. Where has she gone, I have always looked up to you.'

Mary wiped her eyes.

Marie turned to Mrs Chambers. 'Can you ring this number please,' she wrote a number on a napkin 'when you get through tell them that Marie requests information on the history of this town. If they give you any problems just call me through.'

Mrs Chambers wandered back through to the lobby.

Marie sat with her sister in peace.

Twenty minutes passed before Mrs Chambers came back into the bar/lounge. 'What a lovely polite gentleman I spoke to Marie,' she gave a slight chuckle 'He says the information you require will be collated and sent to you by courier.'

Marie smiled 'Thomas is one of our historians at the University he loves looking up details and has always been kind enough to do favours for me. When this information arrives will you kindly place it somewhere safe Mrs C.'

Mrs Chambers smiled 'Of course my dear.'

Marie stood up 'Now I am going to get changed and have a shower, and then were going to get some answers to some questions.'

Mrs Chambers looked from Marie to Mary then shook her head and left the bar/lounge.

Mary just sat at the table in a trance like state.

Marie came down the stairs half an hour later wearing blue jeans, a long sleeved slightly cropped black top and her hiking boots. She slung her backpack on her shoulder and wandered into the bar/lounge, touching her sister on the arm she slowly led Mary outside and back to the car.

Marie knew where she wanted to go first, she was determined to see what all these keys had in common and who the maker was, and (if it was possible) speak to the original maker.

All these thoughts wandered through her head as they drove through the village.

Charlie McCormack lay dozing in his chair at the age of 76 he deserved to relax when he needed. He had had a busy life with owning his own business and when the time had come he had sold the business and retired to a cottage in the town he had been brought up in.

Hearing a knock on the door he slowly got up, he hobbled to the door with the aid of a walking stick and opened the door keeping the chain on.

'Can I help you ladies?' he enquired

Marie smiled, 'I believe Mr Patterson rang you, we have come to ask you about the keys you made.'

Charlie smiled 'Yes he did.' he removed the chain and let them both in.

Charlie led them into his sitting room. 'I do not get many visitors let alone people asking about keys.' he chuckled.

Marie reached into her bag and pulled out the cellar key. 'I need to know if you made this key.'

Charlie reached over and took the key from Marie, turning it over, studying it.

'This is one of my keys, albeit in a dreadful state, where did you find it?'

Mary glanced over 'My Niece and Nephew found it in the well at our property, the Whippletree on the outskirts of the village.'

Charlie put the key down. 'You bought the property?'

Marie sat up 'Listen if you know anything about that house, we would really appreciate knowing.'

Charlie looked from Mary to Marie.

'It is not what I know that matters about the property, but what I know about the past that matters.' he slowly got back up.

Marie glanced as Charlie got up 'We need your help, whatever is happening has something to do with that key.'

Charlie laughed 'Young lady, a key is nothing more than an access portal for another room, just like your keys start your car.'

He passed the key back. 'I did make that key, and I have made keys for the village...'

Marie stood up 'Then explain how the library door key is identical to this!'

Charlie smiled. 'I suggest you both follow me.'

Charlie led them outside and down to his garden shed; he unlocked the shed door and led them both in. Keys hung from hooks and Charlie pulled several down caressing them before returning them to the hook. 'This is what is left of the keys to the village, just like when you need a spare key you go and get one cut.'

Marie glanced around, and felt like this was getting her nowhere.

'You said inside that what you know doesn't matter, but the past did...'

Charlie smiled. 'Very astute, the past is very important, we learn from the past to perfect our future.'

Mary looked around 'This doesn't explain why the key to my cellar is still identical to the key in the library'

Charlie looked at Marie 'I worked at the old hardware store, making the locks for the doors, there were times when we made locks the same.'

Marie nodded 'I can understand that, but this key is different...'

'In what way,' Charlie retorted.

'In the way it opens not only a cellar door but another door in the cellar itself.' replied Marie candidly.

'I see...' Charlie rubbed his chin. He locked the shed door and started back towards the house.

Mary looked at Marie 'This is getting us nowhere.'

Marie nodded and walked down the garden path followed by Mary.

Mary and Marie thanked Charlie for seeing them and they bade their farewells.

Charlie locked the door behind them. Picking up the phone he dialled a number.

He waited listening to the ringing tone 'It's me; they have been asking questions about the key.'

Charlie listened nodding his head. 'I think they will be visiting you soon.'

Making his goodbyes, Charlie went back into the living room; he looked at the books on his shelf.

He pulled one down, opening it up he searched for a page. He looked at the title on the aged newspaper clipping stored inside the book.

Strange Goings On: Couple Never Found.

Reading the passage he closed the book and replaced it back on the shelf.
Wandering slowly to the window he glanced out.

Chapter 22

(1969)

It was Monday, and Maureen had just kissed her husband goodbye and watched him drive off to work. She smiled as she closed the door and walked into the study.
She busied herself tidying and cleaning with the radio on.
With the housework out the way and the washing hanging on the line she made herself a drink and sat in the garden.
The Dorking Chickens were running around in the chicken coop, closing her eyes she listened as the wind blew across the garden. Life had never felt so good.
She got up and fed the chickens and collected 5 eggs. Continuing down the garden she reached the fence and glanced at the bubbling stream as it trickled slowly. She slowly made her way back up the garden and into the house placing the eggs in the bowl.
She glanced at the cellar, almost tempted to see the trapdoor, but knowing that she needed to go to the shops she grabbed her coat and locked up.
Ten minutes later and Maureen reached the church; she waved at the Reverend and walked across the green.
Naomi walked out of the butchers and saw Maureen.
'Mrs Farley... Mrs Farley...' she called.
Maureen waved and walked to Naomi.
'Morning Miss Horncastle, glorious day today.'
Naomi touched Maureen's arm 'enough of the Miss Horncastle dear it's Naomi.'
Maureen blushed slightly. 'Sorry Naomi, my mind has been occupied today, such glorious weather.'
Naomi chuckled 'How have you both been?'
Maureen mentioned that they had been out of the village just yesterday, and that Tony seemed so healthy and more alive when he wasn't working too hard.
Naomi laughed 'Don't all men.'
Mr Barstow stood looking out of his hardware store window. Maureen waved and he moved away.
Naomi turned, 'Was Mr Barstow looking out that damn window again!'
Maureen nodded
'He is worse than any woman for news or gossip.'
They both laughed.
Naomi noticed Charlie walking across the green, 'Excuse me Maureen, I want a word with Charlie.'
'Charlie you rogue,' Charlie whirled round and almost groaned when he saw Naomi striding towards him.
'What can I do for you?'
'The lock in the Library is stuck again, can you be a dear and pop in and fix it.'

Charlie tipped his hat 'Pop in later.'
Naomi made her way to the library.

Maureen started to walk back home, laden with her shopping bags, the sun shone brightly making the walk back even more enjoyable, the slight breeze gently wafted the trees.
Maureen let her mind wander, the joys of yesterday. Tony had been such fun almost like a teenager again. Chuckling to herself she walked past the fields and into the garden.
Unlocking the door she stooped down and picked up the mail, she set her bags down and closed the door; making her way through to the kitchen she set the bags on the table.
As she unpacked she noticed the cellar door was ajar. Strange she thought I am certain it was locked earlier? Maureen opened the cellar door and peered into the darkness. Closing the door she shook her head. As she packed the shopping away her mind kept thinking about what they had discovered. What was that inscription all about? What or who had put that shining orb under the house? What did it all mean? Chastising herself she finished off putting the shopping away.
As she glanced out the kitchen window the cellar door slowly creaked open. Maureen spun in surprise, 'who... who is there?' she stammered.
Grabbing the torch from the shelf she edged towards the cellar. Tentatively she peered down the steps, shining her torch around, hearing and seeing nothing she shivered. Maureen walked into the lounge and unlocked the bureau; she found the cellar key and walked back into the kitchen and towards the cellar. She slowly edged her way down the steps, feeling the cold clammy wall on her hand as she descended.
Her breathing was ragged as she slowly descended, the light from the torch shone around, each step quickened her heartbeat as she finally reached the last step and stood at the bottom of the cellar.
She looked up at the flight of stairs and shivered.
Slowly and cautiously she edged her way round and followed the dank dark walls, shining her torch around, turning occasionally, she looked at the trap door and its inscription.
Kneeling she reached in her pocket for the key. The key shone, eager to be reunited with the lock and Maureen slowly inserted the key and removed the padlock. The padlock turned a golden hue. Lifting the trapdoor she slowly descended into the cavern. Her heart beat faster. She slowly descended knowing the cavern was just beyond the atrium, reaching the opening she turned and glanced around the cavern.
She stood transfixed before she turned to the pedestal and the orb which shone brightly, hovering above the pedestal.
'What... what are you?' she asked her voice quivering.
The room was silent. Maureen chastised herself for asking a question to an object.
She felt transfixed by the orb, but, she knew she shouldn't be down here. No one had been down here since they had discovered the cavern.
Maureen turned; she knew she had to get out. Turning once more she looked at the orb.
Fighting an inner conflict she felt compelled to know what was going on. She slowly moved back towards the orb her fingers slowly reached out. The orb was beautiful. Her fingers neared the orb.
Maureen watched as she saw another couple in the cave. She shouted out to them, yet neither of them looked in her direction. She felt like she was in the wall unable to move yet transfixed as the couple reached the orb. She yelled at them 'Do not touch it...' yet they were unable to hear her.
She watched in horror as the couple touched the orb and watched them fall to the ground.

Unable to move Maureen shouted again. She watched a shadow move slowly towards the couple and envelope them. Maureen closed her eyes blinking.

Maureen glanced around the cavern. What am I doing down here she thought. The orb still glowed and hovered above the pedestal. Her torch was on the floor, picking it up she ran out the cavern and made her way up the steps.

She closed the trapdoor and locked it, the key turned back to its dull lifeless colour. Maureen ran up the steps and reached the safety of the kitchen. She locked the cellar door and ran in the back garden.

Deep in the cellar the shadow reached the trapdoor and disappeared through it, it slowly descended the steps and entered the cavern.

'She is yours master.'

Chapter 23

When Tony arrived home from work he found Maureen in the kitchen, he could smell the chicken in the oven, he kissed her and she smiled. Placing his cup of tea on the table he started on about his day at work.

'More contracts to sort through tomorrow...'

Maureen half listened, she was still feeling confused of why she had been in the cavern, let alone worrying about her husband's day.

'If this keeps up I may have to work at the weekend.' Tony mentioned. He rustled his newspaper.

Maureen opened the ovens door and checked the chicken. The potatoes were boiling and the veg was almost ready too.

'What is good for business will be good for all...' he lowered his newspaper and glanced at his wife.

'Feeling under the weather? Tony enquired

Maureen turned half smiling. 'Sorry, yes I do feel slightly groggy.' she sat at the table and watched as he drank his tea.

Tony became more engrossed in the newspaper and Maureen slowly got up, she set both plates out and dished up.

Tony smiled as he ate, they then washed up.

Maureen half listened to the radio as they sat in the living room after they had finished in the kitchen and Tony never wanted to pressure her into talking about it.

The evening seemed to drag on but finally they both decided to go to bed.

Tony checked the doors before he headed up.

Tony kissed Maureen goodnight and rolled over to sleep.

Maureen stared at the shadows cast on the ceiling and sighed. Why didn't I mention anything to my husband when he asked?

What on earth was I doing down their?

The questions went round and round in her head.

Finally she drifted off to sleep.

Tony was standing in the kitchen, he walked to his bureau opened the draw and removed the cellar key. Unlocking the door he stood at the top of the stairs, he turned on his torch and shone the beam down.

Maureen crept up behind him with a wild look in her eyes; she lunged pushing Tony in the back, losing his footing Tony fell down to the bottom of the cellar cracking his head on the stone floor. Maureen crept down the steps looking at her poor husband, 'you poor pathetic man.' she said. She looked around, her eyes adjusting to the darkness. She walked to the boxes which were lying around the cellar and opened one.

Pulling out the rope she knelt by her husband, slowly she wrapped it round his neck. A small pool of blood started to form from his head.

Maureen smiled and grasped the rope in both hands and pulled hard. The rope tightened around his neck. Maureen kept pulling, harder and harder.

Maureen sat bolt upright in bed, bathed in sweat. She turned and looked at her husband, snoring away. She slowly got out of bed and splashed water on her face.

Looking in the mirror she sought some explanation from her reflection. Nothing came to mind.

Just a dream she thought, just a dream.

Climbing back into bed she slowly drifted back to sleep.

Maureen was up at first light and started to organise the breakfast. Tony came down dressed in his suit. Kissing him she made their breakfast and then kissed him again when he left the house. Once he had driven off she picked up the phone. She waited impatiently listening.

'Hello Naomi...' she started to sob.

'Maureen what on earth is wrong?'

'Please I need to speak to you...' she said as tears started to fall.

'I will come straight over,' replied Naomi.

'No... no I will come to yours.'

'Come straight over.' Naomi said in her calm way.

Maureen put the phone down and put on her coat and left the house.

Naomi put her phone down and finished off her breakfast. Whatever has happened she thought, Maureen had been in such high spirits only yesterday.

Naomi glanced out the window seeing Samuel walk past. Running to the door she called him over.

'Samuel I have just had a distressed phone call from Maureen,' she stated in a matter of fact way. 'I suggest you come in, as she may need moral support.'

Samuel followed Naomi inside and sat at the kitchen table. 'What happened?' he enquired.

Naomi shook her head. 'I wish I knew.'

Twenty minutes later Maureen knocked on Naomi's door.

Naomi ushered her into the kitchen. She could clearly see that Maureen was in distress.

Samuel stood up.

'I have just made a fresh pot and then you can tell us what has happened.'

Maureen sat at the table, glancing outside at the lawn and peonies.

'Last night I had a dream that I killed Tony...'

The sentence hung as Naomi looked at Samuel.

Naomi reached out and put her hand on Maureen's 'Come... come that is nothing more than stuff and nonsense and in a dream.'

Maureen looked at Naomi. 'You fail to see the point, both of you do. It felt... felt...felt so... real.'

Naomi patted Maureen's hand, 'let me make this drink.'

Samuel looked at Maureen 'What do you mean it felt so real?'

Maureen looked back out the window. 'I mean I killed him, I took the rope and wrapped it round his neck....'

Naomi looked aghast 'oh my stars.'

Naomi placed the tray on the table and poured three teas.

Maureen took a sip. 'I saw my husband standing in the cellar doorway and pushed him down the steps and then took a rope from one of the boxes and then strangled him.' Maureen paused 'it... felt so real.'

Naomi patted her hand 'and did you see your husband this morning?'

Maureen nodded.

'Did you send him off to work?'

Maureen nodded again.

'Then he is well and you had nothing more than a nightmare.'

Maureen exhaled. 'It was the reality of the dream; I knew he had to die.'

'Have you ever experienced anything like this before?' Samuel asked.

Maureen shook her head.

'I... have another confession.' She looked at Samuel. 'I found myself yesterday in the cavern.'

Samuel pushed his chair back making it scrape across the floor.

'How on earth.... Maureen how... we all said we wouldn't venture...'

Maureen nodded hanging her head low. Naomi looked from Samuel to Maureen.

'What are you both on about?'

Samuel looked at Naomi 'You remember I mentioned the trap door in the cellar.'

Naomi nodded vaguely remembering.

'We opened the trapdoor and it led to a large cavern with a pedestal and a floating orb.'

Naomi stifled a laugh 'That sound preposterous.'

Maureen looked at Naomi 'Yet it exists under the cellar.'

Naomi stood up. She felt excitement and nervous at the same time.

'I want to see this with my own eyes. I trust you both, but you have to see it from my point of view. How on earth can a cavern exist under the house?'

She grabbed her coat.

Samuel stood up as did Maureen.

'This is not to be talked around the village.' warned Samuel.

Naomi nodded. 'I can understand that' she said 'but.... I just have to see.'

Maureen looked at Samuel.

They walked back to the house, with Naomi asking questions about the cavern and the trapdoor.

Maureen felt her pulse quicken. She didn't want to go back down but at least she wouldn't be alone.

Maureen unlocked the door, the house felt colder; she walked into the living room and removed the key from the bureau.

Naomi and Samuel followed Maureen into the kitchen. Tentatively she unlocked the cellar door.

Samuel grabbed two torches from the side and passed one to Maureen.

Maureen turned on the light using the wall she steadied herself as she took each step down into the cellar. Naomi followed next and Samuel walked down last.

Maureen shone her torch round the corner. Naomi glanced around, shocked by the size of the cellar. 'How far does this go back?' she enquired.

Samuel laughed 'it seems bigger than it was, it never went this far back when we first came down here.'

Naomi looked bemused 'bigger, how is that possible?'

Maureen snorted. 'Nothing in this cellar is normal.'

Maureen walked farther into the darkness of the cellar, Maureen followed close by. Maureen paused and shone the light at the floor. The trapdoor and padlock came slowly into view. Naomi looked stunned as Maureen shone the torch at the ground.

Samuel shone his torch at the inscription.

Naomi peered at the inscription; slowly she read it out loud.

"You will be but be unseen,
The past is here but in a dream,
Touch me once and you'll see all,
Treasures of the mind now hear my call"

'What the blazes does that mean? Naomi shook her head.

Samuel looked at the trapdoor. Maureen knelt down and placed her torch on the floor. Removing the key she could almost feel the key longing to be reunited with the lock.

Inserting the key into the padlock they turned a golden hue colour.

Naomi took two steps back. 'What the blazes was that?'

Maureen and Samuel both looked at Naomi. 'Imagine our shock and confusion when that happened the first time...' Maureen mumbled.

Naomi looked shocked.

Samuel put his torch down and slowly lifted the trapdoor. Picking up his torch he descended through the trapdoor and started down the steps which led to the cavern.

Naomi entered next; taking everything in, none of this is possible she kept thinking to herself.

Maureen entered last, knowing that they shouldn't be descending back into the cavern.

Chapter 24

(2011)

Samuel had just put the phone down, why oh why didn't they listen? He pondered. The house, that house! He walked outside into his garden.

If only they had never discovered that chamber under the cellar.

He knew they would return. He also knew that Tom was in Hospital.

He stormed inside slamming the door, strode into his lounge and looked at the library of books he had.

Studying them, he reached up and removed one. He flicked through the pages and found the newspaper cuttings.

Strange Goings On: Couple Never Found.

Today an inquest into the disappearance of Cecil and Edna Hamilton was finally ended and the property will go to the estate of Cecil's Brother Reginald.

Cecil and Edna hadn't contacted their brother in over a month and Reginald decided to pay them a visit.

After arriving at the house he found the house in perfect order, but with no sign of his brother or sister in law.

Concerned he contacted the local police.

After a thorough investigation and with nothing missing the police were baffled.

It is only guessed upon that they visited the lake at the end of the garden and vanished.

The lake was drained and no bodies found, the well was also checked.

The whereabouts of Cecil and Edna Hamilton remains a mystery to this day.

The house on the outskirts of town will, according to Reginald, be sold.

Fire Destroys House.

On Thursday last a terrible storm broke out. Lightning struck the top most part of the Whippletree property and started a fire of such intenseness that the property was severely damaged.

The owner one Reginald Hamilton was informed.

The property had belonged to his Brother and Sister in law who both vanished.

Mr Hamilton claimed that this house is to be restored to its former state and sold.

Asked upon whether he had heard from his Brother or sister in law, he commented that neither had been seen since he heard the tragic news.

Couple Found Dead.

Tony and Maureen Farley were discovered dead in their house. Their bodies were discovered by Samuel Henshaw who was a close friend of the family.

Mr and Mrs Farley had spent some considerable time away from the property, and had only returned the week previous.

It is believed that Mr and Mrs Farley died from old age, as both were found sitting in the living room.

Samuel Henshaw spoke about the loss of his two dear friends. 'Tony and Maureen will be sorely missed around the village.'

A post Mortem on Mr and Mrs Farley will be carried out later this month.

Where the couple had been is unknown.

The couple had no children and no family.

Funeral will be Monday at 2pm.

Samuel placed the cuttings on the table. He alone knew the truth. At that moment the doorbell rang. Startled Samuel glanced out the window.

Yes he thought... they want more answers.

He made his way to the hallway and opened the door.

'You better come in,' he said as he led them both to the living room.

Mary and Marie followed Samuel through.

'So was your conversation with Charlie fruitful?' Samuel enquired.

Marie looked at Samuel. 'He is an enigma...'

Samuel chuckled. 'That is one way of putting it,' Samuel sat in the chair 'just heed his words.'

Mary glanced at the table noticing the newspaper clippings.

Samuel looked at Mary 'So any news on your husband?

Mary shook her head 'he is in a coma Samuel and only time will tell if he recovers.'

Marie reached in her bag, 'Your books.'

Samuel took the books back thanking Marie 'were they of any use?'

Marie nodded 'oh yes they were, but with Tom in hospital we haven't had chance to get all the information sorted.'

Mary kept reading the newspaper clipping on the table.

Samuel looked at Mary 'I suggest picking it up, you can read them better.'

Mary reached over and read the clipping; she looked at Samuel 'So you found the previous owners?'

Samuel nodded.

'But...'

Samuel looked at Mary 'but I know more than that.'

Mary lowered her head.

Marie reached in her bag.

She pulled out the cellar key and the padlock.

Samuel looked at Marie. 'What are you doing with those?'

Marie ignored him and inserted the rusted key into the padlock.

The key and padlock turned a golden hue.

Samuel looked aghast. 'What have you done, I warned you, no...no...no.'

Marie removed the key, 'So you have seen that happen before?'

Samuel looked down and nodded.

Marie carried on relentless 'Did the previous owners?'

Samuel nodded again.

Marie felt satisfaction coursing through her. She picked up the newspaper clipping. Laughing she put it back on the table.

'Not sure about natural occurrences, but I think what is under that trap door is the key to all of the mysteries surrounding the house.'

Samuel stood up.

'I have one last book for you.' He pulled down a small book; 'This book contains information on what happened one fateful day.' He passed the book to Marie. 'If I may suggest, look at the books first. One last request put the lock back on the trap door.'

Mary looked at Samuel. 'Okay we will.'

Samuel ushered them both to the hallway. 'One day I might be able to live with what has happened in this village.'

He closed the door.

Samuel watched as Mary and Marie got in the car and drove off.

Marie was elated as she drove 'did you see his face... obviously been talking to Charlie...'

Mary seemed pensive, going back to the house, filled her with dread.

Marie knew Mary was preoccupied, with her husband in hospital, the house being different to say the least, but Mary was strong and would come through this.

Five minutes later they pulled up outside the house.

Mary glanced out the window. Our dream home... she thought. The house looked different to Mary, so much had obviously happened that it had lost appeal in her eyes.

Knowing she had to face this house gave her some strength, and with her sister she was a rock.

Mary turned to Marie. 'We go in, we put the padlock back, and then we leave.'

Marie nodded.

They both got out the car; Mary pulled out her keys and unlocked the door. Picking up the post she placed several letters in her bag.

Removing the keys they made their way through to the kitchen. Marie unlocked the cellar door and opened it, wedging the door open.

Mary grabbed two torches, ensuring they worked they slowly made their way down into the cellar.

Mary could feel her heart quickening as she moved down the steps. Fear enveloped her. She just wanted to run.

Marie placed her hand on Mary's shoulder. Mary jumped. 'Come on sis, let's just do this and get out.'

Mary nodded, chastising herself for being scared.

They cautiously made their way round the corner. They shone their torches into the darkness of the cellar. Marie reached the trapdoor. She felt exhilarated and nervous. Pulling the padlock out of her bag she locked it in place.

Mary and Marie turned and hastily made their way out of the cellar and back into the kitchen.

Mary removed the wedge and closed the cellar door and using the key she locked it.

Marie returned the torches to the sideboard and they both walked back through to the hall.

Opening the front door they both left the house. Mary locked the door and walked with Marie to the car.

Sitting in the passenger seat she exhaled.

She looked at the key. 'When we get back to the hotel, this goes in the safe.'

In the darkness of the cellar the shadow glided effortless to the trapdoor. 'She will be yours master...' it whispered and slowly it descended through the stone into the cavern.

Chapter 25

They drove back to the hotel and asked Mrs Chambers to put the key in the safe. Mrs Chambers placed the key in the main safe and locked the safe door.

Feeling slightly relieved Mary and Marie made their way upstairs to their rooms. Both needed a shower and change of clothes.

After showering and changing they had there evening meal. Although Mary wanted to go back to the hospital the image of seeing Tom lying there in a comatose state was not going to help her get to the bottom of the mystery of the house.

Mary walked round the hotels garden, hoping it would distract her and her thoughts or at least give her a sign. Disgruntled she made her way to her room.

By morning, and, after breakfast both Marie and Mary met in the bar/lounge, Marie was laden down with paperwork. She had all the files from the museum archives and the information from Samuel. Mary brought down her laptop and the information about the history of the property.

Marie worked methodically, using the information she had collated she built up a basic timeline.

1953 – Property owned by Mr Hamilton.
1957 – Mr and Mrs Hamilton died – *Newspaper clipping.*
1959 - House damaged in severe storms.
1960 - House renovated – *Newspaper clipping.*
1963 - Property unwanted.
1968 - Property purchased by Mr and Mrs Farley.
2006 - Mr and Mrs Farley found – *Newspaper clipping.*
2006 - Property on market.

2011 - Property bought.
2011 – Key for cellar found in well – Check well.
2011 – Tom coma – Cellar key fits padlock in cellar.
2011 – Letters received – *Sent by Samuel Henshaw.*

Mary watched as her sister built the basic of all profiles 'At least we have a timeline.'
Marie concurred 'The information you found out was the starting point, we now have to fit in the information from the books we got.'
Marie read the letters that Tom had found in the books in the bureau. The letters were to Maureen from her parents and her sister.
Nothing in the letters gave any indication that something strange had happened.
Marie reached the last letter.

Dear Maureen,

It has been a while since we last spoke on the phone, and I have to wonder if you and Tony are well.
The children want to visit to see their aunt again and we would love to know if we could visit in the spring.
I feel that I have distanced you, you were preoccupied on our last visit and you know if you need any help that I would dearly be there for you.
Please let me know if we can visit and if anything is troubling you.

Love always

Abigail.

Marie passed the letter to Mary, who read it over and over. 'Does it give a date?'
Marie shook her head. 'No envelope.'
Marie added the letter to the timeline placing it before the Farley's were discovered.
Mary was skim reading through the small books that Mr Peterson had lent her.
Every so often Mary made a note.
Marie was busy checking the maps of the area from the present to the past.
Mary put the book down.
'These books...' she started '...the curator of the time was...' she turned to the inside page '...a Naomi Horncastle.'
'Naomi was a historian, and she mentions...' Mary gasped.
Marie looked up. She reached for the book.
Mary sat slumped as Marie read out loud.
'...the passage was dark, yet my fear and exhilaration compelled me to carry on...'
Marie read through some more of the page.
'...the cavern itself was amazing, the pictographs on the walls the pedestal and the strange object that floated above it...
Marie put the book down. 'So...this' Marie flipped pages 'lady is describing...'
Mary stopped Marie. 'She mentions a pedestal and a floating object. Don't you remember what the nurse in the Hospital told us, Tom was screaming don't touch the orb.'
Marie looked at her sister. 'Do you think this has something to do with the trap door?'
Mary glanced out the window. 'I think it has something to do with the house.'

Marie opened her laptop. She opened the file she had made on Samuels Notebook. Reading through she paused.

'I feel the pull of the object, the orb, the bright light driving inside me, making me... no... no... do not touch the orb, please... I beg you... '

Marie looked at her sister.

'Looks like Samuel and this Naomi had a visit to the orb factory and got sucked right in.'

Marie looked at the other books on the side.

'I suggest we concentrate on these for now.'

Mary passed Marie two more books.

'If this has something to do with the house sis, how are we going to stop ourselves from making the same mistake?'

Marie laughed 'Were going to learn from Charlie...'

Mary looked confused.

'...from the past, we learn about the future.'

Mrs Chambers was sorting out the bookings for the week. With everything going on she had booked Mary and Marie for another week.

Something was wrong, with her husband in hospital and the house...

Listing the menus she looked up as a young man came to the desk.

'How can I help you my dear?' enquired Mrs Chambers.

'A package for Miss Beresford,' the young man replied.

Mrs Chambers signed the document, and walked through into the bar/lounge. 'Marie this package just arrived for you.'

Marie thanked Mrs Chambers and opened it.

The package contained topological maps, 2 discs and a letter.

Marie read the letter.

Dearest Marie,

Please tell me you haven't moved into the back of beyond and become a hermit in a sleepy village. The information you required was fun to find, and the researchers have found some interesting areas in the village.

We have pinpointed several dark marks on the maps, and used the latest technology to try and figure what they are.

The discs contain a brief history of the village, which may or may not be of any use.

I would like to remind you that the resources at this university could benefit from another lecture, if you so wish.

Let me know.

Thomas.

Marie passed the letter to Mary, who chuckled as she read it. 'He sounds charming, and what do you lecture?'

Marie stood taller, almost teacher like 'boredom 101' she replied.

Putting the maps to the collated information showed nothing unusual; Marie had noticed the dark marks but couldn't think of what they were. She looked at them searching for a pattern.

Mrs Chambers suddenly appeared, 'Mary the phone, come quick, it's the hospital.'

Mary followed Mrs Chambers and picked up the phone.

'Hello…'

'Mary Plant?' the woman said.

'Yes,' replied Mary her voice quivering.

'This is Sister Charlotte your husband…' the nurse started.

Mary faltered for a second 'Tom, what has happened?'

'He has come out of the coma.' replied Sister Charlotte.

Mary dropped the phone and cried.

Mrs Chambers picked up the receiver. 'Hello yes Mary is still here but not able to talk.'

Mrs Chambers listened and made a note. Putting the receiver down Mrs Chambers led Mary back to the bar/lounge.

Marie looked up as Mrs Chambers led Mary back in. 'What has happened?'

Mary flung her arms around her sister. 'Tom has come back to me.'

Marie and Mary cried.

Once more they tidied the information up. Marie made her way up to her room and placed it all on the dresser.

Grabbing a jacket she made her way into the bar/lounge. Mary dried her eyes and they walked out to the car.

Marie drove Mary back to the hospital; they parked and made their way to reception.

Mary found which ward he was on and made their way up.

Mary stopped at the nurse's desk and asked which bed Tom Plant was in.

The Nurse smiled' Bed 2, main ward.'

Mary thanked her and they both wandered through.

Tom was sat up in bed, he smiled as Mary and Marie entered the ward.

Mary ran and kissed him. 'You…' she sobbed 'you scared me…' tears ran down her face as Tom hugged her.

Marie walked over and smiled.

'Still not sure what has happened.' said Tom.

Mary sat down and Marie pulled up a chair.

'You were going to be discharged, and then started ranting and raving about orbs, and people, yet no one was there, and then you were sedated and fell in a coma.'

'Wow…' replied Tom.

'Can you remember anything at all?' enquired Marie

Tom shook his head. 'Sorry… nothing,' he replied.

Mary smiled, 'Listen I am going to find out when you can be released.'

Marie watched as Mary left the ward.

Tom looked at Marie 'anything been happening?'

Marie laughed. 'Yes loads, but when you are feeling better.'

Tom smiled, grasping Marie's hand he smiled. 'Thank you for being here.'

Mary knocked on the ward Sisters door. 'Come in…'

Opening the door she found Sister Kilpatrick behind the desk.

'Mary, please take a seat. I was beeped when your husband came round, and I have checked his vitals.'

Mary nodded 'So when can he come home?'

Sister Kilpatrick lowered her glasses. 'He has been through some traumas and normally I would suggest a couple of weeks rest and observation.'

'Couple of weeks!' exclaimed Mary

Sister Kilpatrick carried on. 'He has suffered a fall, a coma, visions…'

Mary started to cry.

Sister Kilpatrick came round the desk. 'I understand the frustrations you have suffered as of late. I know you want him home.'

Mary exhaled 'I do... he is my rock.'

Sister Kilpatrick walked back round the desk. 'If his vital signs are good for the rest of today, and he eats and proves to me he is on the mend.' She exhaled 'I will consider releasing him in the morning.'

Mary wiped her eyes; she thanked Sister Kilpatrick and walked back to the ward.

Tom was the first to notice Mary walking back in the ward. His smile faltered.

'Well...' he enquired.

'If your vitals remain stable, if you eat something, and if you go...' she smiled and pointed 'on your own and have a walk around, then possibly tomorrow.'

Tom exhaled. 'I need some fresh air.'

He pulled back the bed sheets and slowly got out of bed. He took some tentative steps, walking to the end of the ward and back. Mary smiled.

Marie smiled and fetched a wheelchair. 'I can accommodate a walk in the grounds.'

Tom sat in the wheelchair 'Lead on Marie'

Mary laughed.

Chapter 26

Two days had passed since Tom had awoken from his Coma; he sat in the chair next to the bed. He had made great progress and was being released.

Mary had been called and was on her way. Reading his book he glanced at the clock watching the seconds tick by. He hated hospitals, they just... he struggled to remember.

Putting the book in the bag he walked to the window. He looked out, the countryside view and then the nurses and visitors arriving.

His mind drifted. He had been asked several times if he remembered what he had been screaming, he wished he did, but nothing came to the forefront of his mind.

He remembered being told about the fall in the shower and that was about it. He felt frustrated.

A hand touched his shoulder and Tom turned.

Mary smiled and kissed him 'You ready to get out of here?'

Tom Laughed 'Please, before Nurse Hitler returns with her groupies.'

Mary picked up his holdall and they left the ward.

Marie waited patiently in the car, '...listen I will be back when things are sorted here...'

She listened to the voice on the other end. 'Call it my damn well holiday then.'

She listened more as the voice barked and bawled. Marie laughed. 'You make me laugh Greg.'

She looked out the window seeing Mary and Tom leaving the hospital. 'Got to go Greg and will be back soon.'

Mary and Tom reached the car, Tom climbed in the back of the car whilst Mary got in the passenger side.

Marie placed her phone on the dashboard 'right,' she said 'back to the hotel.'

Marie drove through the village and back to the hotel.

Mary got out carrying Tom's holdall, Tom got out and breathed a sigh of relief. They walked to the entrance and were greeted by Doris.

'So glad to see you back Tom,' she kissed him on the cheek,

'Lovely to be back here Doris,' he replied.

She ushered them into the bar/lounge.

'Can I fetch you anything?'

Tom shook his head 'Not at the moment Doris, just need to rest.'

Doris nodded and wandered back to the lobby.

Mary set his bag down.

Marie walked into the bar/lounge carrying the keys.

Mary smiled at her sister; she had been a rock while everything had been going on.

Mary and Marie spent the rest of the day reading the books about Naomi and the village. Tom rested trying to remember what had happened over the past few days.

He felt like he was fighting an inner battle, if only he could remember. Exasperated he got up.

Mary smiled, 'feeling better?' she enquired.

'No, just wish I could remember...' he replied.

Marie looked at Tom, 'Well take this book and have a read.'

Tom looked at the book 'What's it about?'

Marie turned. 'It's the history of the charming village and your house,' she replied.

Tom opened the book.

June 1969.

The village has an eerie feel to it today, yet the day is bright. I wish I could recall my entire dream, but I get so far and then nothing.

This has infuriated me. I know it has something to do with what I saw yesterday.

Maureen was so upset, she has been having nightmares.

Is it due to that property, or is something in the air?

I wish I knew.

Tom read it several times. Turning the page he saw a picture. He looked at it. Something stirred inside him, he struggled to remember, but he felt like he had seen something like this before.

Turning more pages he read more of Naomi's journal.

The history of this town has been collated at the Library. We have received several interesting artefacts and we thank the village for the donations.

As the historian I am grateful to learn more about our town's past.

Tom skipped some of the pages.

I had the nightmare again last night. I am in a large cavern with pictographs on the walls. The pedestal stands at the side with the large silver shining ball floating above it.

I can feel the intense power as it draws me near. I am unable to stop myself from touching it.

I now feel weightless, like I am in the past. I can see the cavern and Mr and Mrs Hamilton, they are both in the cavern.

I call to them both, but they cannot hear me.

Mr Hamilton keeps looking around, Mrs Hamilton is crying. He takes her hand and they touch the silver shining ball.

The light blinds and I blink.

I am back in the cavern without knowledge, not knowing what I am doing there.

Tom put the book down.

'This historian really has the low down on the village and the house.' He looked at Mary and Marie. 'Have either of you been to the house lately?'

Mary turned away, 'We have...' she paused looking at Marie for moral support.

'When you fell in the shower and then started seeing things…'

Marie butted in. 'We thought the cellar held the answers as that was the only place you were found and trapped to be fair.'

Marie reached in her bag and pulled out her camera. 'Look at the cellar key and this padlock.'

Tom looked at the photo and shrugged his shoulders. 'Old cellar key and a padlock so…'

Marie turned to the next photo. Tom gasped.

'Same key same padlock, but they are that colour.'

Tom looked at them both.

'Do you think the cavern mentioned in these books is under the cellar?'

Marie smiled. 'Welcome back Tom.'

It took Mary and Marie another hour to go through everything that had happened whilst Tom was in the hospital.

After everything had been told he just looked dumbfounded.

'I need a drink,' he said.

Mary looked at the clock. 'Forget the drink; we better get some food in us before Doris gets angry.'

After a quick wash and change they went down to dinner.

Doris was bustling around the dining room as they entered. She led them to a corner table and took their order.

After another delicious meal they spent the evening in the bar/lounge area talking to Doris.

Tom looked at his watch. He felt tired and decided he was going up.

Mary and Marie watched him leave, 'With what he has been through I am not surprised he is tired,' said Marie.

Mary took another sip of her drink. She was glad Tom was back, but she felt like he wasn't fully himself. Chastising herself she had to remember he had been through an ordeal.

Once they had finished their drinks they bade Doris goodnight.

Tom was snoring as Mary entered the room, she got undressed and climbed into bed. She watched Tom for what felt like an eternity but was only a few seconds.

Mary drifted off to sleep.

Samuel turned on his torch and slowly entered the house. He made his way through to the kitchen and unlocked the cellar door.

He descended into the cellar, feeling the damp cold wall. Slowly he reached the bottom and walked towards the trapdoor.

He inserted his key into the padlock and removed it.

Lifting the trapdoor he followed the steps down and into cavern.

He knew this was wrong. Yet he was compelled.

He shone his torch around the cavern, he looked at the pictographs. His breathing was ragged.

He turned and looked at the pedestal and the orb.

He felt a cold chill around him.

He turned looking around as if someone was in the cavern with him.

The shadow glided slowly in the cavern, it knew Samuel would come. The dreams, the fears, the darkness it caused, fed the evil within.

It slowly reached Samuel and wrapped itself around him.

Samuel tried to escape; he froze, trying to move. He tried to scream but couldn't.

The shadow wrapped itself around his neck. Samuel reached up trying to pry it off with his hands. His hands gripped nothing. The shadow tightened its grip, the fear coursing through Samuel. He stumbled and fell.

Samuel thrashed around in his bed, his nightmare consuming him, his screams rang out in the night yet no one could hear them.
He lashed out knocking his lamp to the floor and suddenly laid still.
His eyes closed.

Chapter 27

Local resident dies in sleep.

Samuel Henshaw was today found dead in his cottage. The postman rang for the Police when he noticed several bottles of milk had not been taken in.
The Police searched the house and found Mr Henshaw in bed; his lamp was on the floor broken.
The coroner was called and cause of death was a Heart Attack.
It is believed that Mr Henshaw tried to reach for his tablets when he knocked the lamp on the floor.
Samuel had been part of the village and will be sorely missed.
With no family he will be laid to rest in the local church.

Chapter 28

(1969)

Samuel was first to enter the chamber, he shivered. Naomi gasped when she entered; she had never seen anything like this in her life. She walked to the walls looking at the crudely drawn pictographs.
She could make out the pedestal and the ball of light above it, lines drawn from the ball to emphasise the light emanating around.
The crudely drawn people stood back from the pedestal.
Moving along to the next pictogram she saw one of persons touching the light. The lines drawn from light were thicker; she had studied art and knew this illustrated a brighter fiercer light. What did this all mean?
Taking her notebook from her bag she drew the first pictograph and then the second.

Maureen stood at the entrance of the cavern; she had no reason to be back down here. She shivered.
'I do not like this place.' she said.

Samuel looked around the golden pedestal. He seemed almost enthralled by its presence.
Naomi walked further along the wall, she kept feeling the wall as if willing it to come to life and
divulge its secrets to her.
She came to another pictograph. She studied it carefully. The person who had touched the ball
of light was laying on the floor its hands by its head. The light was shining like it had in the first
picture.
Naomi drew this in her book and walked along the wall.

Glancing up she saw another pictograph higher on the wall.
It had the person lying on the floor by the pedestal but what could only be described as a ball
on the floor turning into a shadow person watching him.

Naomi called over to Samuel. 'Samuel what on earth do you make of this?'
Samuel walked over and looked at the pictographs; he had seen them when they had first come
down to investigate. He looked at the fourth one and could make out the pedestal and the ball
shining above it, he could see a body on the floor and a dark shape like ball and a shadow type
person. Lines led from the person on the floor to the shadow type person.
Samuel shivered. Yes he thought. I understand. While we are down here we are being watched.
Naomi drew the fourth picture in her book and moved along the wall.

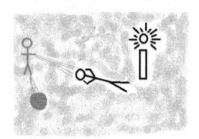

She stopped at the end looking at a fifth pictograph.
She dropped her book.
Samuel walked over.
The picture depicted the shadow man killing the person on the floor.
Naomi picked up her book and drew the picture.

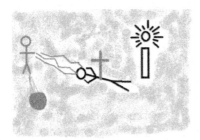

She felt disgusted by the pictograph. Yet, she also felt like she understood.

She walked over to Maureen 'please tell me you haven't touched that...' she pointed to the orb floating above the pedestal 'thing.'

Maureen looked at Naomi. 'I have never touched it, yet I feel drawn to it.' Her voice quavering as she spoke.

Naomi looked at the golden pedestal.

Walking towards it she could feel an unknown presence drawing her closer to the orb. The light it emanated was almost hypnotic making you feel like it was part of you.

She glanced at the writing around the pedestal. The inscription was the same as around the trapdoor.

She touched the pedestal. Questions ran through her mind. Where did this come from? Who had put it here? What was its purpose?

Naomi felt the pull of the light; slowly she backed away.

Samuel studied the pictographs; he ran his hands over the etchings, as if to get some insight into who had drawn them and why.

The coolness of the cavern had preserved the colour and texture of the pictographs.

The shadow silently moved down the steps and into the cavern, it rose and wrapped itself around Maureen. As Maureen gasped it entered her body.

The shadow used Maureen as its vessel. Walking slowly into the cavern it controlled Maureen edging her closer towards Samuel.

Samuel turned 'Do you feel the pull of that...' he pointed at the orb.

Maureen smiled. 'I think it will answer all our questions.'

Samuel looked puzzled.

Maureen turned, 'I can prove it too.' She walked towards the orb, Samuel watched her and realised what Maureen was going to do.

He reached out to stop Maureen, Naomi watched in horror as Maureen reached out and her hand touched the orb.

The blinding light filled the cavern.

Maureen, Samuel and Naomi fell to the floor, each having the same vision. The shadow slithered out of Maureen and entered the orb.

The orb soon returned to a glow.

Maureen sat up and looked around. Where am I? She thought. Looking around she saw Naomi on the other side of the pedestal.

Samuel groaned behind Maureen, he sat up confused and dazed.

Naomi slowly sat up, glancing at Maureen and Samuel with a bewildered look on her face.

Samuel helped them both up. 'What happened? He asked.

Maureen shook her head. 'What are we doing down here?'

Naomi walked around the pedestal to Samuel 'Where are we?'

They all turned and looked at the orb.

Maureen rushed out of the cavern and up towards the cellar. Samuel watched her leave, shouting her name he rushed up after her.

Naomi walked out the cavern holding her bag. She turned and glanced at the orb.

As she walked quickly up the steps the shadow slid out of the orb.

'Feed on them master.' it whispered.

Chapter 29

Maureen sat at the table crying as Naomi and Samuel climbed the steps from the cellar and locked the cellar door.

Naomi sat and reached in her bag, pulling out her notebook she looked at the drawings she had made. 'We were down there and I made these.' She passed the notebook to Samuel and then Maureen.

'Whatever happened, according to the pictographs, we have touched that ball of light. Did we all do it though?'

Samuel looked from Maureen to Naomi. 'I don't remember touching it, but then again I don't remember anything.'

Maureen looked at them both. Picking up the key she walked through to the main lounge and placed it back in the bureau.

She walked back into the kitchen and dried her eyes on her apron. 'We weren't down there; I am not letting Tony know what happened.' She paused and looked at them both. 'I am not sure why either of you are here.'

Naomi stood up, glancing out the window. What am I doing here? She thought to herself.

Mustering her energy she turned to Maureen. 'I cannot explain what has happened to us. I suggest we go Samuel.'

Samuel stood and looked at Maureen. 'Will you be fine here?'

Maureen stifled a smile. 'Yes.'

Naomi walked to the hall and looked back. Is this what happened to the Hamilton's? She wondered.

Samuel joined Naomi and they left.

Maureen watched from the window as they walked out of view.

Naomi and Samuel walked down the road, neither of them speaking. Neither understanding what had happened down in the cellar or why they went down to the cavern.

Naomi knew that she had drawn those pictures in the cavern, and something had to have happened since that point.

They walked to Naomi's cottage. Naomi invited Samuel in. Walking through to the kitchen Naomi noticed three cups on the table. So something had happened here too she thought.

Samuel closed the door and walked through to the kitchen. Naomi smiled. 'Look at the table Samuel and tell me how many cups.'

Samuel counted three cups, Naomi waited for Samuel to come up with some sort of conclusion. Exasperated she sat down. 'Samuel we have three cups and how many of us were in that cavern.' She let it sink in as Samuel looked up. 'Maureen was here.' He said quietly.

Naomi nodded.

Naomi made a note in her notebook. She also walked into her living room and found the articles of the previous owners.

Samuel watched as she poured over the information.

'Here we go!' she exclaimed 'the previous owners,' she passed the information over to Samuel so he could read it.

Samuel read the articles about the previous owners and the strange goings on. Naomi then remembered what she had said to Maureen, about Mrs Hamilton looking drawn and constantly looking at the cellar.

Samuel looked at Naomi. 'Do you think they went down into the cavern?'

Naomi nodded 'I think this goes back further than we originally thought.'

Naomi remembered that Cecil's brother Reginald had had the house restored after the fire, had Cecil and Edna tried to destroy the floating ball?

Samuel looked at the time. 'I better get off, some jobs to finish, but keep me informed.'

Naomi kissed him on the cheek and watched as he walked down the road.

Placing her folder and book into a large bag, she set off for the library. The walk did nothing to improve her day; what with the images she had drawn and the memories... she couldn't remember... it was going to be difficult to collate the information.

Naomi walked past the church and across the green, exchanging pleasantries with various members of the community.

Unlocking the library door she placed her bag on one of the tables. She opened the main door and made herself a drink.

Not many people visited the Library, Naomi volunteered her time as and when she could. She had seen many things happen in the village and in one particular place.

Opening her folder she poured over the information she had, making notes in her book.

Naomi glanced at the clock, almost closing time. Charlie had been in and fixed the lock in the library, several people had looked around.

Packing her books up she wandered into the back room, the archives of the library held information and Naomi wanted to see if she could find anything about Reginald Hamilton.

The musty archives held everything in chronological order and Naomi was lucky to find Reginald's phone number. Making a note she placed everything back and locked the library up.

The weather had changed, dark clouds had filled the sky and the imminent feel of rain was hanging in the air as Naomi walked across the green.

She walked hurriedly determined to get home before the heavens opened.

Walking along the country lane she felt the rain slowly fall, pulling her collar up she made it back to her cottage before the downpour really started.

She busied herself in the kitchen, and after having her evening meal and cup of tea she made her way into the living room.

Gathering her information she looked at Reginald's phone number. Did he know anything about the trapdoor and the cellar?

She picked up the receiver and dialled the number.

She waited several seconds before someone answered the call.

'Good evening, can I speak to Mr Hamilton' she enquired.

'Speaking,' he replied. His voice sounded crackly.

'Hello its Miss Horncastle, I wanted to ask you about the Whippletree property.'

A lengthy silence hung before Reginald replied 'I have no dealings with that property.'

'I knew your brother and sister in law, and wanted to ask about the fire,' she added hastily.

Reginald exhaled 'A tragic loss, but...' the sentence hung unfinished.

'I wanted to ask if you found anything strange with the house.' She asked.

Naomi heard Reginald chuckle. 'I had the house rebuilt for one reason only.'

'May I ask why?' questioned Naomi

'The house and the grounds had been in the family for thirty years,' Reginald paused for a moment. 'It was rebuilt in memory of my father.'

Naomi made a note.

'My father was a good man, a learned man, he understood the house, the delights of the grounds, he knew what the house meant, and...' Reginald paused.

'Did you or your father know about the pedestal and glowing light in the cavern?' Naomi questioned.

'I knew as did my brother and my father... as obviously do you.' Reginald scoffed.

'Yes I was introduced to it earlier today, but don't remember much,' she replied.

Naomi heard Reginald laugh. 'The inscription obviously wasn't heeded.' he laughed again

Naomi remembered the inscription she had written in her book. What happened in the cavern many years ago? Where did the pedestal come from and what was its purpose?

'Miss Horncastle, I cannot divulge the secrets of my forefathers. That part of my life destroyed when my brother failed to heed our warnings. The pedestal and the orb of light have sat in that position longer than any of us will live.'

Naomi listened intently.

'My father God rest his soul, was able to channel the past and control the orb of light. It takes a special person with the gift of sight to see what truly lies beyond.' Reginald paused briefly.

'For those who do not hold this, then it is only time before...' his sentence hung.

'Mr Hamilton... Reginald...' Naomi waited for him to answer, and then the line went dead.

Putting the receiver down Naomi went through the brief notes she had made.

Little did she understand the information she had written.

The wind blew during the evening and into the night, rain lashed against the windows, the wind howling as the storm gathered momentum.

Naomi turned off the light and checked the doors ensuring they were locked. She made her way upstairs. Yawning she got into bed.

The smashing of glass woke Naomi; she put her glasses on and glanced at the clock. It was three in the morning.

Slowly she got out of bed and reached for her dressing gown. She peered round the corner of the staircase and glanced down the stairs, hoping to hear something, the house was silent.

She slowly walked down the stairs and turned on the hallway light. Nothing happened; she flicked the switch several times. She made her way into the kitchen and grabbed a flashlight from the pantry.

Turning it on she glanced around the kitchen, nothing seemed out of place, ensuring the door was still locked she moved through the hall into the living room.

Instinct made her reach for the light switch; she shone the light around the room, the light dancing across the walls. Nothing was broken or out of place.

She turned and gasped. Samuel held a knife; he lunged forward slashing her arm. Naomi fell, blood gushing from her arm. 'Samuel what are you...' he lashed out again the knife plunged into her chest. Naomi screamed and sat up in bed drenched in sweat.

She walked through to the bathroom; her breathing ragged from the nightmare and glanced in the mirror.

She splashed some water on her face and walked back to the bedroom. Turning on the bedside light she made a note of the nightmare as best as she could remember.

She placed the book on the table and turned off the light. Taking a few deep breaths she fell back to sleep.

Samuel got up and washed and then changed. He felt so tired still; he had spent half the night tossing and turning, dreaming if that's what you could call it of the cavern.

After his breakfast he went for a walk in the village and collected his newspaper.

His thoughts felt consumed by yesterday's visit to the cavern. Was Naomi right that Maureen had been at Naomi's? Why had they visited the cavern? Had they touched that silver floating ball?

None of yesterday had made sense. He had been chased down the cellar by nothing in his dream, then forced to open the trapdoor and descend into the cavern, before... before. If only he could remember.

He had made a note of the dream and would show Naomi when he next visited.

Samuel spent the day working in the church yard, as a gardener he loved to keep the grass mown and the bushes trimmed back. The storm the previous day meant he could tend to the flowers and trees.

By lunchtime he was sat on the church wall, he looked at the weather beaten church. The dark upper walls, the lighter lower walls, the ivy climbing up giving it a more foreboding look.

Just looking at the church gave Samuel a feeling of contentment, and, he had to admit after yesterday he needed it.

He packed his lunch away and carried on with the weeding of the flower beds.

The rector walked out of the church and walked to Samuel.

'Lovely day, especially after all that rain last night,' said the rector.

Samuel wiped his hands and stood up 'Yes going to turn warmer by the weekend.'

The rector smiled. 'Good news for the wedding on Saturday.'

Samuel laughed.

The rest of the day passed with no incident. The flower beds looked tidy, the paths were clear and the trees trimmed back.

The rector thanked Samuel for the extra work.

Samuel left the church and walked down the lane, with Naomi living close by he decided he would see if she had found anything new out.

Naomi was busy in the kitchen, her hands covered in flour as the doorbell rang. Cursing slightly under her breath she wiped her hands on her apron and opened the door.

Flashbacks of her nightmare flooded back when she saw Samuel standing there.

Naomi ushered him in and through to the kitchen.

She stuck the kettle on and made them both a drink. Sitting down she looked at Samuel, he looked dreadful, his eyes slightly red.

'You look like you haven't slept,' she finally spoke.

Samuel nodded. 'Been doing the churchyard today for the wedding on Saturday, but hardly slept last night.

Naomi watched intently as Samuel reached into his bag and pulled out a notebook. 'Remembered as much as I could from my dream last night...' he said handing over the book.

Naomi took his notebook and handed him her book. 'My dream was no better.'

Samuel looked bewildered, taking Naomi's book he read what she had written.

'I also spoke to Reginald Hamilton last night; the details are at the back.'

Samuel read in silence as did Naomi.

Once they had finished they looked at each other.

'What did Reginald mean with' Samuel read down '...he knew what the house meant...'

Naomi shook her head. 'I have no idea.'

After a lengthy conversation Samuel made his farewells and walked home.

Naomi had been interested in his dream too.

Only one question remained in her mind. Did Maureen suffer the same?

Chapter 30

(2011)

Mary read the headline from the local paper about Samuel dying. She put the paper down, several questions running through her mind. Had he died from a supposed Heart Attack? Was what had happened in the past in the cavern had anything to do with his death?
Nothing made sense.
Tom had gone for a walk around the grounds of the hotel. He was getting stronger, but didn't need to get too excited.
Marie had been preoccupied. Mary knew she was needed back at work.
Finishing her coffee she folded the newspaper and walked in the lobby.
Doris was going through the guest lists.
'Morning Doris, can I book us in for two more weeks please, and can I pay you now.'
Doris looked up 'not a problem Mary.'
Doris worked out the price and handed Mary the invoice. Mary smiled and paid.
Marie came down the stairs wearing her beige slacks and white t-shirt.
'Mary, finally...' she said 'have convinced my boss that I cannot leave and have two more weeks holiday.'
Mary hugged her sister. 'I have just booked Tom and myself in for two more weeks, and will organise yours.'
Marie touched her arm. 'No need, I pre-booked it with Doris before I rang my boss.'
Mary laughed. 'What tactic did you use this time?'
Marie laughed. 'Doris, yes can finalise that booking.'
Doris looked up. 'Wonderful my dear,' Marie pulled out her bank card from her purse. Mary put her hand on Marie's. 'I'll pay.
Marie mouthed thank you to her sister.

Mary walked outside; the slight breeze did nothing to cool down the heat of the morning.
She caught sight of Tom sitting on one of the benches.
He looked deep in thought.
Marie joined her sister. 'Need to go home, check the mail, get some more clothes etc.'
Mary nodded 'See you tonight.'
Marie walked to her car and Mary watched her drive off.
Sighing she took a walk around the garden, finally joining Tom on the garden bench.
Tom could sense Mary's sadness. He put his arm around her, and she leant her head against his shoulder.
Mary felt everything she had kept pent up dissolve around her. The tears rolled down her face.
Tom kissed her. 'You have been a tower of strength. We will solve whatever has happened at our dream house.'

Doris finished off tidying the dining area and walked towards the foyer. She glanced at the gentleman looking through the leaflets of local attractions.
'Good morning, can I help you?' she asked.
The gentleman turned and smiled 'Good morning,' he tilted his hat 'I was hoping to speak to Mr and Mrs Plant. Are they in?'

Doris smiled. 'I believe they are both still here, I saw Mrs Plant…' Doris refused to use first names to strangers 'walking round the garden area. Would you like to take a seat and I will check for you.'

The gentleman took a seat.

Doris walked outside and saw Tom and Mary on the garden seat.

She called them both.

Tom and Mary got up and walked to Doris.

'What's up Doris?' Mary asked.

'Gentleman in the hotel would like to speak to you both,' she said slightly breathless.

Tom glanced sceptically at Mary. 'Not many people know we are here.'

Doris started to walk back to the foyer, Tom and Mary followed.

The gentleman was still sat in the foyer, his overcoat over his arm, briefcase by his feet.

Doris smiled as she entered 'They will be with you momentarily.'

The gentleman smiled and thanked Doris.

Tom and Mary entered the foyer. The gentleman stood. 'My name is Edward Greenwood; I was Samuel Henshaw's solicitor, terrible tragedy.'

Tom shook his hand 'How can we be of help Mr Greenwood,' he asked quizzically.

'Mr Henshaw bequeathed some books to you in his will; he came to see me two weeks ago and changed his will.'

Mary glanced at Tom. 'We really didn't know him that well!' exclaimed Mary.

Edward smiled. 'If I may have five minutes of your time, I will explain.'

Doris smiled 'you may use the bar/lounge area.'

Edward tipped his hat at Doris and walked through to the bar/lounge. Tom and Mary followed.

Edward sat; he placed his overcoat over a seat and reached in his briefcase for his paperwork.

Tom and Mary sat at the table and looked at Edward.

Edward smiled. 'Let me explain. Two weeks ago Mr Henshaw came into my office; he looked quite drawn and concerned. He wanted to change his will. He said he had some books which would help you both in the future. He had a will in place and this would only be a minor change to his last will and testament. He told me in the strictest of confidence that several of his books should be bequeathed to you both.'

Tom looked dumbfounded. 'We only met Samuel once,'

Edward laughed. 'Samuel was a great judge of character, if he wants these books to be bequeathed to you, then that is his choice, he also left you a letter.'

Edward passed Tom and Mary an envelope addressed to them both.

Tom opened the envelope and removed a letter, he started to read.

Dear Tom and Mary,

I knew the past would catch up with me sooner or later.
I have left you both all my books regarding the dreams or nightmares.
Please use the information written inside.

I wish I had had the strength to finish it myself, but this old body would never be strong enough.
Miss Horncastle and I visited the cavern; her books are in the library, albeit one.
I have held onto this last book for so long and I hope it holds the key to this horrid affair.

I have changed my last will and testament and my Solicitor will let you have the books in due course.

I want to ask you both to speak to Charlie again. He has answers you need.

Samuel.

Tom passed the letter to Mary.

Mary read the letter a tear fell onto the letter. 'We will Samuel, we will.'

She put the letter back in the envelope and wiped her eyes.

Edward watched as Mary put the letter away. 'So I take it you know what Mr Henshaw was on about?' he enquired.

Tom answered 'Yes, fully aware.'

Edward smiled 'Good, You can pick up the books in the morning.'

He shook Tom's hand and bade farewell to Mary.

They both watched as He bade farewell to Doris, thanking her for the use of the room. Doris smiled as he tipped his hat at her.

Mary laughed at Doris. 'What was with the hat tipping and the smiles Doris?'

Doris blushed 'Lovely to see a man with such good manners.' she retorted.

Mary laughed 'We won't tell your husband.'

Tom laughed and they both wandered back outside.

Doris watched them leave and smiled. Picking up some napkins she walked through into the kitchen.

Tom and Mary spent the whole day walking through the village. They visited the church and several shops. Mary had never felt so relaxed since coming to the village. Tom felt back to his old self.

As they walked across the green they noticed a sign about a village fete.

After what had happened over the past few weeks they could do with getting to know the community.

They made their way back to the hotel. After showering they got changed ready for dinner.

Mary had noticed that Marie had returned as her car was in the car park.

They left their room, knocking on Marie's door as they passed.

Marie opened the door and smiled. She hugged her sister and kissed Tom.

She ushered them both in 'sorry not fully unpacked,' she said. Mary looked at the pile of clothes on the bed. Tom stood open mouthed. 'Booked in for two weeks Marie, you have more clothes here than I own.'

Marie blushed 'A lady needs to look her best at all times.'

Mary laughed and the left her room, Marie was quite chatty as they walked down the stairs to dinner.

'...so I said I can sort out half the problems they have in two minutes...'

Tom laughed.

'...let's just say, these two weeks will be holiday...'

They reached the bottom stair and walked through to the dining area.

'...he will get a shock when I return and he is removed to a different department.' Marie opened the door and greeted Doris and her husband.

They all sat and looked at the menu. Tom and Mary opted for the Lemon Chicken; Marie fancied the Salmon.

Doris bustled around all the tables, welcoming guests, fetching drinks, fetching the meals, and just being her charming self.

She loved being a hostess. This hotel was her life.

She brought the meals out for Tom, Mary and Marie. 'Enjoy your meals and lovely to have you back Marie.'

They thanked Doris. After dinner Marie excused herself, she was determined to get her clothes packed away.

Mary and Tom sat in the garden area as the sun slowly set.

It had been a strange day, with the Solicitor and the letter from Samuel but it had been a day of rest for them both.

As the light slowly vanished they went inside and up to their room. Mary made two coffees and they sat in silence, enjoying what was left of a perfect day.

Tired they both soon fell asleep.

The coolness of the night drifted across the village. Mary walked barefoot through the grass. Her dressing gown huddled around her as she stopped by the swing.

She sat. Her mind occupied by the events that had led them to this. Her feet brushed against the grass blades, tickling the soles of her feet.

'You know, I used to sometimes sit there,' said a voice from behind.

Mary jumped off the swing.

Samuel walked slowly towards her. 'This is a perfect spot for bringing calm where there was chaos'

'You're dead!' Mary exclaimed.

'I am that Mary,' he emerged from the shadows, the elderly Samuel was young once more.

Mary stood looking at him. 'How...'She stammered, lost for words.

Samuel smiled. 'This time of night is the best.'

Mary scowled. 'You died; your solicitor visited us today.'

He smiled. 'Use the book I have left you both. It will help.'

An owl hooted in the trees, Mary looked up.

'Listen Samuel...' Mary looked around but Samuel was gone.

Mary woke up startled, sitting up slowly in bed she looked around the room. The book... the letter mentioned a book. She rubbed her eyes. Was I dreaming?

She looked at the clock. Three A.M. She groaned and settled back to sleep.

The house had been silent for weeks. The cellar door opened ajar. The shadow slowly made its way upstairs and into the study.

It was home.

Chapter 31

Marie woke with a start, pushing back the duvet she slowly got out of bed. She brushed her hair back and slipped her gown over her nightie.

She put the kettle on and picked up her mobile. No messages. Then she remembered. I'm on holiday.

She made a cup of tea and drew the curtains back. She glanced out. Dark menacing clouds filled the sky. She yawned. She curled up in the plush chair and sipped her tea.

She finished her tea and walked into the bathroom. After her shower she looked in her wardrobe at her clothes. She took her blue jeans from the hanger, found a cream top and a white jumper. She got changed and applied her meagre amount of make-up.

She opened the door and walked into the corridor. She knocked quietly on Mary's door.

Mary opened the door inviting her sister in.

'Tom won't be long,' she said laughing 'he is attempting to make himself look handsome.'

Marie laughed as Tom walked out of the bathroom.

'Oh Mr handsome!' she exclaimed laughing.

Tom smirked. They made their way down the stairs and into the dining area.

Mr Chambers walked out of the kitchen with two plates and placed them down. He exchanged a few pleasantries with the other guests then ushered Tom, Mary and Marie to a table.

'Good Morning' he said. He handed them all a menu each.

They all decided on the full English. Mr Chambers walked into the kitchen and brought out a coffee pot and tea for Marie.

After breakfast they walked back to Marie's room. They had to decide on a plan of action.

Tom knew he had to visit Samuel's solicitor to retrieve the books which claimed would help them solve the puzzle of the house.

Mary and Marie said they would go through the historian's books in case they had missed something.

Tom left the room and Marie passed three books to Mary.

Tom walked to his car. He pulled out the letter the solicitor had given them. He glanced at the address.

He started the car and drove through the town and parked up opposite the church.

Walking across the green he exchanged some pleasantries with villagers.

He walked past the Butchers and found the Solicitors.

Mr Greenwood's secretary told Tom to take a seat. He glanced around the room. The secretary appeared round the corner. 'Mr Greenwood is free, please follow me.' Tom followed the secretary into a plush office.

Mr Greenwood stood 'Mr Plant, take a seat... coffee... tea... water?'

Tom declined. 'Right the books.' Mr Greenwood rummaged in his draw. 'If you can just go through the list and sign at the bottom please.

Tom looked at the list of books. Unsure if any were going to be of any use, he signed the form and handed it back.

Mr Greenwood signed the form and pressed a button on his intercom. 'Caterina, can you bring the books in please for Mr Plant.'

'Certainly Mr Greenwwod,' she replied. Getting up from her desk she walked through into the back room. This place gave her the creeps, the light never worked properly. She found a box with the clients name on and carried it to her desk.

She knocked on Mr Greenwood's door and entered carrying the box.

Mr Greenwood smiled and thanked Caterina. After she left and closed the door, he took the lid off the box.

The box contained fifteen books of various sizes. Tom glanced at them all. 'So Mr Henshaw left me all these books?'

Mr Greenwood nodded 'I am unsure of his reasons but what was in the will has to be dealt with, and I hope you enjoy them.' Mr Greenwood stood up and replaced the lid.

He shook Tom's hand and Tom carried the box out and back through the village to his car.

Placing the box in the boot he got in the driver's seat and rubbed his forehead again.

He drove back through the village to the hotel.

Mary slammed the book down hard on the table 'enough is enough!' she exclaimed.

Marie looked up. 'Tedious or what sis...'

Mary laughed.

They were sat in the bar/lounge area of the hotel. Books and files lay strewn across the tables.

They had tried to make sense of what they had read.

Marie had set up a brain storming sheet to see if any of the pieces fitted together.
She scribbled away frantically on the sheet.
'One more time...' she said exasperated.

The Whippletree

Present	Resolved	Unresolved
Letters	Resolved	
Dreams (Mary)		Unresolved
Tom Accident / Coma		Unresolved
Key and Lock in cellar		Unresolved
Under the trapdoor		Unresolved
Books		Unresolved
Files from Museum		Unresolved
History of town		Unresolved
Books from Solicitor		Unresolved
Samuels Death		Unresolved

Marie stood back looking at the details she had written down. She sat dejected.
Mary stood up and looked at it.
She picked up Marie's pen and started writing.

The Whippletree

Present	Resolved	Unresolved	Possibilities	Actions
Letters	Resolved			
Dreams (Mary)		Unresolved		
Tom Accident / Coma		Unresolved	Stuck in cellar	Cellar/House
Key and Lock in cellar		Unresolved		Cellar/House
Under the trapdoor		Unresolved		Cellar/House
Books		Unresolved	Read - Clues?	
Files from Museum		Unresolved		Been Through
History of town		Unresolved		Been Through
Books from Solicitor		Unresolved	Being Collected	
Samuels Death		Unresolved		Cellar/House
Previous Owners				Cellar/House

Mary stood back.
Looking at it now, it had purpose. They could work out answers. The one thing which struck them both was the fact the cellar held a lot of the answers. They knew they had to return.
Doris walked through the door. She looked around 'What in...' she started.
Mary stood up. 'Sorry Doris we got distracted.'

Doris seemed transfixed by files on tables. 'You ladies better have this tidied up before this afternoon.'

Marie looked apologetic 'we will Doris I promise.'

Doris walked out shaking her head.

Marie looked at her sister. 'Well that is some sort of headway.'

Mary nodded. Marie started moving files and books. This way the room would resemble the categories they had made.

Mary started to prioritise them. Grabbing a fresh sheet she wrote out the list again in priority order.

The Whippletree

Present	Resolved	Unresolved	Reason	Actions
Tom Accident / Coma		Unresolved	Stuck in cellar	Cellar/House
Key and Lock in cellar		Unresolved		Cellar/House
Under the trapdoor		Unresolved		Cellar/House
Samuels Death		Unresolved		Cellar/House
Previous Owners				Cellar/House
Books		Unresolved	Missing Clues	Read Again
Books from Solicitor		Unresolved	Being Collected	Read

Mary smiled at the end list. Now she could see what had to be done. The books Tom would bring back would hopefully help them understand the cellar and what lied beneath.

Marie started packing the files that were no longer of any use away. This would give them scope for what lay ahead.

Tom walked into the room carrying the box. He placed it on the table and wiped his brow.

'Samuel left us these,' he indicated to the box.

Marie and Mary walked over and looked inside. They both groaned.

Marie decided to remove the files they no longer needed. She took them to her room and put them in the bottom draw of her bedside cabinet.

She walked back down and placed the books they had to check into the box along with the notes they had previously made.

Tom lifted the box and took it to Marie's room.

He walked back down and followed Doris into the bar/lounge area.

Tom looked at Marie and Mary. 'So, what's next?' he enquired.

'We're going to the house.' replied Marie.

She picked up her bag and walked towards the foyer.

Tom glanced at Mary. His expression said it all. Mary turned to Doris 'Can we have the key from the safe please.'

Doris walked with them to the foyer; opening the safe she passed Mary the key.

Marie reached her car and unlocked it, Tom and Mary got in as Marie climbed in the driver's seat. They drove in silence through the sleepy village and out to the countryside, the menacing sky had darkened more, grey clouds covered the sky with rain imminent.

They drove past the fields, all of them deep in their own thoughts. It didn't take long for the house to come into view.

Marie pulled up outside the house. The clouds above made the house look more sinister than it was.

Mary shivered and looked behind her at Tom. He just stared at the house. So many things had gone through his mind on the way.

Marie turned off the engine and got out the car. Mary and Tom got out and stood next to Marie.

Marie suddenly walked to the boot of the car. 'Hold on,' she said.

She rummaged in the boot pulling out a video camera.

'This time we can have video proof of everything,' she smiled and walked towards the gate.

Chapter 32

Tom unlocked the door and slowly pushed it open. The house was still as he entered the hall.

Mary stooped and picked up the post, placing the letters in her bag she followed Tom into the hall.

Marie walked in last and closed the door. The stillness sent a shiver down Mary's spine.

They walked through the hall into the kitchen.

Marie turned on her video camera and followed Tom and Mary into the kitchen.

Mary took the cellar key out of her pocket. 'Tom can you pass me the torches and the door wedge please.'

Tom reached up and grabbed the torches and the door wedge. He passed the torches to Mary and rubbed his forehead.

'What's up Tom?' enquired Mary.

'Just a slight headache coming on,' he smiled 'I'll be fine.'

Marie recorded everything including Tom rubbing his head. Nothing was going to escape her attention.

'Okay I am going to unlock the cellar door,' Mary said trying to sound confident.

She unlocked the door and Tom wedged it open.

Turning on the torches she passed one to Tom.

'Wait one moment,' Marie put the video camera down and reached in her pocket, pulling out a mini head torch she turned it on and placed it on her head.

Picking up the video camera she resumed recording.

Mary glanced down the steps. Her heart pounded, her skin prickled, this was the last place she wanted to be. Slowly taking a step at a time she descended into the darkness. The beam of light shone from the torch showing the dust floating she steadied herself placing her hand on the cold damp stone wall.

Tom reached the steps he could see Mary half way down. He felt her pain, and he felt his emotions boiling inside. Last time I got trapped down here he thought.

He took his first step; his hand felt the dampness of the cold stone as he followed Mary down. His breathing became heavier as he descended. His heart pounded, the memories flooding back. His temple throbbed. He wanted to scream.

Mary reached the bottom and walked a few steps; she turned watching Tom come down. A beam of light pierced the dusty cellar as Marie descended. The light from her head torch combined with the light on the video camera gave the cellar an eerie glow.

Tom reached the bottom step, taking a deep breath he tried to relax. Mary touched his arm.

'You okay?' she enquired, worry clearly in her voice. He feigned a smile 'yeah, just the last time I was here...'he paused. Mary nodded, she remembered all too well.

Marie reached the last step.

She turned off the video camera and looked from Tom to Mary, 'let's go then,'

Taking the lead she filmed the walk to the trapdoor.

Mary and Tom followed; as they reached the trapdoor Marie filmed the inscription. This inscription had always bewildered her. The padlock lay dormant. Mary removed the cellar key from her pocket where she had put it once she had unlocked the door and knelt down; she inserted the key into the padlock. They key slowly changed from a dull grey to gold like the padlock.

Tom gasped 'That is...' his sentence hung. Mary nodded knowing exactly what he meant.

Tom bent down and removed the padlock from the lock.

It took Mary and Tom to lift the trapdoor they coughed from the dirt and dust they had disturbed.

Tom shone his light down where the trapdoor had been. He could see steps leading into the dark abyss.

'Marie filmed what she could, the darkness in the cellar causing her problems even with the extra light her head torch gave off.

'I do not want to find out where that leads,' Mary stated adamantly.

Marie felt her skin prickle, she felt the same. Tom exhaled. He hesitated before building up the courage to enter the abyss. He used the wall to steady himself on the old stone steps as he slowly descended.

'Not sure how far this goes down...' he shouted up 'so dark... and narrow.'

Mary went next, she slowly descended taking a step at a time, her torch giving her enough light and using her other hand she followed Tom.

Marie exhaled; turning off the video camera she took her first step and followed the steps down. She could see the feint light from Mary's torch, but no sign of Tom.

Tom flashed his torch from side to side; he could see a wall ahead of him. What in God's name was this place?

He slowly reached the wall, and saw the steps descend to his left. 'You will come across a wall ahead of you...' he shouted 'the steps carry on down to your left.'

Mary shouted a reply back the words muffled but he was sure she had heard him.

Tom walked down the steps he felt claustrophobic the walls felt like they were closing in on him. He tried to control his breathing; his heart racing faster, a cold sweat broke out across his body. He shivered.

He descended farther down eventually entering the atrium. He could see a light in the near distance.

He waited for Mary and Marie to catch up with him.

Mary coughed as she reached the bottom step. 'What in...' Tom nodded, he felt transfixed by the large opening, but that light seemed to beckon him forward.

Marie reached the bottom and turned on her video camera. She turned round so that she could film the steps she had just come down. Turning, she filmed the atrium area as best as she could. The light in the distance captivated her.

'Well let's follow the light,' she said, as she took the lead once more. She walked cautiously towards the light slowly entering the large cavern.

She stopped and lowered her video camera. Nothing had prepared her for this.

Tom entered next and gasped. Mary brought up the rear and stood dumbstruck.

The cavern housed the pedestal and the shining orb hovering above it.

Marie filmed the walls from the entrance of the cavern. She could make out some rough drawings. She turned her attention to the pedestal and orb. Turning off her torch she could make it out clearer.

Tom rubbed his head once more; he seemed to be struggling to remember. Mary walked slowly in. her mind taking in the details but she remembered her dreams.

Marie walked closer to the pedestal, filming it on all sides and noting the inscription was written into the gold coloured pedestal.

'Mary... Tom... that inscription on the trapdoor is also on this pedestal.'

Marie stood back her head pounding, feeling the pull of the orb. 'What are you?' she said out loud.

Mary walked along the walls, she had read about the historian's visit, but, when you got down here, it was much more than just pictures.

Mary could almost reach and touch them. She felt something touch her shoulder and screamed. She turned to see Tom 'Sorry you seemed preoccupied.' Mary nodded. 'These drawings, they are the same what was drawn by the historian.'

Tom rubbed his head once more.

Mary looked at the first pictograph; she felt a compulsion to touch it. Her hand touched the cold damp wall. She felt like she knew the past. She could see the past!

Mary felt transfixed by the images in her mind.

She turned looking at the orb. She walked towards it, feeling her fear dissipate and courage return. She touched the pedestal, feeling drawn to it, the immense power it held.

'Do not touch this orb' she said her voice slightly different. Tom and Marie looked at Mary 'the orb of light is too powerful for you.' She slumped to the ground.

Rushing to where Mary had fallen he knelt down and felt for a pulse. 'She's alive...' he said the relief in his voice.

Marie looked at Tom. What was she going on about?'

Tom shook his head. 'I want to get her out of here.' He picked his wife up and carried her out of the cavern.

Marie had one last look around. She paused, what was that? She turned round and looked around the cavern. Nothing looked any different. She walked back to the steps and up into the cellar.

Tom carried Mary carefully up the steps, without his torch he struggled to know where he was in this labyrinth of steps. Cursing himself he concentrated on getting his wife to the cellar. His eyes became accustomed to the darkness as he struggled up the steps. He had to be close he kept thinking to himself.

He could feel the air changing and finally reached the cellar. Placing Mary on the floor he climbed the last few steps. Turning on his torch he shone the light down aiding Marie.

'Marie...' he shouted 'Marie...' no reply. He felt torn, should he leave his wife and go back down for Marie? Had Marie fallen? He started back down the steps and saw a feint light growing brighter. Marie climbed the steps. 'Tom is that you?' she cried. 'Yes Marie, are you okay?' he replied relief present in his voice that Marie was fine.

'The light grew stronger and they both left the steps and entered the cellar. They replaced the trapdoor and put the padlock back on. The key faded from its golden hue back to a dull lifeless colour.

Tom felt a wave of relief flood over him now they were back in the cellar. He picked his wife up. Mary murmured. Tom carried her up the steps and back into the kitchen. He placed Mary on the floor. Marie clambered up the steps and removed the wedge. Tom closed the cellar door and locked it.

Tom carried his wife into the living room and set her down. He grabbed a blanket. Marie carried two glasses of water into the room. Passing one to Tom she took several gulps. Tom drank his and set his glass down.

'How is she?' asked Marie.

'She just keeps murmuring occasionally.' he replied.

'Do you want to get her to hospital? Marie enquired.

'No...' replied Tom. 'We wait.'

Mary was floating. She could sense everything. The courage she had shown in the cavern seemed to reside in her. She could feel people around her, people from the past, places she had never been, it was all combined.
'Mary... Mary... can you hear me?' Mary groaned the voice seemed distant yet so near. She slowly opened her eyes; the light blinded her as she struggled to focus. 'Tom... the light...' She said her voice felt distant too.
'Mary...' she struggled to sit up. Two hands pushed her back 'lay still Mary.' Mary opened her eyes, she gasped 'Who are you?' she looked frantically around 'where's Tom and Marie? She could hear voices behind her, she turned. 'Where am I?'

Chapter 33

(1969)

Maureen sat alone at the kitchen table, Tony had gone to work, the plates from breakfast still unwashed on the side.
The nightmares she had had the night before resurfaced. She stared at the cellar door. The memories stirred inside her. She stood up, looking out to the garden.
Restless, she walked outside and down the garden. Reaching the fence at the end she looked across the fields.
She turned and glanced at the house. How can anything so beautiful cause so much pain she thought? She needed to speak to Naomi and Samuel.
She closed her eyes, taking a deep breath she walked back into the house.

Naomi finished off in the kitchen, wiping her floured hands on apron. She had spent most the morning making cakes and sponges for the church fete.
She looked more drawn than normal, her sleep being interrupted by more nightmares; she just wished they would pass. She made sure she kept a journal of them and anything else that happened. It was difficult, once she woke up she hardly remembered.
She sat down at the kitchen table and surveyed the delights.
At least the money raised from the fete would help towards restoring the church.
She let them cool and boxed them up, storing them in her pantry.
Naomi intended to meet Samuel in the village this afternoon, his phone call she had received sounded like it was urgent.
Her thoughts drifted briefly to the cellar, and that cavern.
She had spent ages trying to figure out what Mr Hamilton had meant.
Was he the only survivor of a previous time? She picked up the book and looked at what Reginald had said.

Orb of light.
Father had been a learned man.
We failed to heed the inscription.

The inscription she thought. She flicked through the pages until she came across the inscription she had scribbled down.

"You will be but be unseen,
The past is here but in a dream,
Touch me once and you'll see all,
Treasures of the mind now hear my call"

Naomi read it to herself several times.
You will be but be unseen. Does that mean being somewhere but being hidden, therefore being unseen? Surely that made no sense.
The past is here but in a dream. This made no sense, the past cannot be here, because now is the present, but in a dream. Does that mean dreaming about the past?
Touch me once and you'll see all. Touch what once, the pedestal? Naomi thought, or the orb of light as Reginald called it.
Treasures of the mind now hear my call. Treasures of the mind... memory... knowledge... Now hear my call. Hear my call? Will someone be talking?
Nothing made sense, exasperated she put the book in her bag.

Samuel was sat on the church wall. He looked troubled as Naomi approached him, clambering from the wall they walked together across the green.
Samuel explained his latest nightmare (or what he could remember) to Naomi.
'... and I remember the cave and something in there with me,' he gestured wildly with his hands.
'... the light surrounded me and then...' he struggled to remember.
Naomi listened intently, hoping to find a link between what Samuel had said and the inscription on the pedestal.
'Samuel, these nightmares only started after we were in the cavern.' Samuel nodded.
'I can only assume that whatever happened to us, is the reason we have these terrors.'
For a split second Naomi thought she was onto something. Shaking her head they carried on past the Butchers and towards the Library.
'Have you had any nightmares since?' enquired Samuel
Naomi nodded. 'I write what I can remember in my book,' Samuel knew what Naomi meant.
'We really need to see Maureen she was with us when it started.'
Samuel nodded in agreement.
Naomi opened the door of the Library and saw Mrs Castlethorpe behind the desk.
After exchanging some pleasantries Naomi confirmed details of the upcoming fete.
'...if you can arrange the flowers and the tables...' Naomi nodded as Mrs Castlethorpe droned on.
Finally they left, Samuel had been surprised that Naomi could concentrate on anything else, let alone make cakes etc.
Naomi had only visited Mrs Castlethorpe for one reason. She had asked if she could get Maureen to help her on the cake stall.
Mrs Castlethorpe had thought it was a splendid idea.

Maureen had finally got on with the housework, ensuring the house was perfect for when Tony arrived home.
She was cooking Leg of Lamb for tea as Tony walked in; placing his briefcase on the chair he kissed Maureen. He smiled and sat down.
Maureen poured the cup of tea, placing it on the table she turned back to cooking the lamb, humming a tune she had heard on the radio.
Tony put his paper down. 'I noticed the church is having a fete this weekend in aid of the church itself.'
Maureen turned, 'not this weekend, they have a wedding booked.'

Tony looked at his wife. 'You mean that new couple?' Maureen nodded. 'So when is the fete?' He asked.

'Weekend after.' replied Maureen.

Rustling the newspaper he carried on reading.

Maureen finished cooking the meal, she was tired, she felt irritable and she wanted to go out and scream.

Taking a deep breath she asked Tony to slice the Lamb whilst she dished up the potatoes and veg.

Maureen had just finished stacking the dishes away when she heard a knock on the door. She walked through to the hallway and opened the door.

Naomi stood outside, she was unsure how she was going to find out if Maureen had had any dreams but first she would go with the fete.

The door opened. Maureen looked at Naomi 'Can I come in please?' asked Naomi.

Maureen seemed almost scared to open the door fully.

'Who's at the door.' shouted Tony from the living room.

Maureen opened the door and let Naomi in. 'Just Naomi,' she replied.

Maureen led Naomi through to the kitchen. Maureen glanced at the cellar door. 'We will come to that later. First of all Mrs Castlethorpe would like to know if you want to help with the fete this weekend at the church.'

Maureen looked puzzled 'Not this weekend surely its next weekend, the young couple...' her sentence drifted as she tried to remember.

Naomi sat. 'The young couple are getting married next weekend, total mix up.' she said shaking her head.

Maureen looked relieved. 'Can we talk?' Maureen said quietly as she led Naomi through to the garden.

Naomi walked down the garden listening to Maureen as she unburdened her nightmares or what she could remember.

'...several times I have killed Tony in my dream...' she said worried. She carried on '... with a rope, I can feel it cutting into him...' Naomi nodded solemnly. '...then I wake up.'

Naomi nodded. 'Samuel and I keep having these nightmares too. It has something to do with when we were all in the cellar.'

Maureen lowered her head, she couldn't deny the fact they had started with the cellar and the cavern.

Naomi carried on relentless. 'I spoke to the brother of the previous owner. He wasn't very helpful.' Naomi struggled to remember what Reginald had said.

Maureen clasped her hands 'what can we do to stop this happening?' she asked almost pleading for Naomi to hold the answers.

Naomi shook her head. 'I wish I knew.'

They spent the next half hour talking more about what they had gone through as they walked up the garden path towards the house.

Tony opened the bureau and smiled. He took the cellar key and made his way to the kitchen. Unlocking the door he turned on the miniscule light and slowly walked down into the cellar. He felt like he had two choices. One voice told him to go down into the cavern whilst the other told him to get the hell out of there.

He reached the trapdoor and bent down, inserting the key into the padlock he watched as the key turned a golden hue.

He struggled to lift the trapdoor but finally managed. He slowly descended down the steps; he knew he was safe even without a torch. Nothing could harm him, it needed him.

The chill bit at his arms as he reached the corner of the steps and resumed to his left.
He reached the bottom seeing the light from the cavern cast shadows around the atrium.
He entered the cavern and slowly moved towards the orb, he could feel its power, he called to
him. He reached out with his fingers and touched the orb.

Maureen and Naomi entered the kitchen. Maureen saw the cellar door open and gasped. She ran
from the kitchen to the living room. Tony was not there. She reached the bureau and saw the
draw down.
'Oh god!' she exclaimed. She raced into the kitchen her heart pounding. Naomi looked at her
'What is wrong?' she enquired.
Maureen moved towards the steps of the cellar. 'Tony has gone down into the cellar.'
Naomi looked at her, her eyes widened 'do you think...' she didn't need to finish the sentence as
Maureen grabbed two old torches and rushed into the dark cellar.
They clambered down the steps and rushed around the corner. Maureen flashing her torch light
around looking for her husband. 'Tony... Tony... you down here?' she shouted.
No reply came. Maureen reached the trapdoor and saw the padlock and key glowing gold, the
trapdoor was up.
Naomi gasped in shock. Maureen started down the cellar. Naomi followed her as they descended.

Tony could see the past, he stood captivated watching as Mr and Mrs Hamilton touched the orb.
He struggled not to blink.
Finally his eyelids closed and he was back to the beginning. Mr and Mrs Hamilton entered the
cavern. Mrs Hamilton seemed scared to go near the pedestal and orb, but Mr Hamilton led her
to it and made her reach out and touch it.
Tony felt spellbound.

Naomi finally reached the bottom of the steps, running she reached the cavern and stopped.
Tony was on the floor. Maureen ran to his side.
Naomi entered the cavern breathless; she saw Tony on the floor and Maureen next to him. She
started to move towards them and felt a shiver. She watched for a moment. Naomi closed her
eyes; surely she was seeing things, a shadow. She watched as Maureen held her husband's hand.
The shadow slowly drifted across the floor and moved towards Tony.
Naomi was sure she could see something. She opened her mouth to warn Maureen and felt
invisible arms push her into the cavern wall. Naomi screamed then fell like a ragdoll to the floor.
Maureen heard Naomi scream and turned. The shadow entered Tony's body.
Tony opened his eyes, the shadow controlling him. He groaned. Maureen looked at her husband
and then at Naomi.
'What...where am I? Tony asked almost feebly. Maureen hugged him and helped him to stand.
'We have to help Naomi.' she said frantically.
Tony grabbed her arm. 'You have to join me,' he said forcefully. He wrenched Maureen forward
and shoved their hands into the orb.
Maureen screamed.
The cavern filled with light as the orbs light intensified.
The shadow slithered from Tony and entered the orb.
Maureen and Tony slumped to the floor.

Samuel had been waiting over an hour and a half for Naomi to call. She had been adamant that
she visit on her own.

Samuel wished he had now gone with her. Angry and impatient he put his jacket on and walked down the road to Naomi's cottage. He banged on the door several times but Naomi either wasn't home or was still at The Whippletree property.

Samuel ran up the lane, he felt the burn in his thighs and the burning in his chest, his body needed to replenish the oxygen.

He saw the house in the distance and ran harder. He reached the gate and took a deep breath. He knocked on the door. Waiting what felt an eternity he knocked again.

No answer.

He walked round the side of the house and saw the door leading to the kitchen was open.

'Hello… Hello' he said 'anyone here?' the silence was deafening.

He turned and saw the cellar door was open.

No…no he thought, surely they hadn't gone down.

He looked on the sideboard for the torches but they were gone.

Samuel raced down into the cellar, shouting their names. Where the hell are they? He walked round the corner and towards the trapdoor using his hands to guide him. He saw a miniscule light low on the ground and scrambled towards it.

He lost his footing and fell to the floor, as he slowly got up he felt a sharp pain in his foot.

He saw the padlock and key. He found the steps; he slowly entered and used his hands to steady himself as he descended.

He kept shouting their names, hoping they were alright. 'Tony… Maureen… Naomi…' he got no reply. Trying to get down faster he cracked his shoulder into the wall and realised the steps bared left.

He struggled down the steps and reached the entrance to the cavern.

He entered and saw Tony and Maureen slumped on the floor. Where was Naomi? He turned.

Naomi was still slumped against the cavern wall. He touched her shoulder. 'Naomi…' Naomi was motionless.

Samuel heard Maureen moan, she was coming round rushing over he grabbed her hand. 'What happened down here?'

Maureen was dazed, she tried to focus.

'Where am I?' she asked Samuel. Samuel helped her up. 'You're in the cavern but Naomi needs help.' Tony murmured and opened his eyes. 'Samuel?' he said groggily. Samuel slowly helped Tony up.

Tony looked at Samuel to his wife and then saw Naomi slumped against the wall. 'What happened?' he exclaimed.

Samuel slowly heard Naomi groan. 'My head…' she said her voice weak.

Samuel helped her up and led her slowly from the cavern.

Chapter 34

(2011)

'Who are you? Mary asked, she felt panic rising within herself. The bright light hurting her eyes she squinted trying to understand where she was.

The man came into view. He had a kind face. His skin was tanned but his eyes were captivating. The blue pierced into her… causing her to feel calm.

'Mary you need to take deep breaths. Everything will be explained in due course.' His voice was soft but held authority.

'My name is Lucas Raven, and where you are… that will take some understanding.'

Mary relaxed slightly. 'How did I get...' she gestured with her arms 'to where I am?'
Lucas smiled. 'That question will be answered later.'
Mary became accustomed to the light, she sat up slowly. She could make out images in the light which surrounded her. 'One question...' Mary paused and touched Lucas's arm 'am I dead?'
Lucas laughed 'Mary you are alive and well.'
Mary looked down; she could see nothing beneath her feet and nothing above her. The light surrounded everything. She felt at peace.
'Come with me Mary.' Mary took his hand and found herself surrounded by trees in a field. She turned round 'How...' she backed away from Lucas.
Lucas smiled. 'This is where I come when I need guidance.' He said his voice soft and calm.
Lucas sat cross legged on the grass. He closed his eyes letting his mind wander. Mary watched. This is bizarre she thought to herself.
Lucas laughed. 'Bizarre at first, but were not here,' Mary looked puzzled. 'This,' he gestured with his arms 'can be anywhere or everywhere.'
'So how did I end up here?' she asked 'with you.'
Lucas stood up. 'That is the question...'
'Listen Lucas is it?' Lucas nodded 'Where are we? How did I end up here? And Where's Tom and Marie'
Lucas took Mary's hand. 'Before I can help, what were you doing before you entered this meditative state?
Mary remembered 'I was in a cavern under my house,' Mary sat on the grass 'Tom and Marie were with me, we have this pedestal with a floating orb light above it.'
Lucas stepped back. 'Not possible.' she watched as he started chanting and mumbling.
Lucas stopped chanting and looked at Mary. 'Please do not touch the orb.'
Mary looked at Lucas. 'Can you explain what it is?'
Lucas touched Mary's hand 'In time...' his voice drifted and Mary sat up.

Tom looked as Mary sat up. Mary put her hand to her head. 'What happened?'
'You shouted something and then collapsed,' replied Tom.
Marie walked in the room and hugged her sister. 'That was quite a fright you gave us.'
Mary rubbed her head. 'What time is it?'
Tom looked at his watch 'its four p.m.' he smiled at his wife and brushed the hair from her forehead. 'You've been murmuring for an hour, but we were unable to wake you.'
Mary looked around the living room. 'I thought I had died, I dreamt I was in clouds, then in a field with another man.'
Tom stiffened slightly 'another man?' He asked.
Mary looked at her husband. 'Not letting you go.' Tom smiled at Mary.
'LUCAS RAVEN,' she shouted. She got up and grabbed a piece of paper. 'His name was Lucas Raven.'
Marie looked at her sister. 'And he is...'
Mary scowled at her sister. 'Someone you can find out about.'
Tom laughed 'Who is he?'
Mary turned 'Someone who saved all our lives today.'
Mary walked purposely out the living room and towards the door. 'Come on we have work to do.'
Tom looked at Marie 'She's fine.'

Marie drove them back to the Hotel. The storm clouds had passed letting rays of sunshine burst through.
Mary sat deep in thought, struggling to remember where she had been, let alone who Lucas Raven was and his connection to the pedestal and orb.

Marie spent the afternoon looking through records to find anything on Lucas Raven, having just a name had given her little to go on. She felt tempted to ring work and use the search system they had, but with being on holiday and after the conversation with her boss she felt it was best not to push her luck.

She rung her friend at the university, maybe he could find something out on her behalf.

Tom felt concerned as he watched the video footage of them in the cavern. He rubbed his head once more. The feeling of dread he had experienced had left him nauseous. He watched the footage in the cavern. He could quite clearly see the images on the wall and had picked up the historians notebooks. Naomi had a keen eye, whatever had happened was clearly still in the cavern.

He carried on watching, Marie was filming the pedestal and orb, he could clearly make out the inscription on the pedestal and then he heard his wife's voice. *'Do not touch this orb... the orb of light is too powerful for you.'* He watched as the video camera focused on his wife and then she collapsed.

Tom wrote what Mary had said. *'Do not touch this orb,'* bit strange he thought, if it had been the orb it would make sense. Was there more than one orb? *'The orb of light is too powerful for you'.*

Again Tom considered the wording, too powerful for you. Was this a warning? He rewound the footage and listened again. He noticed a different tone in his wife's voice. It was like someone else was speaking through her.

Marie walked over to Tom. 'Any luck? She asked.

Tom shook his head. 'Just something else to add to the ever growing list of unsolved' he sighed.

Marie sat down. She felt dejected. 'Have a listen to this.' Tom said.

He rewound the footage. Marie watched the pedestal and then heard Mary's voice. *'Do not touch this orb... the orb of light is too powerful for you.'*

Marie asked Tom to play it once more. She listened intently. Tom played it back three more times for Marie.

'I know my sister...' she said with confidence 'and that isn't Mary talking.' Tom nodded solemnly.

Mary walked into the bar/lounge room and looked at Tom and Marie. 'Any progress?' she asked.

Tom nodded. 'We know it isn't you talking before you collapsed.' Mary gave her husband a quizzical look. 'Who was it then?' she looked down for a second 'Sorry,' she said. 'Okay you say it isn't me, but it was neither of you two, and I am the only one left.'

Marie looked at her sister. 'Watch this.' Marie replayed the pedestal scene and then Mary's warning before collapsing. Mary looked at her sister 'Yes it was me.'

Marie shook her head. 'Listen to the words.'

Mary watched the footage twice. 'This orb' she questioned. Tom nodded 'Too powerful for you.' She looked at Tom 'for who exactly.' Tom looked at Mary then Marie. 'I need some air,' he got up and walked out of the room.

Marie watched Tom as he left. 'Have you talked to him yet?'

Mary looked at her sister. 'No, he seems distant of late. He keeps rubbing his forehead yet claims he is okay.'

Marie smiled 'Men for you.' Mary gave a half laugh. 'Give him time and when this is all over he will be back to normal.'

Mary hugged her sister.

Tom sat outside on the old wooden seat. He rubbed his temple again. Nothing seemed to ease the tension he felt inside.

The trip to the house had reawakened the fear he had felt when he was trapped. He sighed. Whatever was going on at the house was not going to be sorted overnight.

Tom got up and walked around the grounds of the hotel, he found it helped him to focus.

As he walked back in the hotel he realised he had two choices. He could put the property on the market and let it be someone else's problem or he could face what was happening.

He walked back into the bar/lounge area and smiled at Marie and Mary. 'We better get this lot packed away.' he said.

Marie looked at the clock and realised it was almost six.

They cleared the tables and walked up to their rooms.

Mary walked into the bathroom first. She undressed and turned the shower on. As she stood under the shower she tried to gather her thoughts on what had happened.

She felt the grime of the cellar and cavern wash away as she applied the shower gel. As she washed herself she reached for the shampoo. She reached round the curtain and felt a hand grab hers. She screamed.

Tom rushed in. 'What's up?' he said.

Mary peered round the curtain 'Someone just grabbed my hand.'

Tom looked at her. 'No one entered the bathroom after you did and no one left either.'

Mary tried to steady her breathing, her chest rose and fell. 'I know what I felt Tom.'

Tom walked over to her and kissed her. Mary kissed him back, she wanted reassuring. Tom looked in her eyes. 'What were you after?' Mary pulled at her straggly hair. 'Shampoo to sort this tangled mop.' Tom laughed and picked up the shampoo. He then picked up a small rectangular card.

The orb is too powerful for you.

Do not touch the orb.

L.R.

Tom read it twice and took it into the main room.

His mind flooded him with questions. Had this mysterious Lucas been in the bathroom? How did he get in? What in god's name did he want?

Putting the card on the dresser he glanced out the window.

Mary walked out wrapped in a towel and one round her head.

'Nice look.' commented Tom.

'Do you fancy a quick brew before we go down?' she asked. 'Tom nodded. 'Let me get showered.' Tom closed the door and peeled off his shirt.

As he undressed he felt conscious that someone might be watching. He got in the shower and turned it on.

Mary set the cups and boiled the mini kettle. She sat down at the dressing table and plugged in her hairdryer. She dried her hair first with the towel and then finished off with the hairdryer. She was still adamant that someone had grabbed her hand while she was in the shower. And nothing anyone said was going to make her feel like she was going mad.

After she had done her hair she made the two coffees.

She noticed a small rectangular card on the side, turning it over she read.

The orb is too powerful for you.

Do not touch the orb.

L.R.

Mary dropped the card.

Tom finished his shower and walked back into the main bedroom. Mary was sat at the dresser. He could tell by her demeanour that something was troubling her. 'You okay?' he asked. Mary smiled. Tom knew that smile. He had learnt in the relationship quickly that when she smiled and never spoke he was in serious trouble. Normally it was over not discussing a purchase or the furniture or going behind her back.

Tom sat on the edge of the bed and reached over for his coffee. As he lifted the cup he saw the rectangular card. He closed his eyes. This was not good.

Mary was stubborn. She knew Tom was thinking on how to approach the subject.

'You remember when you screamed...' he said as he turned the card in his hand. Mary nodded, 'this card was under the shampoo.' as the words left his mouth he knew it sounded lame.

Mary chuckled. 'Please tell me that wasn't the best you could come up with.'

Tom looked down at the card. He passed it to Mary. 'Sniff it.'

Mary looked at her husband, feeling angry. Yet sensibility compelled her to do as he said. She sniffed the card catching the feint scent of her shampoo.

'You said someone grabbed your hand,' Mary nodded 'how would I get this underneath the shampoo?' Mary struggled to think of a rational explanation.

'So you took the card instead of telling me in the shower?' Tom nodded solemnly. Realising that was mistake number one.

'You then left it on the dresser for me to find?' Tom shook his head. 'No, I was wrong to not tell you straight away. I admit that.' Mary nodded accepting his apology. 'Look at the wording.' Mary read the words. Tom reached over for his book. He had made a note of what Mary had said in the cavern.

Mary took the book off him. *Do not touch this orb... the orb of light is too powerful for you.* She then looked at the card. *The orb is too powerful for you. Do not touch the orb. L.R.*

Mary then looked at Tom.

Tom looked at his wife. 'I cannot comprehend to understand what is going on,' he said as he rubbed his temple again. 'I have been locked in a cellar, I have been in a coma, and I have witnessed my wife saying something strange and now this card.' He rubbed his temple again.

Mary got up and sat next to him. She placed her arm around his shoulder. She could feel the tension along his shoulders.

She slowly started to massage his shoulders; she kneaded into them trying to break his tension down.

'If someone did grab my hand...' she said as her hands worked into his back 'what would they gain by leaving the card?'

Tom shook his head. He felt some slight relief from the massage. Her hands were so soft and gentle. He closed his eyes relishing the experience.

Mary finished the massage and kissed her husband. 'We will get through this,' she said taking his hand in hers 'but, we must be strong' Tom nodded kissing Mary.

They finally got dressed for dinner and knocked on Marie's door.

Marie noticed a slight change in Tom; he seemed to be more relaxed. As Tom walked down the stairs Marie glanced at Mary. Mary understood the unasked question and smiled.

Claudia waited outside the hotel for the car to pick her up. She had done what had been asked of her. She glanced at her watch.

The black BMW drove into the car park and she got in the rear of the car.

'Did you do as I asked?' Lucas asked.

Claudia nodded.

'Good.' He replied.

The Black BMW turned out of the car park and drove away.

Chapter 35

After dinner Tom, Mary and Marie drove into the town. They walked across the green to towards town.

Mary explained to Marie about the card they had found under the shampoo bottle and how the wording was slightly different to the one she had said in the cavern.

Marie was also concerned about Mary feeling a hand grab hers.

Tom felt slightly better his tension had eased. He kept thinking how someone, if they were real had managed to evade him when his wife screamed in the shower.

Mary wouldn't have screamed for any reason. He knew her too well. It nagged at him. Marie seemed puzzled by the newest of events too.

They looked around the town itself and strolled through the sleepy village.

As the sun started to set they made their way back to the hotel. Mary felt more relaxed, she felt she had got through to Tom and whatever was happening they would get through it.

When they got back to the hotel they made their way up to their rooms. Marie looked at them both.

'I have an idea,' she said smiling. Tom had seen this smile. He groaned, 'behave you' she said. Mary laughed. 'What is your idea?'

Marie walked with them into the room. She purposely walked into the bathroom. 'Mary...' she shouted through the closed door 'go for that shower again and Tom can you rush in when Mary screams.' Mary smiled at Tom 'let's humour her.'

Mary opened the door trying to remember what she did first. She looked around the bathroom but couldn't see Marie. 'Marie?' There was no answer. Mary pretended to undress. She climbed into the shower. She reached out for the shampoo and felt someone grab her hand, she screamed as she did before. Tom came into the room and looked around. Marie was nowhere to be seen. Mary stepped out of the shower and walked with Tom back into the bedroom. Marie was sitting in one of the chairs.

Tom and Mary stood open mouthed. 'How did you...' Marie smiled. 'It was simple.'

Marie led them back into the bathroom. Mary stood where she had when she had walked in.

Marie walked over to the wall by the door. The wall jutted out enough for Marie to crouch down. 'Your mysterious friend was actually in the room' she said purposely. 'When you got in the shower, they could stand up. If like me, you normally keep the shampoo inside the shower area you would never reach out to the side area to reach for it.'

Mary nodded, 'You were made to reach out, and they grabbed you. Instinctively you would scream. I would too.' Marie looked at Tom; he had watched her move from her crouched hidden area into plain view to grab Mary's hand. He watched Marie move back to the hidden area. 'Now Tom when you rushed in, you would be only conscious of getting to Mary this gives the mystery person the advantage to slip out of the room and out.

Mary and Tom watched as Marie reconstructed her movements for them both to see.

Tom was dumbstruck. 'So when did you figure that out?' he asked.

Marie grinned. 'I have had my fair share of mysteries to solve.' Tom nodded. Both Mary and Tom knew better than to ask Marie what she actually did for a living.

'Suffice to say' she said 'it proves that someone had access to the room in the first place. No one can guess when you are going to go to your room.'

Mary nodded. 'So we better ask Doris if anyone has been asking about us.'

Marie nodded. 'That can wait for morning', she bade them both good night and walked to her own room.

Tom locked the door and looked at Mary.

'If she ever leaves her job, she could go freelance.'

Mary laughed.

Mary made them both a drink and finally got changed for bed.

Mary opened the door and walked into the hall. She closed the door behind her and glanced towards the kitchen. As she started to walk through she caught movement on the stairs. She put her left hand on the railing and started to climb the spiral staircase.

She reached the top of the stairs and looked around.

All the bedroom doors were shut but the study was open. Mary walked into the study and glanced around at the array of books neatly lining the oak bookcase.

Feeling drawn she glanced at the titles. Encyclopaedias, Dictionaries and numerous files filled the top shelf.

Mary looked at the second shelf and noticed one book slightly out of alignment to the others. Removing the book she looked at the title. *"Our shamanic life"* opening the book she read a passage.

"Our shamanic journey begins, as if were new, finding a path to what is true. This book contains our journey as we discover the rituals and ideas of the shamans.
We begin our journey..."

Mary turned another page and glanced at the photographs. She saw three young men sitting on a seat. The clothes were early 1920's with the eldest man wearing a cap and a pipe in his mouth.

Mary continued to flick through the pages. She stopped on another page, whoever had owned the book had written in the margin. She continued to flick through the pages. She found several more pages with comments in the margin area.

Then she noticed several words written around the page clockwise. She turned the book as she read. Mary stepped back, dropping the book. She had seen this before on the trapdoor and the pedestal.

Mary looked at more photographs another caught her eye as she saw the house in its splendour.

Mary pulled the seat away from the desk and sat down.

As she flicked through the rest of the book she found a name scribbled childlike on the back page. C. Raven.

Mary looked at the front of the book and then the spine. She found the authors name. R. Hamilton.

As Mary stood up she sensed movement to her left. She turned instinctively and screamed.

Mary sat up in bed and rubbed her face. She looked at the bedside clock and saw it was four in the morning. She climbed out of bed careful not to disturb Tom.

Switching on her laptop she tried to recall the title of the book.

Wracking her brains she closed the lid down. What she did remember was the book was in the study. She also remembered that the books had gone in storage when they were decorating but should be back in the oak bookshelf.

Mary walked into the bathroom and glanced at the dark reflection. The dream itself had not been evil. It seemed to be pointing her in the next direction. Knowing she couldn't fathom it out at this late hour she walked back to bed.

Lying in bed she glanced at the ceiling. She closed her eyes and sleep took over.

Doris was clearing tables when Tom, Mary and Marie walked in. Doris ushered them to a free table.

'Good morning my dears,' she said cheerily. 'How are we all this morning?'

Marie smiled 'Very well thank you Doris, how are you and your husband?'

Doris leant in closer 'Robert is not feeling his best today; his back is aching from dealing with the garden.'

Mary laughed. 'You will have to give him a back rub later Doris.'

Doris almost snorted. 'He can suffer.'

They all laughed. 'Now what can I get you for breakfast?

After eating breakfast (full English) and numerous cups of coffee they wandered outside.

Tom had listened to Mary's dream and he was sure the books had been put back in the study.

Marie had been quiet, almost deep in thought after everything that had happened she was determined to get this solved.

Mary wanted to go to the house to look for the book in the study. 'Tom,' she pleaded 'it won't take long to go to the house and check the study for the book.'

Tom looked at his wife 'No, no and NO.' he replied adamantly.

Mary turned exasperated. Marie decided to step in and defuse the situation. 'Tom,' she said calmly 'if you start going through the books that Samuel left us, and then I can drive Mary to the house and fetch the book.'

Tom looked from Marie to Mary. He knew if he refused them they would just go anyway. He knew he had no choice.

'Fine,' he replied, his teeth slightly clenched 'but you have to promise...' he looked from Mary to Marie 'just the book.'

Marie beamed.

Tom turned and started to walk back to the hotel. Mary caught up with him and kissed him. 'Be back in a short while,' Tom kissed her back. 'Be careful,' he replied.

Mary ran back towards Marie's car and got in.

Marie turned the car round and Tom waved as he watched them drive away.

Tom walked back into the hotel lobby; Doris smiled as he walked past. He waited as she finished her phone call.

'...as I have mentioned this hotel has lots to offer...' Doris tilted her head to the side.

'Yes, we can organise anything you want.' She replied.

Doris listened to the caller 'I look forward to seeing you...' Doris rolled her eyes. 'Yes... thank you for calling... yes... bye for now.'

Finally Doris put the receiver down.

Tom laughed. 'Doris, do you ever have normal guests?'

Doris laughed. 'Not many.' she replied

Tom laughed. 'Did anyone visit over the past day or two asking about us? Or come to do any supposed work?'

Doris looked at Tom. 'I keep a register of anyone who visits, for Health and Safety purposes.'

'May I?' ask Tom.

Doris nodded 'Be my guest,' she chuckled afterwards 'I have always wanted to say that.'

Doris wandered off chucking; two guests came down the stairs and looked at Doris chuckling. Tom rolled his eyes.

Tom looked at the register.

Name	Company	Time In	Time Out	Signature	Work Done/Comments
Miss Sanderson					Lovely Holiday
Charles Anderson	Brewery	09:00	10:00		Stocked Up
Craven	N.A	15:30			

Tom read the list of names. He looked at the last Name Craven... was that a Mr or a Mrs? He bet Doris and her husband had great fun ensuring this was up to date.

Placing the book back behind the counter area he made his way to his room.

Mary and Marie pulled up outside the house; Mary shivered and glanced up at the windows.

'Every time we return I shiver,' she said out loud. Marie laughed. 'Well you want this book.'

They both got out the car and walked to the house. Mary inserted the key and unlocked the door.

They stepped into the hallway and climbed the spiral staircase to the study. Mary looked around; the bedroom doors were closed like in her dream.

Mary walked slowly into the study itself. The oak bureau had centre place so anyone sitting could look outside at the beautiful scenery. Marie stood by the door. 'Where was this book?'

'In this bookcase.' replied Mary.

She searched frantically starting from the top and working her way down. 'It's not here!' she exclaimed. Marie walked over and helped Mary look. Marie felt partially useless as she had no clue of which book it was.

Mary closed her eyes; she remembered it wasn't the top shelf. It was about... she carried on searching pulling out books and replacing them.

Marie could see Mary getting more annoyed. 'Start at the top.' She suggested.

Mary knew her sister was right. Frantically searching would not do.

Mary removed the files and placed them on the bureau. She then removed each book in turn and replaced each one.

Working methodically she reached the third shelf. She pulled the books out, looked at the title and placed them back. Marie stood by the bureau looking at the folders. She opened them in turn and glanced at the paperwork.

Mary reached the bottom shelf. She had to find this damn book. Pulling another out she glanced at the title. No she thought. Maybe it was just a dream. Maybe the book didn't exist.

She pulled out another and another. She finally reached the last book and put it back.

Marie turned and looked at her sister. 'Listen maybe it was a dream and nothing more.'

Mary nodded. She felt stupid. She stood up and looked at the bookcase once more.

Marie placed her arm around Mary. 'Listen let's go back to the hotel.'

Mary nodded.

They both turned to leave. The Study door slammed closed. Mary and Marie tried to turn the handle, the door wouldn't budge.

Marie pulled out her mobile phone. As she pressed Tom's number into the keypad the phone battery died.

Mary looked around. This was insane.

Mary moved to the window and glanced outside. She tried to open the window. The handle was stuck.

Pulling out the chair she sat down.

Marie looked around the room; she wanted something to use to break the window.

Mary stared out the window. 'Marie,' she said quietly. Marie was still looking around the room. 'Marie...'

Marie looked at her sister. 'What is it?'

Mary pointed outside.

Marie moved towards the bureau and looked down towards the garden.

She looked at Mary and back outside.

A man and a woman stood in the back yard.

Marie turned to Mary 'Who are they?'

Chapter 36

Samuel helped Naomi up the steps and back into the cellar. 'Wait here,' he said as he sat Naomi down against the wall. Samuel rushed back down and helped Maureen up the steps. Tony was right behind her. Samuel let them both pass and entered the cavern, he picked up the torches and left.

He climbed the steps back into the cellar and helped Tony lower the trapdoor. He watched as Tony put the padlock on and removed the key.

Tony slipped the key in his pocket.

'What the hell were you all doing down there,' shouted Samuel, anger clearly in his voice.

Tony looked down 'I don't remember.' Samuel looked at Maureen and then to Naomi.

Samuel helped Naomi up 'We need to get to the kitchen and look at this injury.'

Tony led the way and Maureen helped Samuel with Naomi.

Once they reached the kitchen they sat Naomi down. Tony locked the cellar door.

Maureen fetched a flannel and soaked it in water. Samuel placed the flannel on the back of Naomi's head. Naomi flinched as she felt the flannel touch the back of her head.

Samuel looked at the wound. It wasn't too bad, but he thought Naomi best go to hospital.

Tony reached for his car keys. 'I will drive.'

They helped Naomi into the passenger seat and watched as Tony drove off towards the hospital.

Samuel walked back into the house with Maureen.

He sat her down and stared at the cellar door.

'It's no good,' he finally said. 'Whatever happened...'he paused 'no one will remember.'

Maureen looked at the table. She had no idea how she had ended up in the cellar again.

Samuel sighed. The silence felt deafening, the waiting felt worse.

'I need some air.' he said. Maureen looked at Samuel. She didn't want to be alone in the house.

They walked down the garden, just to pass time. Samuel reached the fence at the bottom and looked at the stream.

This felt normal. No worries, or concerns down here. Maureen stood next to him.

'Do you know why Naomi visited you tonight?

Maureen shook her head.

'Fete on Saturday to help with the sale...' he said hoping it would remind her.

Maureen looked at Samuel. She felt a flicker of memory come back. 'We were outside.'

Samuel looked at Maureen. 'We talked.' The memory faded. Maureen sighed.

'I keep having nightmares about the cavern and...' Samuel paused for a second 'and killing people I feel closest too.'

Maureen looked at him. 'I have nightmares too.'

'Naomi told me she had been having nightmares.' Samuel said quietly.

Maureen looked at Samuel. 'Its... it's the cavern isn't it?'

Samuel nodded. 'I think we all have to go down one last time, and destroy that light.'

Maureen faced him. 'Do you think that will stop us having the nightmares?'

Samuel smiled. 'I hope so.'

They turned and started to walk up the garden path. Samuel looked up at the house.

'They say that this house was built on an ancient burial ground,' he said as they passed the chicken coop.

Maureen laughed. It felt so good to laugh at such nonsense.

Maureen looked up at the house. 'Samuel...' she pointed upwards. 'Can you see people in the study?'

Samuel stopped and looked up. For a fleeting moment he thought he had seen movement.

They ran back to the house through the kitchen and into the hallway.

They made their way up the stairs and stood outside the study room.

Samuel listened at the door. He couldn't hear anything. He opened the door and rushed in. He looked around but no one was there.

'Does anything look out of place?'

Maureen looked around; everything seemed to be where it should be.

Samuel led her out and back to the kitchen.

Naomi groaned in the car. Tony glanced at her 'You'll be fine,' he said. He drove along the country roads and into the village.

Naomi opened her eyes. 'Doctors...' she murmured.

Tony looked at her. 'We're going to the hospital.'

Tony drove past the church and the green and through the village. His head was aching and his mind was reeling from being in the cavern. His brow furrowed in concentration.

Pulling up outside the hospital he ran to the door. He rushed into the hospital. Visitors were just leaving.

Tony stopped a nurse. 'You have got to help me,' he said his voice frantic.

The nurse looked startled. 'Visiting hours is over sir.' Tony grabbed her arm. 'My friend is in the car and injured.'

The nurse struggled. 'Let go.' she screamed. She pulled away and ran down the corridor.

'What is going on?' Tony whirled and saw the matron approach.

'My friend is injured...' he babbled trying to make sense.

The matron looked at him. 'Show me where.' she said sternly.

Tony ran back to the door and towards the car. He opened the passenger door. He helped Naomi out and led her up the steps.

The matron took hold of Naomi and led her inside.

Tony watched as she ordered two nurses to fetch items.

'Thank you.' he said. His voice seemed to be a whisper.

'Sit in the waiting area.' the matron ordered.

The matron took charge as they checked the severity of the injury. One of the nurses took Naomi's details and took it to the main desk.

Tony waited anxiously.

His head ached from everything; he couldn't remember what had happened or how they had all ended up in the cavern.

He rubbed his face. 'Are you alright sir?' Tony looked up at a nurse. 'You don't look well.' Tony smiled at her. 'Just waiting for a friend.' he replied.

The matron looked at the wound and cleaned it up as best she could. 'How on earth did this happen...' she asked in a matter-of-fact tone.

Naomi couldn't remember. 'I... I am not sure.' she replied

The matron carried on working. 'It doesn't need stitches, your very lucky.'

The matron finished off and informed Naomi to do nothing but rest for a few days, and if she had any headaches to return.

The matron left the room and walked back into the waiting area.

'I have cleaned it up and she is to rest and return if she has any headaches or feels nauseated.' she stated in her matter-of-fact tone 'It would help if I knew how it happened.'

Tony's heart skipped a few beats 'I am unsure of how it happened.'

The matron glared at Tony. 'You can take her home, but she needs rest.'

Tony smiled and thanked the matron. The matron turned on her heel and walked off.

Naomi was wheeled into the waiting area. Tony was pleased see her and helped her back to the car.

They drove back through the town and back to the house.

Tony pulled up outside and led Naomi back in the house. Maureen rushed to the door after hearing the car pull up.

Samuel waited till they got Naomi in the living room.

Naomi had some colour back in her cheeks but couldn't remember what had happened. Tony walked to the drinks cabinet and poured himself a scotch.

He looked at Maureen and then Samuel, what had happened? He listened as Naomi told them what the nurse had said. '...they told me to rest and return if feeling nauseated or have headaches.' Samuel smiled. He was just glad it was nothing too serious.

Maureen glanced at her husband. 'I think Naomi better stay here tonight.'

Tony nodded. Samuel looked at them. 'I want to stay too.'

Tony nodded again.

Maureen walked out of the room; making her way up the stairs she went into the spare rooms and made the beds up.

Maureen finished off the beds and walked past the study; she glanced back in the room and closed the door. Making her way down the stairs she walked into the kitchen and put the kettle on.

She walked back into the lounge 'I am sure we could all do with a drink.'

Tony nodded he was very quiet; Naomi said she was parched and Samuel nodded too.

After the drinks Samuel looked at Tony. 'I think it would be a good idea that we all decide on what we should do about the cavern and that light.'

Tony put his cup down. 'What did you have in mind?'

Samuel looked at Naomi 'We should destroy it.'

They debated for an hour if it could be destroyed and what the consequences could be. Everything ended in ifs and buts.

Maureen had listened as they argued their points across.

Naomi finally spoke. 'We have to try something, before it destroys us all.'

Samuel nodded. 'I have nightmares.' Tony looked at him. 'I do too.'

Maureen looked at her husband. 'That's settled then. We destroy the light.'

Tony knew they had good reason. He himself felt different, his work performance had slipped and people were concerned about him.

Maureen looked at the clock. She was tired. Naomi was also yawning. Maureen looked at them all in turn. 'We will discuss this in more detail but not tonight.'

Samuel helped Naomi up the steps he felt like he had failed in protecting her. She walked into the room and Samuel walked along the balcony to the next room.

Maureen and Tom checked everything was locked downstairs before heading upstairs themselves.

It was 2am. The coolness had returned, and a slight breeze blew through the branches.

The owl blinked as it sat on the branch of the Whipple tree searching for its next meal.

The shadow slowly drifted out of the cellar and up the stairs to the study. The door slowly creaked open as it entered. The shadow drifted off into the bookcase and found its resting place.

The book slowly edged out of the bookcase and thudded dully on the carpet. The shadow left the room and glided towards the balcony.

The owl sensed movement and ruffled its feathers. The shadow looked at the owl and then glided towards the window.

The owl hooted and flew off into the night.

The shadow entered Samuels's room, it watched as Samuels eyes flickered as he dreamt.

It glided out and into all the other rooms watching them dream.

Slowly it descended the stairs and entered the kitchen. The cellar door creaked open and it vanished into the depths of the cellar.

Naomi woke up. She looked at her watch and groaned. Half past five. Her head ached and she felt sore, but she knew who she was and where she was.

She slowly got out of bed and walked to the bathroom. She had a wash and walked along the balcony. She stopped by the study and glanced out the window. A few rain drops fell against the window. She saw the book on the floor, she bent down and winced. She picked the book up and glanced at the title. "*Our shamanic life*". Naomi looked for the author's name. *R. Hamilton*. Naomi made her way back to the room. Could this be the same Reginald Hamilton?

Hearing noises outside Naomi slid the book under the pillow.

Maureen was down stairs cooking breakfast when Naomi entered the kitchen.

Yesterday's events had cemented a new bond between them all. Maureen smiled and poured two cups of tea. They both sat down and talked about the upcoming fete. Maureen wanted to help; it would at least take her mind off the house.

Tony wandered in and yawned. He glanced out the window and noticed the rain. 'I hate the rain,' he said out loud to no one in particular.

Maureen laughed and poured his cup of tea. 'Drink that.' She kissed him and got up to finish the bacon.

Tony looked at Naomi 'how do you feel this morning?' he asked sympathetically.

Naomi smiled 'a little sore but better.'

Maureen set the plates out and the cutlery and started to serve as Samuel walked in.

'Cup of tea for you,' she said and ushered him to the table.

Maureen served up bacon, eggs, sausages and toast. She finally sat down and they all ate.

They discussed the upcoming fete and decided it would be best to get that out the way first.

Tony got up from the table and kissed his wife. 'I better get to work.' Maureen kissed him back and watched as he left the kitchen.

Samuel also decided he better get off, he had a few jobs to do at the church before the weekend.

Naomi smiled as Samuel left, 'kind man.'

'He cares deeply for you.' Maureen replied

Naomi knew this 'he will be fine, I am his motherly figure.'

Maureen started to pack everything away. Naomi helped her clear the plates and wash up.

After it was all done they had a second cup of tea.

Maureen certainly didn't want to spend time in the house today. Naomi needed to go into town. She could do with the company.

As they left the house, the cellar door opened.

Chapter 37

Maureen and Naomi returned home laden with shopping bags, Maureen unlocked the door and carried them through to the kitchen while Naomi shut the door.

Maureen packed the shopping away and made them both a cup of tea. Naomi knew she had done too much, but, in many ways, the trip had cleared her head.

Maureen offered Naomi some headache tablets to ease the pain.

Before they had returned they had popped into Naomi's cottage and picked up an overnight bag. Maureen was adamant that she should stay one more night.

Naomi didn't want to be a burden but Maureen insisted. Naomi finished her tea and took her bag to the guest room.

She reached under the pillow and pulled out the book, placing it at the bottom of her overnight bag, if it was the same Reginald Hamilton, then maybe it held answers.

She made the bed up and walked back down the stairs.

Maureen insisted that Naomi laid down to rest.

Samuel returned to the house mid-afternoon, after speaking to Naomi he then got on with the gardening. Maureen was so happy; it had been a while since she had visitors. Whilst Samuel was in the garden she did some dusting.

She called Samuel in and asked if he wanted to stay for dinner and overnight. Samuel accepted the dinner invitation gracefully and agreed one more night would do no harm as long as Tony agreed.

Maureen chuckled, she wanted the company, and was sure Tony wouldn't mind.

When Tony got home he looked slightly surprised that Naomi and Samuel were still at his house. Maureen took him aside explaining that it was just for one more night.

Tony kissed his wife. He had to admit, it did get quite quiet in the house with just the two of them.

Maureen busied herself in the kitchen accepting no help from Naomi or Samuel. Tony looked through the local paper.

Maureen saw him smiling at something. 'What's funny?' she asked.

'Not funny,' he replied 'just something I have been after for a while.'

He put the paper down and showed Maureen the advertisement about a snooker table.

Maureen looked at him. 'You're not serious surely?' she said.

Tony looked almost hurt by the remark 'It means Samuel and I can play snooker, you and Naomi can gossip, and also we can have parties.'

Maureen could see the prospects. She kissed him and told him to get washed for dinner.

Maureen knew how to cook a feast. The beef was succulent, the roast potatoes were crispy yet fluffy inside and the carrots, peas and runner beans were perfect.

Naomi felt much better since resting and helped Maureen wash up.

Tony had rung the number in the newspaper and could fetch the snooker table anytime, he was eager to fetch it that Samuel went with him.

Maureen finished the last of the plates and started wiping the worktops down they then moved to the Lounge.

It was a good hour later before Tony and Samuel returned, laden with snooker table and everything.

Naomi laughed as they both struggled with everything. Maureen couldn't help but laugh as they put it back together in the next room.

It took another hour before they had it set up.

Maureen made them all a drink and watched with Naomi as Samuel and Tony attempted to play snooker.

The evening was full of laughter that Maureen almost wished it wouldn't end. Naomi yawned on the Sofa while Maureen finished off her glass of wine.

She had to admit she too felt tired.

Tony and Samuel finished their beers and entered the Lounge.

Samuel yawned also and decided it was time to go up. Naomi also decided to retire for the evening.

Maureen thanked them for stopping. Tony looked at the grandfather clock. It was almost ten in the evening.

They took the glasses into the kitchen, checked all the doors and walked up the stairs to bed.

The rain lashed against the windows when Tony woke up; he almost groaned as he got up. Walking through to the bathroom he gazed in the mirror rubbing his stubble chin with his hand.

After a wash and a shave he showered. His mind wandering over the past few days, sure it had been wonderful having Naomi and Samuel over, he had noticed a difference in Maureen too.

He turned off the shower and dried himself off, he got dressed and walked down the spiral staircase to the kitchen

Naomi sat at the breakfast table also dressed, Maureen had looked at the back of her head and since she had suffered no ill effects she felt strong enough to go home.

She sat talking to Tony whilst Maureen finished off the breakfast.

Maureen finished setting the table and poured her husband a cup of tea. He smiled as she started plating up.

Samuel walked through he also looked smart and wanted a lift into town if Tony was driving that way. Tony nodded. Samuel explained he needed to get some things in town and then home.

Naomi explained she needed to visit the library as she had a few last minute preparations to sort.

Maureen started passing the plates round 'I wouldn't mind coming along Naomi if it would benefit you...' she enquired.

Naomi smiled 'Please do Maureen and then you can try one of the cakes.'

Tony looked up. 'How come I have never heard of your cakes?'

Samuel swallowed 'Her cakes are wonderful.'

'I will save you a cake Tony.' replied Naomi.

After breakfast Tony gave Samuel a lift into town and then drove to work.

Naomi helped Maureen wash and pack away; they left the kitchen and walked up the stairs and stripped the beds.

Naomi took her overnight bag and walked down the spiral staircase. She felt conscious of her movements due to the book that was in the bag.

She felt the house was watching her; Maureen followed her down the stairs and offered to carry the bag until they got to Naomi's cottage.

Naomi smiled but declined the offer. Maureen opened the door; the rain was lashing down harder as it danced off the pavement and roads.

Picking up an umbrella from the underneath the coat rack she opened it up as she stepped outside.

Naomi followed her outside and held the umbrella while Naomi locked up.

Maureen and Naomi made small talk as they walked along the country lane; they walked quickly and soon arrived at Naomi's cottage.

Naomi unlocked the door, picked up two letters and walked into the kitchen. She placed her holdall on one of the chairs and closed the door.

Maureen followed Naomi through. Naomi offered Maureen a cup of tea and fetched a selection of the cakes she had made from the pantry.

Maureen had to admit they were delicious and took a selection home for herself and Tony.

'Thank you for letting me stay for the past two evenings, and Samuel too,' Naomi said gratefully.

'I feel partially responsible,' replied Maureen 'it was our fault that you ended up injured.'

Naomi smiled and knew exactly what Maureen meant.

'We will pick you up Saturday morning, and help get these cakes to the church.' Maureen said as she turned towards the door.

Naomi let her out and watched as Maureen headed into town. Naomi walked back into the kitchen and made herself another drink. She opened her holdall and removed the book. Her cheeks reddened slightly, as if she had been a naughty child stealing a sweet.

She headed into the living room, placing the post on the small table along with the book.

She opened the post first. One was a letter from a friend with her news and gossip. The second was a letter from her Bank manager.

She slowly stood up and reached for her other books. Maybe there will be something about how to stop all these nightmares she thought to herself.

She sipped her cup of tea and opened the book. The book itself had several photographs of the house and explained the basics of their Shaman journey.

Her eyes felt heavy as she tried to read the book, the book slowly fell from her hands to the floor.

Naomi opened the cellar door and shivered, the cool moist cellar enveloped her as she descended. She used the wall to steady herself.

Her eyes became more accustomed to the darkness as she reached the bottom step.

She felt her pulse quicken as she rounded the corner she walked steadily toward the trap door. Reaching in her pocket she fumbled for the cellar key. She knelt and inserted the key into the lock watching as the key changed to its golden hue, she removed the key and padlock and with some effort lifted the trap door.

The darkness surrounded her as she slowly made her way down the steps using her hands to steady herself as she descended, she could hear her heart thumping as she moved father down towards the cavern itself. The wall she knew should be coming up where the steps veered to the left. Each step she took edged her closer to her goal. She knew the wall would be coming up, her eyes adjusting to the dark. Feeling the wall she veered to the left and carried on her descent towards the cavern.

She took several deep breaths when she reached the bottom. Her goal was ever closer; she entered the cavern and looked directly at the orb and the pedestal.

The orb floated just above the pedestal; to Naomi it called out to her, she could sense more with the orb than what it was. Naomi reached out her fingers inching closer to the orb. She felt compelled to touch it.

The shadow watched from a distance willing Naomi to touch it, it glided effortlessly towards her. Sometimes people needed help to understand.

Naomi sensed movement behind her and turned. She glanced around the cavern; she walked back towards the entrance but still saw no one.

She walked purposely to the orb again. As she reached out to touch it she felt a sense of sorrow wash over her. She put her hand down and just stared at the orb.

The shadow moved silently towards her, it wrapped itself around her before she could scream, controlling her it made her reach out again towards the orb.

Knock. Knock. Knock. Naomi opened her eyes. She looked at the book on the floor and put it on the table. Knock. Knock. Knock. Naomi slowly got out of her chair and walked towards the door Her mind still fuzzy from the dream, opening the door she saw Samuel standing outside.

'Come on in Samuel.' she said. Samuel stepped over the threshold and Naomi led him towards the kitchen. 'I was about to make a cup of tea,' she said as she filled the kettle.

'How is the head? Enquired Samuel, a look of concern written across his face. Naomi ushered him to sit. 'Feeling better,' she replied 'but I have something to show you,' she walked back to the living room and fetched the book. 'I want you to have a read of this book.'

Samuel looked at the book and then back at Naomi.

'Where did you get this?' he said puzzled.

'I found it at Maureen's on the floor of the study.' she stated.

Samuel flicked through the first few pages. He recognised the house but no one in the photos.

'What is a Shaman? He asked.

'Shamans can be healers, they meditate and they have been known to see into the future, and or cure people including themselves.' Maureen said as she poured two cups of tea. 'Reginald who had the house rebuilt was a Shaman, and I think he knew how to control the orb.'

Samuel gasped as he took the information in. He turned to the back page. 'Who is?' he looked again at the childish scrawl 'C. Raven?' he asked.

Naomi shook her head. 'I have no clue,' she said 'maybe just what a child wrote in the book.'

'The reason I want you to read it,' she said earnestly 'it might hold answers to stopping our nightmares.'

Samuel placed the book on the table.

Chapter 38

(2011)

The industrial estate lay on the far end of town, most of the businesses had gone under due to the recession.

Claudia sat in the small office/warehouse. The office/warehouse was sparse to say the least. Claudia didn't care. It was her business knowledge that had expanded the business. She designed the website, she organised the events and she kept the books.

The office/warehouse was leased for six month. Lucas had been having dreamscapes about the village.

Claudia had organised the finances for the lease, the owner of the office/warehouse was pleased to get some revenue from one.

He had admitted it had been a disaster and not many companies wanted one.

She finished typing up the information on her computer and walked out the back to make a drink. She could hear the rhythmic drums and knew that Lucas was escaping her reality.

Claudia had asked him what was so important about this village. Lucas just smiled. He never divulged the information he saw.

Claudia sat back down at her desk with her coffee. Lucas wanted to hold another seminar close by. He found nature to be very intuitive when helping people discover there hidden paths.

The drumming stopped. Claudia knew that Lucas would walk through energized. He had been learning the shamanic ways for several years, as well as learning the shaman life from his fore fathers.

Lucas stepped into the office and smiled at Claudia 'I can still sense the disturbance.' he said as he reached for a bottle of water.

Claudia knew not what he meant. 'You have a booking in two weeks.' Lucas walked and peered over Claudia's shoulder. He read the information and nodded.

'Just going into town.' he said as he slipped on a sports jacket. Claudia watched him leave.

Tom reached in the box for the last book; he had spent the past hour going through books which hadn't held any insight into understanding what was happening at the house.

He took out the old book and looked at the cover. '*Our Shamanic Life*' he dropped the book and reached for his mobile. He dialled Mary's number and listened as it started to ring. The sound from Mary's mobile made him jump as he heard it ringing in the room.

Cancelling the call he dialled Marie's number. '*I am not able to take your call, leave a message after the tone.*' Tom hung up. Concerned he grabbed his coat and keys. He locked the room and ran down the stairs. Tom raced out the foyer and towards his car. He drove out the car park waiting for a black BMW to turn in and then drove through the town, he felt he was wasting time as he drove through the streets of the town, the 30mph seemed slower than ever. As he passed the church he sped up to 50mph almost leaning forward to make the car travel faster. He gripped the steering wheel tightly. He felt the tightness in the chest. Had something happened to them?

He passed the farms and drove another mile before he saw Marie's car come into view. He pulled up behind and rushed from the car running towards the door.

He found the door unlocked and ran into the grand hall. 'MARY…' he shouted 'MARIE…' he rushed into the living room and then into the kitchen. There was no sign of them downstairs. He rushed up the spiral staircase and onto the landing. 'MARY…MARIE…' he shouted again.

Marie was first to hear the noise she rushed to the door and banged on it 'TOM…' she shouted waking Mary from her thoughts.

Mary got up and joined her sister.

Tom rushed to the study door 'STAND BACK.' he shouted.

Mary and Marie stood back.

Tom rushed at the door putting his full weight behind him as he slammed into the door 'NO TOM,' Marie shouted 'KICK THE DOOR, USING THE FULL FORCE OF YOUR HEEL BY THE LOCK.'

'YOU SURE?' he shouted

'YES,' she replied 'IT IS THE WEAKEST PART OF THE DOOR.'

Tom kicked at the door; it took six well placed kicks for the door to give.

The door eventually splintered and opened inwards.

Mary ran to Tom 'Our hero.' she said as she kissed him.

'I found the book you were on about in the box of books left to us by Samuel.' he said as he tried to get his breath back.

Mary looked at Tom 'Where is it?' she exclaimed, she stood excited, eager to read it. 'It's at the hotel.' he replied.

Marie watched as Mary rushed towards the landing. 'Let's go.' she cried. Tom rushed out after her and then stopped. Marie was glancing out the window. 'You coming Marie?' he asked quizzically.

'Tom before we rush off, Mary and I saw people in the garden when we were trapped in here.' Tom rushed to the window and gazed out; he looked around but saw no one. 'No one there Marie.' he said contritely

Marie put her hand on Tom's arm. 'No you don't understand,' she said 'they were outside but they were dressed in olden day type clothing.'

Tom looked at her dumbfounded. 'They then vanished from sight as if they belonged here but in the past.' she said earnestly. Marie sat on the edge of the bureau and looked at Tom. 'I do not believe in ghosts,' she paused for a moment 'but I think they belonged here.'

Tom put his arm around Marie. 'You're not going mad Marie…' he said sincerely 'this is just another chapter of…' he waved his hand around the house.

Marie smiled and stood up. 'Are you two coming or do I have to rush to the hotel on my own.' They both looked up at Mary, her hands on her hips.

Tom reached in his jacket pocket 'missing something?' He tossed her phone towards her. Mary smiled as her cheeks blushed slightly.

'Let's go then,' said Tom.

Mary made her way down the stairs and opened the door. Marie followed Tom down the stairs and outside.

'That house,' she started 'has some serious issues.'

Mary couldn't help but smile.

Tom locked the door and walked to the Peugeot. Mary was right behind him, she got in the passenger side and they followed Marie back towards the hotel.

The drive back was quiet. Mary was thinking about the book Tom had found, the mysterious people in the garden.

Tom could understand the frustration Mary must be feeling. The house was definitely turning out to be out of control.

They drove through the village and towards the hotel.

Mary exhaled. 'Barbados...' she said smiling 'let's go Barbados.' Tom laughed. 'Once we get this mystery sorted, I promise a long holiday anywhere you desire.'

Mary smiled. 'I like the sound of that, so any idea how we solve the mystery?'

Tom glanced at his wife. 'The book,' he said 'it must hold some clues.'

They drove into the car park and waited for Marie to arrive.

Marie pulled up next to the Peugeot and got out, together they all walked back into the foyer.

Doris was at reception when they walked in. 'Afternoon my dears,' she said in her cheerful voice.

'Afternoon Doris,' they replied, as they walked towards the stairs and up to their rooms.

Tom unlocked the door and they all entered.

Mary looked at the books strewn everywhere. Tom pulled the seats round the bed and Marie closed the door.

Mary picked the book up and looked at it. The book was old. She glanced through the book and looked at the photos. She skimmed through the rest of the book and looked at her sister and then her husband.

'Every-so-often there are some notes written in the margin,' she said 'I remember from my dream that the inscription on the trapdoor was also written around one of the pages.'

She passed the book to Tom who glanced through the book, noticing the photos and how majestic the house used to look. He turned to the back page and noticed the childlike scrawled name. 'Is that C. Raven?' he passed the book to Marie who glanced at the name. 'Looks like it to me.' she replied.

Tom got to his feet. 'I will be right back.' he left the room and closed the door behind him. Mary shrugged her shoulders.

Tom rushed down the stairs and into the foyer. 'Doris...' he said as he caught his breath back 'the visitor's book?'

Doris reached behind her and passed the book to Tom. He found the entry marked Craven and looked at Doris. 'Do you remember this person coming in?' he asked.

Doris looked at the entry. 'She was a young lady; she wanted to look at the size of the dining area for party bookings.'

Tom thanked Doris and ran back up the stairs to the room.

'Sorry, the name was also in Doris's visitor's book I...' he paused '...long shot he said.'

He sat down and looked at them both.

'I find it strange,' started Marie 'you have a name in a book, a card with the initials of someone who Mary saw in a dream. These are not coincidences.'

As the hours wound away they realised that they needed to find out who Lucas Raven was and the C. Raven who had visited the hotel, and was there a link to the Hamilton's and the book with C. Raven scrawled on the back page.

Mary heard her stomach growl. She was getting hungry and they weren't getting any closer to a solution.

Marie wanted to shower before dinner and went to her room. Tom put the books away and made them both a drink.

Mary went for a shower. Ever since she had been touched on the arm she made sure she checked all areas of the bathroom. She came out ten minutes later wrapped in her gown and watched as Tom went for his shower.

She finished her coffee and walked to the wardrobe, she rummaged through the clothes settling on dark blue trousers and her cream top.

She checked her emails and phone for messages.

Tom strolled through with a towel wrapped round his waist; he looked in the wardrobe and found his black trousers and blue shirt.

Once they were both ready they knocked on Marie's door. Marie wearing a lemon coloured top and navy blue trousers smiled as she locked the door.

They walked down the stairs and into the diner.

After dinner they strolled around the grounds finally sitting on the wooden bench watching the sun set.

Marie felt restless, she needed to organise herself better. She wanted to solve the puzzle and get back to normality.

Feigning tiredness she headed back in, Mary watched as she walked into the hotel.

Tom watched as the sun disappeared from view and yawned.

'Maybe a good night's sleep will help us tomorrow.' Mary nodded she was feeling tired also.

They walked inside and upstairs to their room.

It didn't take long for sleep to take over.

Marie looked at the clock, it was 11p.m. She slowly got out of bed and unlocked her door. She crept down the stairs and walked through the foyer. She glanced up at the windows and saw no light on in Tom and Mary's room.

Getting in her car she drove out of the car park and through the village. She felt guilty for not informing her sister. Her mind was preoccupied as she drove. She finally pulled up outside the house and gazed up.

The house was still, no lights, no noise.

She stepped out the car and felt her arms prickle with the cool wind. She shivered. The house had been a bane in her sister's life for so long. It ended now.

She opened the boot and pulled out her headlamp and an axe. She closed the boot and walked towards the house. She pulled out the door key that she had borrowed from Tom. Borrowed she thought. That was a blatant lie. She had stolen the keys.

She unlocked the door and entered the hallway. She closed the door and locked it. She didn't require any unwanted visitors.

She walked slowly through to the kitchen and unlocked the cellar door, placing the door wedge down to keep the door open.

Slowly she started to walk down into the cellar. She reached the bottom step and turned round the corner and walked towards the trapdoor. Kneeling down she inserted the cellar key into the padlock and watched the cellar key turn a golden hue. She removed the padlock and on her fifth attempt got the trapdoor up.

She peered into the dark expanse below. Her heartbeat quickened. Her skin crawled. She held tightly to the axe as she descended into the abyss.

The meagre light from the headlamp just shone a few metres ahead and she could see the wall ahead of her and knew the steps carried on down to her left. Once she reached the final step she exhaled.

The axe felt so good in her hand. It felt almost like a friend. She hefted it. This would end all misery this house had seen.

She slowly entered the cavern and turned off her headlamp. The orb floated above the pedestal unaware of what was on Marie's mind.

Marie glanced around; it was like someone was watching her. He skin crawled just at the thought. The axe she thought. This is all I need to do she kept thinking to herself.

The shadow entered the cavern and watched. It silently moved towards Marie.

Marie took another step closer and stopped. The energy from the orb was almost enticing.

Marie shook her head, her arm dropped to the side and the axe fell to the floor.

The shadow moved closer to Marie. It was right behind her.

Lucas was tossing and turning in bed 'no… no… behind you…' he cried. Claudia woke up and looked at her husband. She watched, beads of sweat was on his face 'NO' he screamed. Claudia screamed also.

Lucas sat bolt upright wiping his brow. He looked at his wife. 'We need to go and warn them now.' he said urgently.

He quickly got dressed as did Claudia. He grabbed his car key and they left the office. Claudia could see the concentration on his face. 'Do you know where you're going? She asked as they swerved around another corner. Lucas drove through the village and past the church and out to the countryside. Claudia held on tight not wanting to break his concentration.

She could see a car up ahead and Lucas slowed down. He looked at the house and cringed slightly. He could almost taste the suffering. 'Bang on the door quickly.' he instructed.

Claudia ran to the front of the house and started banging on the door.

Lucas closed his eyes trying to sense anything else. He felt almost helpless and realised he was being consumed by whatever was in the house.

Lucas ran round to the side of the house and started banging on the kitchen door which led to the garden. Don't let me be too late.

Marie felt the pull of the orb. She felt her arm starting to reach out. She closed her eyes momentarily and snapped out of the captivation.

She listened. 'DUM DUM DUM' she turned her head and looked around. What was that noise? She thought to herself. She moved back to the entrance of the cavern.

'DUMDUM – BANG' She left the cavern itself and listened harder.

Someone is breaking in the house she thought. Turning on her headlamp she rushed up the steps from the cavern and reached the cellar.

'BANG… BANG… BANG… BANG…' slightly concerned she shut the trapdoor and locked it.

She slowly walked up the steps out of the cellar and back into the kitchen.

Claudia banged her fists hard against the door, so hard they hurt. Lucas was round the side doing the same.

Marie knelt down and peered round by the door. She could make out an image of someone. Oh God she thought, it's Tom and Mary.

She quickly ran to the door. 'Tom stop banging I can hear you.' she shouted. The banging stopped and she unlocked the door.

Lucas stepped back as Marie opened the kitchen door. She screamed and slammed the door shut.

He heard her locking it. 'NO,' he shouted.

Marie ran through the kitchen and into the hallway and up the spiral staircase.

Who was he? She thought to herself. Opening the bedroom door she peered outside. She could see her car and another right behind it.

Chastising herself she considered her options.

Stuck in a house that is haunted by god knows what, burglars outside, no escape.

Lucas cursed as Claudia walked round the side. 'What happened?' she asked. Lucas walked with her back round the front. 'She opened the door and screamed at me before I could speak.'

Angry with himself he walked around to the front.

'I'm Lucas Raven.' he shouted to the house.

Marie listened what did he say? She could've sworn he said raven. Marie peered round and made out two people standing away from the house.

Lucas shouted again. 'Please let me help you... Lucas Raven.'

Marie heard it that time. She moved out towards the balcony and down the spiral staircase. She put the latch on the door and unlocked it. A little security was better than none.

'Did you say Lucas Raven?'

Lucas watched the door open ajar. Elation filled him. The woman asked a question. 'Yes I am Lucas Raven,' he replied 'can we talk?

Marie listened, still somewhat confused and dubious. 'What do you want? She asked.

Lucas felt exasperated. 'He struggled to think of an answer that would gain her trust. 'We met in a dream,' he responded 'shaman.'

He heard the latch come off the door.

Marie removed the latch. This is the man Mary mentioned she had dreamt about. The book she remembered said Shamanic journey.

She opened the door and stood at the doorway.

'My sister met you in a dream, and we found C. Raven scrawled in the back of an old book.'

Lucas looked at his wife. 'Which book?' he asked

'It is in my sister's room at the hotel.' she replied.

'Can we meet tomorrow at the hotel? He said hope in his voice

'I better get back,' replied Marie. 'Yes tomorrow.'

Marie locked the door and walked towards her car. The woman smiled at Marie.

Marie unlocked her car door. 'I am going to get in a lot of trouble now.' Lucas looked at her.

'Why?' he asked sympathetically.

Marie ignored the question. 'The hotel just past the village centre.'

Lucas nodded and watched as Marie sped off into the night. He looked up at the house.

Claudia got back into the car.

'Tomorrow,' she said.

Chapter 39

Marie woke up the next morning, her head spinning. After a cup of tea and a shower she put on her blue top and jeans.

Her mind was constantly running through ways to tell Mary and Tom about Lucas Raven, let alone what she was doing at the house.

She heard a knock on the door and composed herself. Mary and Tom smiled as she opened the door. She knew the longer she waited the worse it would be mulling it over in her head she decided she would mention it after breakfast.

Doris and Robert were in the dining area talking to guests, it was a ritual for them both when they knew guests were leaving and new ones arriving.

Doris thanked the elderly couple for visiting again and hoped they would meet soon.

Getting up she saw Marie, Mary and Tom enter. 'How are we all this morning?' she asked

Tom smiled 'Very well thank you Doris, and how are you and Robert?'

'Were both well thank you my dear' she said as she led them to a corner table.

'Did you go anywhere nice last night?' Doris enquired. Marie blushed 'Just for a drive to clear my head.'

Mary and Tom both looked confused. 'Robert saw Marie drive off last night.'

Taking their orders she bustled off towards the kitchen.

'I thought you were tired?' Tom said after taking a sip of coffee.

Marie looked at them both. 'I had an idea.' she replied openly 'I will tell you about it after breakfast.'

Robert wandered over and smiled. 'How are we all today?'

Marie smiled 'Fine thank you,' she replied as Doris walked out carrying two plates and then bustled back to fetch the third.

Marie could sense them watching her as she ate her breakfast. She realised that going out last night was, in hindsight, foolish.

She knew they would ask questions and then she still had to explain meeting Lucas and his, well she assumed his wife.

Once breakfast was finished they all walked outside. Once they got to the back of the hotel Mary looked at her sister. 'Where did you go?' she started.

Marie saw the bench and walked towards it. 'I went to the...' she paused momentarily 'the house.' she blurted it out.

Tom sat down on the bench 'What in God's name possessed you to go to the house,' he asked as he tried to keep the anger out of his voice 'that house has locked us in, let alone the cavern.' he hissed.

Marie lowered her head looking at the grass. 'I wanted to...' again she paused searching for the right words.

'Wanted to do what?' asked Mary as she sat next to her sister.

Marie gathered her thoughts as a tear fell onto her jeans. 'I wanted to destroy the orb of light as it has been called.' the tears fell freely as she wiped her eyes.

Tom stood up. He felt angry but – could understand the reasoning. 'Why?' he seethed.

'That is a good question.' someone said behind them all.

They all turned round. Tom looked at the gentleman standing behind them. Mary looked and gasped.

Marie gave a weak smile. 'This...' she started 'is Lucas Raven.'

'Please forgive the intrusion,' he said as he shook Tom's hand. 'Mary...' he said quietly 'lovely to see you again.' he finally looked at Marie. 'I understood what you said last night and decided to come early.'

Marie smiled. 'Where is your...' she let the sentence hang 'Ah.' said Lucas catching on quickly 'Claudia the lady you saw me with, she is my wife.'

Lucas looked at Marie. 'What made you think that you can destroy something so old and...' he paused, closing his eyes 'so trapped.'

Mary finally stood up. 'What do you mean trapped?'

Lucas looked at Mary. 'Honestly.' he spoke softly shaking his head 'I spent the night channelling my energy. I finally have a reasonable hypothesis of what is going on.'

Tom looked at Lucas confused. 'Sorry I must be the only one confused, yet I have been in a coma, my wife and sister-in-law locked in a room...' he rambled on about the numerous problems 'so forgive me when I say that house is evil.'

Lucas turned and watched Claudia walk across the lawn. Tom wide eyed sat down 'you sure this guy isn't a fraud.'

Marie nudged Tom in the ribs.

'He is far from a fraud,' replied Claudia. 'Lucas is a Shaman.'

'What is that if you don't mind me asking,' Mary asked 'and how did I meet you in a dream?'

Lucas looked at them all. 'Let's go somewhere where all your questions can be answered.'

Mary looked dubious but wanted answers, Tom still felt uncomfortable about this. 'Sorry,' Tom looked around at them all 'how do we know we can trust you.' he asked quizzically.

Marie stood 'It's a leap of faith Tom,' she looked at her sister 'I took a leap of faith last night.'

Lucas smiled 'After you screamed at me.' he replied

Marie rounded on Lucas 'dark night... crazy house... strangers banging on doors... you do the math.'

Lucas put his hands up in defence. 'I understand the frustrations,' his voice calm 'if you will give me some of your time, I will answer your questions.'

Marie nodded. 'We have been trying for so long.' Mary agreed she had frustrations. This was supposed to be their dream house.

'Let's go inside.' uttered Tom. He started walking across the lawn back to the hotel.

Doris smiled as they entered. Mary introduced Lucas and Claudia to Doris. Doris smiled. 'Can we use the bar/lounge area Doris?' Mary asked pleadingly.

'Of course my dears.' she replied.

Mary led the way into the bar/lounge area whilst Tom went to fetch the book. Marie followed Tom up the stairs and handed the keys back to him.

Marie sensed Tom's lack of trust. 'If they can aid us in any way towards solving this mystery...' she looked at Tom 'you can start the life you wanted with Mary...'

Tom took her hand 'and you would be welcome anytime.'

Marie looked at Tom; 'anyway...' he said as he locked the door 'we will need an aunty to teach the kids one day.'

Marie laughed and walked down the stairs with Tom.

Mary sat at one of the long tables waiting for Tom and Marie. Lucas and Claudia were seated at another table as Tom and Marie walked in.

Mary almost breathed a sigh of relief and then noticed the book in Tom's hand.

Tom sat next to his wife and Marie sat the other side.

Marie pulled her notebook out of her bag and the list of unanswered questions.

Tom placed the book on the table.

Tom looked across at Lucas 'What is a Shaman?

Lucas nodded 'Shamans can reach an altered state of consciousness. I myself use rhythmic drums to enter this state. Therefore we can interact with the spirit world. Some Shamans are healers depending on…'he looked across at Tom. 'Shamans and rituals can take hours to explain. Some heal, some meditate, and we use the knowledge for the greater good.'

Mary looked across 'So how did I end up in the same spirit world? She questioned.

Lucas closed his eyes briefly. 'I was in my altered state and sensed a lost soul. You were obviously in close proximity to this lost soul. I sensed your presence and interacted if you like with your spiritual form and then helped to heal you in the spiritual world.'

Marie looked confused. 'Tom was locked in the cellar; he fell in a coma, not to forget the missing nurses.'

Lucas smiled 'The lost soul did not cause this. I have sensed another entity which can move around and interact or connect with people. I will go as far as to say it connected with Tom and then at a long shot connected with others whilst Tom was comatose…' Lucas paused momentarily. 'Obviously this entity failed to realise the strength and courage inside Tom which was enough to bring him back. Another hypothesis could be your healing energy brought him back.' Lucas drew breath 'I can tell you that this entity acts like the keeper of the soul yet fails to understand its role.'

Marie looked totally puzzled but made brief notes.

'The key to the cellar and the trapdoor changes colour,' spoke Mary 'any idea why?'

Lucas looked confused 'I apologise I have no knowledge on this.'

'The inscription around the trapdoor and the pedestal what does it mean.' Tom finally asked as he slipped a copy of the inscription over.

Lucas took the piece of paper and read.

"You will be but be unseen,
The past is here but in a dream,
Touch me once and you'll see all,
Treasures of the mind now hear my call"

Lucas read it several times 'this is a warning from our forefathers,' he spoke quietly as he deciphered the riddle.

'You will be but be unseen – If you touch the soul you will witness what the soul remembers almost reliving the soul's memories,' he stated 'but as you are only witnessing you will be unseen.'

Lucas read the second line 'The past is here but in a dream – the dream of the lost soul.'

Carrying on relentless Lucas explained the last two lines 'Touch me once and you'll see all – touching the soul will awaken its past and let you relive momentarily. Treasures of the mind now hear my call – The mind is a treasure we behold. When you relive the soul's last memory then you will suffer the consequence.'

Mary looked over at Lucas. Claudia had placed her hand on his. 'Can you elaborate?'

'This entity which watches over the lost soul feeds off the darkness and the energy you give to the soul it can feed off both,' he paused and stood. 'This entity can control you. It needs your fears to survive;' sitting down again he looked across the table 'don't you see? This is a warning,' his voice rose as he spoke. 'They warned people.'

Lucas closed his eyes.

Tom felt almost afraid to ask another question. 'Does this book hold the answers to everything at the house?'

Lucas laughed he reached across the table and looked at the book. He opened the pages and glanced at the shaman life. He flicked through more pages noticing the inscription and several additions in the margin, when he reached the back page he looked across the table.

'Did you write this? He pointed to the childish scrawl C. Raven.

Tom shook his head. 'That was already in the book.'

Lucas stared at the page. 'Grandfather,' Lucas just kept staring 'could it be?'

Chapter 40

(1956)

It was a cold winter's evening and Edna Hamilton had just finished lighting the coal fire. A tall thin woman yet feisty, she had been to work at the local factory where she was the secretary. Still wearing her Peplum grey suit she picked up her purse and walked through the grand hallway to the kitchen and placed the kettle on the range.

She heard the door open and peered round the corner to see her husband walk through the door. His black overcoat buttoned up he walked straight through and kissed his wife.

Cecil was of average height and fit, his grey single breasted suit looked perfect as he removed his overcoat and walked into the living room.

Edna knew that a woman's place was in the home, but she refused to be tied down with staying home. She loved being out.

The kettle whistled as she turned the gas off and poured two teas, she walked through to the living room placing her husband's drink on the small side table before sitting down.

Cecil closed his eyes for a moment. He worked for an insurance company and although the pay was reasonable he hated the work. He had always had his standards set at a higher level.

After Cecil had drunk his tea he stood up and walked through to the kitchen. He opened the cellar door and turned on the light.

He walked steadily down the steps and walked purposely around the corner. He lifted the unlocked trapdoor and walked down the steps. He knew what his purpose in life was. Reaching the wall he turned and walked down more steps. He stood outside the cavern and closed his eyes, muttering words which sounded like prayer. He entered the cavern and saw the pedestal. Walking up to it he muttered more words. The orb shone above him, yet it didn't draw him in. He walked to the far end and felt the wall with his hands. He muttered more words. He turned and bowed.

The orb sank lower so it rested on the pedestal. He watched the shadow glide into the cavern and nodded as if greeting an acquaintance.

He knew his place on this earth and he knew what had to be accomplished. He strode out the cavern and back up the steps. Once he reached the kitchen he washed his hands. Edna was in the kitchen she had started to cook the dinner. She glanced outside as she saw small flurries of snow fall gracefully to the ground.

'Is it tonight they come?' she asked casually.

Cecil nodded 'My brother will be here tonight.'

'What about the others?'

Cecil looked at his wife, his face sombre. 'They will also be here.'

Edna turned and finished peeling the potatoes. She put the pan on the stove and placed the potatoes in the pan.

'I wish you would tell me what is down there.' Her voice almost inaudible

Cecil kissed her. 'Tonight they will realise.'

Cecil walked purposely out the kitchen and up the spiral staircase. He felt like a custodian of knowledge, yet, tonight that would end.

He reached the last step and walked into the study. He sat down in his chair and opened the book on the walnut bureau.

He picked up his pen and started to write.

The time has come to bid farewell, I sense the change in the orb of light, and the shadow watches me as I acknowledge the power.
I can hear the screams, yet have been unable to let it go.
The shadow I sense is the opposite of me, yet allows me safe passage.
My brother will be here tonight. He is bringing the others. My younger brother will be one and someone who I have yet to know.
Edna becomes more restless. She knows nothing of what is in the cavern.

Cecil read the short passage and closed the book. He looked out of the window and sensed the change in the weather. He wondered if the orb of light could too.
Cecil walked from the study and into the bedroom. He removed his daily work clothes and bathed. He felt the water wash over him as he struggled inside.
After he had bathed he changed into his casual clothes. He walked purposely back down the stairs and into the kitchen. He rubbed his forehead and sat at the table.

Edna took the chicken out the oven; the boiled potatoes were ready as were the carrots, peas and beans. She sliced the meat and dished out the veg and potatoes.
Cecil smiled as she put the plate in front of him. Edna sat opposite and smiled back. After dinner Edna washed the dishes and stacked them away. She then walked through to the hallway and up the spiral staircase.
She had no intention of staying whilst her husband had visitors. She would be back later to see her brother in laws.
She looked at her reflection in the mirror, adjusting her hair and a quick change of clothes.
She glanced at the clock and heard a rap on the door.
Edna rushed out the bedroom and down the stairs. She had never once seen her husband answer the door to anyone. It was her duty.
Edna opened the door and greeted Reginald. 'Edna... my... my,' he said admiringly 'where we off tonight?'
Edna blushed 'Out with a friend,' she replied. She smiled as he stepped into the hallway followed by his younger brother and two strangers.
'Let me introduce you,' said Reginald 'you remember my youngest brother Simon' Simon smiled at Edna 'Been so long.' Edna kissed him on the cheek. 'Charlie McCormack a neighbour from the village who is the locksmith of the town,' Edna turned to Charlie who was in his early twenties and shook his hand. 'And this gentleman' said Reginald 'is Christian Raven.' Edna shook his hand. 'My husband is in the lounge.' Edna opened the door and ushered them in.
Edna walked over to Cecil and kissed him goodbye.

As Edna closed the door she saw Naomi Horncastle walk down the path. 'Shall we go...' said Edna quite quickly. Naomi laughed 'Where are we going?' she enquired.
Edna glanced back at the house 'anywhere.'
They walked quickly down the road. The snow had stopped but the wind was biting. The chatted about the village and the news as they briskly walked into the village, Naomi paused a moment under a streetlight and glanced at her watch. The time was half seven. 'If you like,' said Naomi as she slipped her glove back on 'we can go to the village hall, as they have bingo tonight.'
Edna laughed, 'oh lets,' she replied.
They made their way towards the church and bought their bingo tickets and cup of tea.
Sitting down Edna started to talk more openly. 'Cecil has company tonight,' she started 'his brothers and two others.'
Naomi put her cup down 'boy's night then?' she exclaimed.

Edna half smiled, 'Cecil and Reginald hardly see eye to eye and Cecil refuses to acknowledge his youngest brother.'
Naomi smiled knowingly 'sibling rivalry?
Edna put her cup down. 'Something more than simple rivalry,'
Naomi looked quizzically at Edna 'tell me more.'
'EYES DOWN.' The caller shouted.

Cecil looked at his brother Reginald 'I am fully aware of why you're here,' his voice tinted with disgust.
Reginald smiled 'I am pleased,' he replied his stature tall almost military. 'Simon has joined us tonight. You understand he is here to release the entrapped soul.'
Cecil glanced at Simon. 'I understand but do not agree with the action.'
Charlie moved forward 'I need peace, I hear the calling, the nightmare…'he stammered. He reached in his pocket and removed a padlock and key.
"You believe if the door is locked you will get peace?' scoffed Cecil.
Christian moved forward almost tasting the air. 'Only if we succeed,' he said sombrely.

Cecil strode to the kitchen and opened the cellar door. Reginald watched Cecil walk down the steps, he has done that many a time he thought to himself as he himself touched the damp cold wall and entered the darkness of the cellar.
Simon watched Reginald descend and touched the wall, he could sense the loneliness and the despair, yet, he sensed a darkness too, a malevolent spirit. Simon closed his eyes and relaxed he took a deep breath and walked down the steps.
Charlie looked down the steps and shuddered. He had been suffering for months, he needed closure, and he needed his life back. He felt a hand on his shoulder and looked at Christian.
'Have faith,' said Christian as he led Charlie down the steps.

Cecil stood by the trapdoor and waited for the others to catch up. He felt his anger rise within him as they slowly filtered round the corner.
Reginald helped him lift the trapdoor and looked into the dark abyss. Simon shuddered as he approached 'I can sense so much.'
Reginald put his hand on shoulder 'Deep breaths, remember the training.'
Simon nodded.
Cecil started down the steps and disappeared from view. Reginald looked at Simon, Charlie and Christian. 'I will go down next and watch your step.'
Simon slowly descended followed by Charlie and Christian. Reginald soon reached the corner and turned. He walked down the steps and saw the glow from the cavern. Simon finally joined him and closed his eyes. He could sense the orb of light but more importantly the shadow.
Charlie stumbled on the last step falling to the floor, Simon turned and helped him up, and Christian finally walked down the last few steps and gasped.
He had been preparing himself for the visit but what he had sensed and heard was nothing, he looked around the outer cavern in awe.
Cecil stood at the entrance of the cavern and glanced inside 'this way,' he said his voice sullen.
Christian, Reginald and Simon moved forward and into the cavern itself. Charlie stood at the entrance shaking, his pulse quickened and a cold sweat broke out on his forehead.
Reginald glanced around the cavern taking in the walls before he looked at the pedestal and orb of light.
He walked up purposely. He felt no fear just remorse as he glanced at the soul inside the orb.
'Yes… yes… I sense the entrapment;' he spoke his voice low 'we will help.' He said as he turned and looked at Cecil.

'Look,' he seethed 'this soul has suffered long enough.'

Cecil looked down. 'You know as well as I dear brother,' he retorted 'if the soul hadn't opened itself to us then we would be none the wiser.'

Reginald strode up to Cecil. 'I know brother.'

Simon walked forward and moved towards the orb of light. He could feel the desperation inside. It wanted freedom. He closed his eyes and sent calming thoughts towards the orb.

The shadow moved silently and stopped behind Charlie he had watched them from the darkness of the outer cavern as they entered, it could sense what they wanted to do.

The shadow picked up the vibes from Charlie and slowly wrapped itself around him before entering him.

Charlie gave a gasp and looked at the others as they turned. 'What is wrong?' they asked almost in unison. Charlie looked at them and smiled. 'The shadow slowly controlling him 'Sorry,' he said 'just spooked.'

The shadow forced Charlie to step forward into the cavern. It watched as the others discussed what had to be done.

It influenced Charlie to walk around the cavern. It needed time. It listened intently to the others talking.

'I cannot sense anything else in this cavern!' exclaimed Simon.

'It was here,' started Christian 'I felt a twinge of coolness come close by.'

Cecil looked around he was aware of the shadow. Did it consider the four of them to be far more powerful? He pondered on his thoughts.

Reginald stood closer to the orb. 'We were granted access to its thoughts on several occasions...'

Simon moved closer his hand outstretched.

Charlie still controlled by the shadow turned. He wanted to run across and force Simon to touch the orb that would be the only way to feed off them.

Reginald watched Simon as he sent calming thoughts out. Simon had always had an empathic ability. Simon opened his eyes and lowered his arm. 'I can only sense the soul here,' he calmly said to Reginald.

Reginald placed his hand on Simon's shoulder and looked at the others. 'I suggest we do this now.'

Simon nodded in agreement. Cecil reluctantly nodded as did Christian.

They moved around the orb and stood at 90 degree angles around the orb and started to chant.

'Excuse me,' said Charlie under the influence of the shadow 'what am I supposed to do?'

Cecil felt a fleck of anger enter him 'just pray what we do works.'

They started to chant again, their words nothing more than a mumble. The shadow urged Charlie to move forward slowly.

The shadow watched them chant, he knew he had to act fast. He slithered out of Charlie and glided towards Simon.

Simon gasped as the shadow surrounded him. He chanted more but without avail as the shadow entered Simon and forced him to touch the soul.

Simon screamed and fell to the floor, the light from the orb emanated out knocking them all to the ground.

Simon opened his eyes, he could see nothing yet he could hear the screams as he realised he was lost. He tried to regain his composure as he drifted. He could hear both his brothers shouting his name as well as their names being shouted. He called out, chastising himself he soon realised, they were trapped.

Charlie had been knocked back by the blinding light. He slowly got to his feet and looked around. 'Where... where...' he stammered 'where am I?'

He looked around confused before being transfixed by the bodies on the floor. He stumbled towards them and knelt down by the nearest. 'Can... can...' he stammered 'you hear me?' He looked at the others and heard a murmur. He looked at the person to his right as they moved their hand. 'Do you need help?' he asked cautiously. Simon slowly sat up and rubbed his head. The shadow slowly cowered against the wall and watched. 'Where... am... I? He asked slowly.

Reginald sat up and looked at Simon and then at Cecil. He looked at the soul, the orb. He chastised himself for failing.

Getting to his feet he rushed to the wall. He watched as the wall slowly changed and images began to form in the shape of pictographs in front of him.

Simon slowly got to his feet and looked at Reginald. 'Where are we?' he exclaimed

Reginald grabbed his brother's hand and led him out the cavern. He slowly ran his hands over his younger brother's head and sighed. 'Do you remember me shouting your name?' he asked anxiously.

Simon looked at Reginald and tried to recollect his thoughts 'I can hear screams,' he said slowly 'in my head.'

Reginald hugged his brother and realised it was over.

Cecil slowly appeared at the mouth of the cavern he looked at Reginald and then at Simon. 'What happened?' he spat as the anger rose in him. Reginald let go of Simon and looked at his brother 'He is gone,' he spoke softly 'he will suffer.' Reginald sank to his feet as Charlie stumbled out still confused. Christian walked out and looked at Reginald. He could sense his loss and failure.

Chapter 41

Reginald walked back into the cavern and glanced at the orb, the soul that was trapped. He still felt the pull inside him but fought the link to be enticed.

Christian followed him in 'Can't we try again?' he asked

Reginald shook his head 'if we try again then we could all suffer like Simon and Charlie,'

He looked at the fully formed pictographs on the wall. 'The entity owns this now.' He said quietly as he ran his hand over the wall.

Reginald pointed at the pedestal. 'What the...' he started

The pedestal was glowing slightly as words appeared on the pedestal. Christian walked over totally ignoring the orb.

"You will be but be unseen,

The past is here but in a dream,

Touch me once and you'll see all,

Treasures of the mind now hear my call"

Reginald read the words out loud and looked at Christian. 'A warning for others,' he said 'if people touch the soul,' he pointed at the orb 'they will be consumed by the past and suffer.'

'Is there no way it can be destroyed?'

Reginald looked at Christian, despair in his eyes 'The entity controls the orb now,' he looked round and out at Simon and Cecil 'there is no way we can destroy it.'

Reginald walked out the cavern followed by Christian and slowly they all made their way up the steps and back to the cellar.

As Reginald and Christian closed the trapdoor they noticed the words on the pedestal were also on the trapdoor. Good thought Reginald, a warning for all.

Cecil looked at Charlie. 'Give me that padlock,' his voice tinged with anger.

Charlie removed the key and padlock and gave them to Cecil who locked the trapdoor.

Cecil pocketed the key and they walked up the cellar stairs to the kitchen.

Cecil sat down at the table as the others joined him.

They all sat and Cecil studied each one in turn. He felt slightly pleased it had failed; yet, he felt pangs of despair that his younger brother had been consumed.

Reginald looked at him across the table. 'The entity, the shadow...' he paused as he recollected his thoughts 'it is the keeper of the soul' his voice bitter.

Cecil nodded. 'I have sensed it watching me if I have gone into the cavern' He said regretfully.

Christian watched as Simon got up and walked to the window 'you okay?' he asked softly

Simon turned and put his hands to his ears 'I can still hear the screaming.'

Christian looked at Reginald. He saw the regret in his face.

Edna and Naomi left the church and started walking back along the country road. Bingo had been fun yet neither had won but it had been a night out.

As they reached Naomi's cottage Edna bade farewell and walked along the country road home.

She reached the house and inserted the key in the lock and closed the door behind her and walked into the kitchen.

She sensed the sombre mood as she looked at her husband and around the room.

'Have you had a good evening?' asked Cecil

'Lovely thanks,' she replied and smiled. 'I was going to make a cocoa before bed, can I interest anyone else?'

Cecil nodded and smiled, yet Edna could sense it was false.

Reginald stood up. 'It's late, we must be off' He kissed Edna on the cheek and looked at Cecil.

Cecil rose from his seat and walked towards hallway. Edna looked at Simon as he stood. 'You do not look well Simon?

Simon turned and looked at Edna 'I hear them screaming.'

Edna looked at him confused 'Sorry... I do not understand.'

Simon kissed her on the cheek and walked out the room.

Christian stood and helped Charlie out and smiled at Edna. 'Thank you,' he said as he left.

Edna heard Cecil exchange his goodbyes to the group and closed the door as they left.

He walked back into the kitchen and sat down at the table.

Edna placed the cup in front of him and smiled. 'Was Simon well?' she enquired 'he said he could hear them screaming.'

Cecil looked at his wife. The confusion in Simon had hurt him. 'He thought he could hear screaming earlier,' Cecil looked at the cellar 'but he was mistaken.'

The owl hooted outside at the moon, the wind had picked up and the temperature had dropped.

The shadow drifted out of the cavern and up the stairs to the cellar before gliding up the steps and into the kitchen. It moved silently up the spiral staircase and into the study and looked at the book on the bureau desk.

The pages flipped as if alive and the shadow glanced at the pages before gliding back out and towards the window making the owl hoot once more before flying away.

Cecil sat up restless and glanced out the window as small flurries of snow began to fall slowly.

He got out of bed and wandered onto the balcony and down the spiral staircase. He glanced at the cellar door as he entered the kitchen and shuddered.

He felt preoccupied and made himself a drink. He sat cradling the cup, brooding.

Maybe he could release the soul, which glowed like an orb of light. He thought about it before deciding to go behind Reginald's back.

He quietly moved back up the stairs and into the bedroom and grabbed his trousers and removed the key.

He silently crept out the room and back down the stairs. He opened the cellar door and shivered. He moved down the steps and followed the cellar round and walked towards the trapdoor.

Removing the key from his pocket he inserted it into the lock and fell back. The key turned a golden hue. Cecil gasped. How on earth he thought to himself.

He removed the padlock and lifted the trapdoor up. Placing the key and padlock on the floor he descended into the darkness and towards the cavern.

He had walked these steps several times and never had he had a feeling of uneasiness wash over him.

Reaching the wall he turned and carried on down, his breathing heavier than normal and his pulse quickening.

He finally reached the bottom step and walked towards the cavern.

Edna woke up and yawned; she glanced at her bedside clock and noticed it was 3am. She rubbed her eyes and noticed Cecil was not in bed. Sipping on a dressing gown and slippers she walked towards the study. Cecil spent hours in the study, yet, never told Edna what was going on.

She turned on the light but Cecil wasn't in the room. As she turned to leave she noticed the book on the bureau

She sat at the desk and flicked through the pages. She saw familiar photos of Cecil, Reginald and Simon. Simon she thought... he had been acting odd. He looked almost scared and... she suddenly remembered what he had said about hearing screaming.

She flicked through the pages noticing several writings about drums and spiritual planes. Closing the book she left the room and turned out the light.

She walked down the stairs and noticed the light coming from the kitchen. She also saw the cellar door wide open. She was always getting onto Cecil about closing doors. Shaking her head she opened the lounge door but still no Cecil.

Edna had never been keen on having items stored in the cellar; she considered them to be dank dark places where spiders lived.

She wrapped her dressing gown round tighter and looked in the cupboard for a torch.

The small torch gave out hardly any light but it was a help as she walked down the steps calling his name.

When she reached the bottom step she called louder but still no reply. She became more irate and walked round the corner.

She hated the cellar and felt the cool dampness bite at her throat. She walked further back and came across the lifted trapdoor. She saw a key and padlock on the floor. She pointed the torch towards them. She could swear the key was almost itching to get in the lock.

Chastising herself she peered down the hole and noticed steps.

'Cecil... Cecil...' she said quietly, still no reply.

Cecil entered the cavern and glanced at the newly formed drawings on the walls. He had never seen anything like that in his life, but, even he couldn't deny they had appeared out of nowhere.

He looked at the orb, and felt a stab of sadness. He felt almost responsible for the soul being trapped. The orb hovered above the pedestal silently.

He knew the shadow, the entity, or whatever it was would be watching him. So he moved forward slowly towards the orb of light.

He felt compelled to touch the orb; he knew that is what the shadow wanted. It wanted people's souls to feed upon them, to consume everything about them. Cecil shuddered and turned.

Edna walked down the last few steps and shivered. 'Cecil... Cecil...' she kept saying out loud.

Cecil suddenly appeared out the cavern and saw his wife.

'What is up?' he asked earnestly.

Edna looked at him 'what is this place? What are you doing down here?'

Cecil smiled and led her by the hand. He showed her the pictographs on the wall and the pedestal. Edna gasped when she saw the orb. She had never seen anything like it and took a step back.

She felt her arm rising, she felt a calm feeling enter her; she wanted to just touch it.

Cecil grabbed her arm and dragged her back. He knew the power it held.

Edna felt herself snap out of a trance as she looked at Cecil. 'What is that?' she pointed at the orb.

Cecil took her by the hand and led her out. 'That,' he said forcefully 'is what everyone came to see tonight. It is a soul... trapped yet unable to break free of the holds of an entity which controls people by using the soul.'

Edna looked blankly at Cecil. 'Utter nonsense!' she exclaimed and strode back into the cavern. She looked at the pictographs and felt sick to the pit of her stomach.

The shadow glided past Cecil who was just entering the cavern and noticed Edna. Cecil started towards Edna and then noticed the shadow glide purposely towards her too.

Cecil opened his mouth to warn her, but no words came out. He watched in horror as it slowly reached her feet and started to glide around her.

Cecil reached forward but found unknown hands suddenly pull him back towards the cavern entrance.

He watched helplessly as the shadow surrounded Edna and she screamed.

Cecil screamed out 'No... NO... NO...' he felt physically sick. 'Let her go.' he begged.

Edna turned and walked towards him.

'You are helpless and pitiful,' she spat as the shadow controlled her 'she will soon be mine and you can do nothing.'

Cecil tried to move but felt frozen on the spot. 'TAKE ME.' he screamed out.

Edna turned. Cecil looked at her as tears streamed down his face. 'Take me instead.' he pleaded.

Edna grabbed his hand and walked with him towards the orb.

'Touch it, and be one with me,' said the shadow inside Edna.

Cecil looked at his wife as she lifted their hands up towards the orb.

'I am sorry...' he said.

Their fingers brushed the orb itself and the light emanated around the room and Edna and Cecil fell to the floor.

The shadow glided out of Edna and up into the orb. As the light faded Cecil suddenly sat up and looked around the cavern.

He rubbed his head confused before noticing Edna lying on the ground.

He carried her out the cavern and up the steps towards the cellar. Tears fell freely from his eyes as he took each step. He had no recollection of why he had been down in the cavern, and had always vowed to protect his wife.

He placed Edna on the ground while he locked the trapdoor and then carried her up the cellar steps into the kitchen. He carefully placed her down again before closing the cellar door.

He strained but carried his wife back up the spiral staircase and removed her dressing gown and placed her in bed.

He walked back towards the door and turned before heading into the study. He switched on the light and sat down. Placing his head in his hands he sobbed uncontrollably.

He then reached for a pen and opened his journal.

Dear brother, if this book ends up in your hands, please be aware I have failed you. With Simon lost, I too am lost due to the soul and the entity.

Edna was controlled and due to my love she took me.
He reached the back page and wrote one last word. C. Raven.
He closed the book and placed it on the bookshelf knowing his brother was the only one safe.
Turning off the light he went back to bed.

Chapter 42

(2011)

Lucas Raven just looked at the back page; he felt memories wash over him. Looking up he looked at Tom, Mary and Marie.
'My grandfather was called Christian Raven, I remember stories from my father...' he paused as the memories resurfaced '...he always had a solemn look on his face...' Lucas turned and glanced out the window '...whenever I asked what was wrong; he would smile and say the past.'
Tom listened as Lucas spoke. 'Do you think your grandfather knew the occupants of our house in the past?'
Lucas shook his head. 'I cannot say for sure...' Lucas looked at the book again 'can I borrow this book?'
Mary looked at Tom and he looked back 'We prefer not for the time being,' replied Mary.
Lucas nodded understanding the reasons.
Claudia looked at her husband 'I think we should go.'
Lucas nodded. 'If you need us you can reach us here,' he passed one of Claudia's cards over.
After they left Tom sat and looked at Mary and Marie 'Well that was somewhat enlightening,'
Marie nodded, she looked at the notes she had made and realised they had some more answers to the questions.

Tom walked out of the bar/lounge area and back into the lobby, he rubbed his furrowed brow. How was this information going to help them with... whatever was in the...
Doris walked through and entered the lobby 'You look peaky Tom,' she said and walked behind the desk.
'Can I ask you something Doris,' he spoke, his voice low
'Anything my dear,' she replied
'With all the problems we have faced in that house,' he paused momentarily 'would you fight to keep it?'
Doris laughed. 'If you want that house badly enough my dear, you will fight to keep it.'
She put her book down and lowered her glasses. 'When we first moved here, there were problems galore and my husband, Robert was ready to chuck it all in,' she glanced at Tom her eyes almost piercing into him. 'We fought and you can too.'
She pushed her glasses back to her face and smiled. 'You will do the right thing my dear.'
Tom watched as Doris walked towards the dining area and closed his eyes. He knew her words made sense even if they did cut into him. Was he ready to just give it all in? Tom walked outside the hotel and into the garden.

Mary and Marie spent a further hour going over the information they had received and put it together with the previous information they had dealt with.
Marie looked at the finished work.
The Whippletree

Present	Resolved	Unresolved	Reason	Actions
Tom Accident / Coma	Resolved		The Entity	Cellar/House
Key and Lock in cellar		Unresolved		Cellar/House
Under the trapdoor	Resolved		Soul/Orb	Cellar/House
Samuels Death	Resolved		The Entity	Cellar/House
Previous Owners	Resolved		Soul/Orb	Cellar/House
Books		Unresolved	Missing Clues?	Read Again
Books from Solicitor		Unresolved	Collected	Read

Looking at it with the information Marie started making reasonable hypothesis about everything. She turned to Mary. 'If I have this right I can possibly figure out how to get your house back,' she said eagerly.

Tom walked back in the room after his walk his head felt clear and he looked at the information. 'Just the man,' cried Marie. 'I think I have figured out most of the problems with the house.' Tom sat down next to Mary and waited for Marie to start.

'The Whippletree property is older than anyone believes,' she looked at them both, her eyes gleaming 'so let's start at the beginning.'

Marie picked up the book 'This book has photos of the residents from 1956; this is going to be our starting point. Obviously how the orb or soul as Lucas called it ended in the cellar is unknown but the entity which Lucas mentioned has to be as old as the orb. This book is on a shamanic life, so it is a good hypothesis to assume that either one or more persons back in the fifties were learning shamanism.'

Marie put the book down on the table and resumed her story.

'If you consider this information given, we can then assume that the previous owners would have suffered the same fate as the owners before when they discovered the orb or soul. The temptation would be too great for such people and, also you have to realise that poor Samuel witnessed what happened to the previous owners and the terrors it exhumes has possibly took his life too.'

Marie smiled as she finished her dialogue; she looked for some sort of answer from Tom and Mary.

Mary looked at her husband and then back at Marie.

'One question Marie' she finally said 'if I may.'

Marie smiled.

'Is this what you meant by boredom 101 at the university?'

Marie laughed. 'Actually yes it is,' she said 'but, the information is true, and I suggest we contact Lucas again as he has saved us twice.'

Tom nodded and agreed with Marie. 'To be honest he has answered some of the questions and I think he could help us get our house back.'

Mary glanced at Tom, 'this comes from the man who claimed he might be a fraud!'

Tom looked at his wife 'I want to get back to what we do best. The house is perfect. The cavern and cellar is the downfall.'

Marie looked at them both. 'So do we agree?' she asked as she put her books back in her bag.

Tom and Mary nodded and helped put the chairs back. 'Let us just get this information back in our rooms and then we can decide on a plan of action.'

Marie smiled and the left the bar/lounge area.

'I want to get another answer,' said Marie eagerly 'but I am going on my own, and you two are going to find Lucas.'

Mary looked at Tom 'is this another let her do it moments.'

Tom laughed 'yes it is, but I have two conditions.'

Marie rolled her eyes. 'Which are...?'

Tom put on a stern face 'No going to the house.' Marie nodded. 'And the second is being careful.'

Marie picked up her bag and smiled 'careful is my middle name,' she hugged her sister and kissed Tom on the cheek, as she walked out the door she turned 'I believe I will have an answer to another question when we meet up later.' With that she strode out the door.

Tom looked at his wife. 'So you have the card let's go find Lucas.'

They both walked out the bar/lounge and outside towards the car, they watched as Marie drove away.

Lucas Raven sat in his chair deep in thought. He had been sat thinking about his grandfather for over an hour. Claudia felt concerned. She had never seen him become so withdrawn.

She had attempted to broach the subject when they got back, but he had dismissed the question.

Claudia turned on her computer and opened the web browser; maybe she could find some information online. She knew it might be futile, she had never found information on Lucas when she had first met him.

She tried several variations without any luck. Getting slightly annoyed she closed the web page down.

Claudia glanced at her husband, whatever had happened in his past which left him like this she thought?

Getting more irate she checked her emails and replied to them and then shut the machine down. 'You need to watch that fiery temper building up inside.'

Claudia looked at Lucas 'You need to talk to your wife about your problems too, and then my fiery temper wouldn't invade your relaxation.' She replied bitterly.

Lucas opened his eyes and Claudia could see the sadness behind them. 'What is it about your grandfather,' she demanded.

Lucas looked across at Claudia 'My grandfather was the man who helped teach me the shaman ways,' he said quietly. 'My father would take me to see him weekly; he would sit me on the back step and explain the ways he had learnt. I...' he paused momentarily '...would listen to his teachings as my father had listened, yet...' he looked down at the floor.

Claudia walked across the room and sat next to him 'yet...'

Lucas looked up 'he had a look of sadness and whenever I asked him what was wrong... because... I could sense that much... he would say the past my boy... the past causes my sadness.'

Claudia kissed him. 'His sadness... do you think he was in the property? She asked tentatively

Lucas nodded. 'I think the book, and seeing his name...' he stood and looked at his wife 'I know it is his name... I intend to put right what went wrong.'

Claudia stood and touched his arm. 'You need to know if they need your help first.'

'We need his help,' said Mary as she stood in the doorway of the office. 'Nice place,' she remarked.

Lucas looked as Tom stood behind Mary. 'We weren't expecting you to visit,' he finally said.

Mary walked in and looked around, whilst Tom closed the door.

'Apologies for just barging in... but yes if you can help we would be grateful.'

Claudia smiled and offered a seat to Tom and Mary. 'I was going to put the kettle on.'

'I'll give you a hand.' said Mary smiling.

Lucas looked at Tom. 'Thank you.'

Marie pulled up outside Charlie's house and glanced at his cottage. She knew he had some answers and was determined to get them. He had made keys for the village but had he been more?

She slowly got out the car and walked towards the gate.

She knocked hard on the door and waited. She glanced around at the garden overrun with weeds and turned when she heard the door being unlocked.

Charlie looked older than he did the first time they visited. 'Hello Mr McCormack,' she said as he opened the door ajar 'It's Marie, we met...'

'I know who you are,' he interrupted 'what do you want.'

'Samuel mentioned you might know more to what is happening.' She replied.

Charlie looked down. 'I miss Samuel... a good man... good man,' he opened the door fully and ushered Marie in.

She watched as he used his sticks to walk back to the living room. Once she had entered the room she noticed piles of books on the table. 'Spring cleaning?' she questioned.

'Sit down, and do not be facetious young lady.'

Marie sat her cheeks flushing for a second. She opened her bag and pulled out her notebook.

'I will get straight to the point then,' she said turning the page over. 'Samuel said you can help more than you did when you gave us cryptic clues.'

Charlie cleared his throat. 'Samuel was the key to the answers, since his demise, I suppose it is time I bared my soul.'

He reached over to the pile of books and opened it. 'I have been suffering with the visions of the past. I have witnessed death. I feel trapped.' He said as he read from the book.

He passed it over and watched Marie read the rest of the passage.

'So you have been down in the cavern then,' she commented.

Charlie sank deeper into his chair. 'I have been in that cavern, I know about the soul and I know about the guardian of the soul. A force so dark, it controls people to reach its goal.'

Which would be? She enquired.

'To survive,' he replied 'I do not know if you know, but...' he paused and leaned forward 'when I worked with Mr Hamilton he told me I was suffering, he offered to help and he knew about the soul as he called it. He made arrangements for his brothers to visit to rid me of the nightmares and to release the soul. They failed and lost a brother that night.' He looked at the mantle.

Marie leant forward. 'So they tried and failed. The shamans?' she asked curiously.

Charlie looked at her. 'I suffer daily but they failed too.'

Marie sat back. 'Can anything destroy it?' she enquired.

Charlie coughed into a tissue. 'I need a drink.' He slowly got out the chair and using the sticks walked to the kitchen. Pausing at the door he turned. 'When I shout you can fetch the tray in.' He said as he made his way towards the kitchen.

Marie nodded as she finished making her notes.

Charlie reached into the cupboard and pulled out his Chloral Hydrate. Charlie had been prescribed these to help him sleep. He removed the stopper and placed 4 drops in Marie's cup. He then put the coffee in and finished making the drinks.

He called Marie and followed her back into the living room; he had deliberately left the spoon on her saucer.

Once they were sat down he asked if she took sugar. 'One please.' she replied. Charlie put the sugar in her cup and stirred.

Charlie looked as Marie took a sip. She looked at the cup but before she could say anything Charlie spoke up. 'You asked if anything can kill it.'

Marie focused back on the reason she was here. 'Yes, obviously with so many people suffering...' she took another sip; the coffee to her was quite bitter but didn't want to offend Charlie. 'Surely whatever has happened should be stopped.'

Charlie took a sip from his coffee. 'It has only been the occupants of the house... except the present owners.' Marie nodded and finished the foul coffee.

'You see Marie,' Charlie stood up without his sticks 'I did suffer, but if I provide the soul and the guardian, the entity or whatever you like to call it with new souls then I am free of suffering.'

Marie blinked. Her eyes felt heavy, she dropped the cup and tried to stand. The Chloral Hydrate worked fast causing her receptors to shut down. She slipped to the floor, her vision blurring slightly. 'What... what...' she collapsed.

Charlie stood over her, his thoughts conflicting. He wanted this to end as much as Samuel had, but, he too wasn't strong enough.

He dragged the sedated Marie across the floor and to the open doorway. Leaning Marie against the open door, he reached in her bag and pulled out the keys to her car. He needed to get her to the house. He needed her to touch the orb and become another victim.

He struggled and opened the back door to the house and walked to the garden shed. Unlocking the shed door he looked at the keys, his keys, the keys he had made and... he chuckled, the keys he had been shown to make.

How stupid were people he thought, the guardian in the cellar had shown him how to make any key fit any lock. He had been gifted. He had used this to his advantage, no matter what key it was they were all identical just there perception looked like a regular key.

No matter which key he would always be able to open the cavern.

Reaching up he removed a key and closed the shed door. He hobbled back down the path and into the kitchen and pulled out some twine. His breathing became more ragged from the extra exertion.

Pausing for a moment to get his breath back he looked across the fields. He slowly walked back to the house and dragged Marie through the doorway to her own car. He struggled but finally got her in the passenger seat. Her head slumped forward. He put the seatbelt on and staggered to the driver's side.

It had been years since Charlie had driven a car, let alone a car of this class. He inserted the key and heard the engine purr into life. It was only a short distance no more than a mile or two to the house, but he knew he wouldn't be able to drag Marie that distance.

Beads of sweat formed on his forehead as he drove out the village and towards the property. Marie was still sedated as he pulled up outside the property. He knew he had to tie her hands together to get her co-operation for when she came round. He knew that he couldn't drag her into the house and down the steps alone.

Turning off the engine he removed his seatbelt and took the handkerchief from his pocket, he dabbed his forehead. He could sense the guardian of the soul.

He grabbed the twine from the back seat and leant Marie forward. Carefully he tied her hands behind her back, ensuring that they would be no threat to him.

He walked to the house and opened the front door. He had been in this house many times. He walked to the kitchen and fetched some water. He needed to wake Marie up, if he was to get her in the cavern.

Charlie hobbled back to the car and opened the passenger door dribbling water over her face. It took time but she finally moaned as she slowly came round.

'Where... who... where...' she murmured.

Charlie held the water to her lips. 'Drink this,' he said. Marie took several sips, her throat feeling scratch and dry.

She opened her eyes trying to focus. The light outside felt like someone was shining a torch in her face.

She struggled to remember where she was… what she had been doing. She opened her eyes again as the countryside came more into view. She turned her head and tried to pull her arm from around her back. She struggled more. She felt trapped. Charlie put his hand on her shoulder. 'Stop struggling.' He rasped. Marie glared at him 'where are we…' the sentence unfinished as she glanced at the house behind him.

'Do as I say,' he said 'It's not you it wants.'

Marie aided by Charlie got out the car. She had a feeling she knew where he was taking her. Marie felt a sudden urge of pleasure. 'You cannot open the cellar without the key,' she spat. Charlie pulled a key out of his pocket. 'I can go anywhere.'

He pushed her into the house and closed the door.

Marie started running scenarios in her head. If I try to run he will probably push me down the steps she thought.

Seeing no options she complied with Charlie. He hobbled and opened the Cellar door urging her down the steps. The door closed behind them. There was no way out.

Charlie and Marie walked to the trapdoor. She watched as he unlocked it with his key, watching the key change not a golden hue like before, but a silver colour. Marie was transfixed momentarily.

Marie watched as Charlie struggled to lift the trapdoor. Marie almost believed he was too weak to lift it. After several attempts he got the trapdoor up. Marie glanced down the dark abyss.

'I will help guide you down.' He uttered.

Slowly they disappeared from view.

Chapter 43

(1969)

Maureen and Tony were helping at the church fete. Naomi was serving Teas, Coffees and Cakes after Mrs Castlethorpe had changed the list of helpers.

Maureen was on the raffle ticket table as Mrs Castlethorpe thought it would be good for her to get to know the community. Maureen had tried to object, mentioning they had both been at the village fete, but her words were futile against Mrs Castlethorpe and her desired plan.

Tony was folding the stubs and placing them in a bucket. He found it tedious, but it was an afternoon out.

Samuel walked past the raffle table and nodded at Maureen. 'Had many buyers this afternoon?' He enquired.

Maureen passed another stub booklet to Tony 'I have three dinner parties to attend, I have coffee tomorrow morning with some lady who I do not know, and that woman,' she pointed to an overly large lady with a red shawl over her shoulders 'says that I should join her W.I meetings.'

Samuel tried not to laugh. Tony finished putting the last ticket in the bucket and put his hand on his wife's shoulder. 'Let's not forget you mentioning to…' he looked around the church hall and saw a lady in a blue dress and her husband in a grey suit 'that couple that I owned a snooker table.'

Maureen blushed slightly 'yes they want to come round for drinks and cocktails one evening,' she closed her eyes momentarily and smiled at her husband 'welcome to our humble house, beware it wants to kill you,' she motioned as if taking a coat off someone 'please this way.'

Tony laughed. Samuel looked disturbed for a moment. 'Surely once we destroy that light and whatever you can hold your party.'

Tony and Maureen looked at Samuel. 'Any ideas yet on how we can?' they asked almost in unison.

Samuel leant in closer 'Naomi has been trying to go through the archives and everything, but we will.'

'SAMUEL... SAMUEL...' shouted Mrs Castlethorpe.

Samuel groaned.

Tony laughed 'you better go,' he said 'but, you're both invited for tea tonight.'

Samuel wandered over in Mrs Castlethorpe's direction through the throng of people.

He passed Naomi who was collecting some cups and plates. 'What does she want now,' he whispered.

Naomi glared in Mrs Castlethorpe's direction. 'Can we take her into the cavern and leave her?' Samuel walked off to see what she wanted.

As the fete came to an end, Naomi took the last of the cups and plates into the kitchen and started to wash up. Samuel walked into the kitchen to relay the message to Naomi.

Maureen passed the last of the stubs to Tony and then took the money into the back office where Mrs Castlethorpe was.

'Mrs Castlethorpe looked up as Maureen entered the room. 'Lovely darling,' she said as she took the tin. 'I have heard you are going to be busy, but now you are going to be well known in this village.'

Maureen gave a false smile. 'We really need to get off soon, I have dinner to prepare.'

'Sure darling,' replied Mrs Castlethorpe 'once your delightful husband brings in the ticket stubs you can both get off and it has been a delightful pleasure having you on board.'

Maureen smiled falsely again and left the room. She noticed Naomi washing up and popped in. 'Is she always so sickeningly sweet towards new helpers?'

Maureen chuckled. 'I want you to know something; she is lovely to all at first, once the novelty wears off,' she motioned around 'you will be like Cinderella in the kitchen with just one ugly sister.'

Maureen laughed. 'Well tea is on us tonight Cinderella and make sure Prince Charming isn't late.'

Samuel arrived home and made himself a drink. He sat down and looked through the book that Naomi had given him. The short clips of information held nothing of importance as he read.

He soon began to realise that the shadow that was in the cavern was evil and devilish. It fed on fear.

Was that a clue? The writing became more erratic near the end of the book as the story unfolded and the loss of love was the downfall of the Hamilton's.

Yet he failed to see the significance on how this information could help them.

He knew one thing, they had to contact Reginald Hamilton again and ask him what had happened which went horribly wrong.

Finishing his drink he made his way upstairs and had a wash. He hunted out a change of clothes and glanced at his bedside clock.

By the time he walked to Naomi's they would have time to ring Reginald Hamilton and see if he could shed any light on the situation.

He made his way down the stairs and out the front door. He locked up and walked the half a mile to Naomi's cottage.

Naomi opened the door and asked Samuel in. he explained his idea and Naomi glanced at the clock on the mantle.

Picking up the receiver she dialled Reginald Hamilton's number. She heard the click as it connected and the ringing tone.

'Good Evening,' she heard as someone picked up.

'Hello,' she said 'can I speak to Mr Hamilton please?'

'One moment, who shall I say is calling,' they replied.

'Naomi Horncastle.' She responded.

She listened as the receiver on the other end was put on the side. She waited patiently.

'Hello...' he replied.

Naomi explained the situation to Reginald and heard him exhale several times. '...in the book it mentions...

'The book...' he interrupted.

'Yes, your brother had a book and it has a passage in it, and how he has failed you.'

Naomi waited for a response. 'Reginald...'

'Thank you,' he replied 'I was sure he despised me being the older brother,' he responded. 'I will tell you one thing. The night we attempted to release the soul...' she heard him pause 'we failed and I lost Simon...' she listened as he stopped again. 'He died four months later.'

'I am sorry Reginald' replied Naomi. 'What can we do though?'

'Do not give in to fear. Do not let your emotions take over.' He replied. 'But... do not touch it.'

Naomi felt exasperated. 'Anything else you can suggest?'

She heard Reginald exhale 'I believe you should stop the entity... the shadow... it is the danger.'

Naomi thanked him and put the receiver down.

'No help whatsoever!' she exclaimed. She picked up a bottle of wine 'Let's be off.'

Dinner was roast lamb, potatoes and vegetables, Maureen placed the plates on the side and ushered Tony and Samuel into the lounge whilst Maureen and Naomi washed and dried.

Tony poured two whiskies and sat down in his favourite chair.

They discussed the fete at the church and how they thought it went Samuel wanted to talk about the information they had found out but refrained. He knew the book shouldn't have left the house in the first place.

Maureen and Naomi soon joined them. Tony got up and poured two glasses of wine.

Naomi sat down and had a sip. She looked at Samuel and then decided she should broach the subject.

'Tony, I spoke to Reginald Hamilton today whose brother used to live here.' Tony looked at Maureen and then back to Naomi. 'Would he be able to help us?' he enquired.

'Naomi looked down 'He tried to help the previous owners and failed,' she paused and looked at Maureen 'He said we must not let it feed off our fears.'

Maureen looked confused 'what does he mean by that?'

Naomi felt helpless and unable to answer her.

'The only thing I know if we do nothing then it consumes us all,' She took another sip of her wine 'it feeds on fear.'

Tony took a sip of his whiskey and pondered this information. 'Did he know anyone who could help us?'

Naomi shook her head 'he lost a brother due to the entity or shadow as he called it.'

Maureen sat back on the settee 'So there is nothing we can do.'

Naomi felt awful, the information she had gave no insight into destroying the shadow or orb.

Samuel drained his glass. 'Were damned if we do nothing, so if we can succeed where they failed maybe we can survive.'

Maureen smiled at his optimistic approach. 'The only information he told me was do not touch the orb.'

They spent the night musing over what could work to rid the house of the orb and shadow. No matter what they decided they were unsure if it would work.

By the time darkness fell they had a rudimentary plan of action.

Samuel and Naomi bade Tony and Maureen goodnight and walked along the country lane back into the village.

Tony poured himself another whiskey and glass of wine for Maureen.

'To be honest,' he looked at the mantelpiece 'the sooner we attempt this the better it will be for the both of us.'

Maureen nodded; she had no qualms of having the house back to normal.

After they finished their drinks they checked the doors and walked up the spiral staircase.

They changed and got into bed. Tony was soon snoring but Maureen was restless. It was playing on her mind. She had killed Tony and others several times and it ate away at her.

She slowly got back out of bed and glanced out the window. The stars shone brightly against the dark sky. She knew that the plan had to work.

Yawning she climbed back into bed and drifted off to sleep.

Naomi was still awake. The talk of finally ridding the house of the... whatever-it-was plagued her mind.

She walked down the stairs and made herself a cocoa.

Sitting in her chair she looked at the book Samuel had left.

She flicked through the pages reading the shamanic dreams, visiting other realms and the people who they helped.

She looked at one particular photo and fetched her magnifying glass. She was sure she recognised the very young gentleman in one of the photos.

She then realised... he may be older now... but it looked so much like Charlie McCormack.

She understood now why the writing became harder to read. Obviously after the failed attempt the shadow or whatever-it-was had eaten at Cecil.

It also explained why Edna would sit looking at the cellar door.

Naomi felt a stab of sadness inside.

She read the rest of the passages finding no clue as to what had to be done.

Picking up her own journal she opened it to a new page.

So the time comes for us to rid ourselves of the evil. It has plagued the house for too long. Tomorrow it ends.

I understand why Cecil and Edna became distant. Will this also happen to me?

If we fail tomorrow just know that we tried.

I have been reading "the shamanic journey" book and believe that Charlie McCormack has also been in the cavern. In the picture he looks young, but with a sadness which is written inside him.

She put the book on top of The Shamanic Journey. Both these books had to go back to Samuel in the morning.

She turned off the light and made her way back to the bedroom. She drifted off to sleep the nightmares torturing her mind.

She woke up screaming and bathed in sweat.

Soon she thought. Soon it will be over.

Chapter 44

The alarm went off at 6am and Maureen yawned, she put on her dressing gown and walked down stairs and into the kitchen. She filled the kettle and glanced outside. The sun was shining and it looked like a beautiful day. She glanced at the cellar door and shivered. Hopefully everything would be over after today. She hoped.

Tony walked into the kitchen as she placed his cup of tea on the table. He looked solemn this morning and even Maureen understood that he was contemplating what they were going to do about the cavern.

By the time Maureen had cleaned the breakfast things away both Samuel and Naomi had arrived.

Tony fetched the key from the bureau and unlocked the door and turned on the light. Maureen passed him a torch and hesitantly followed him down. Naomi touched the cold damp wall, she felt apprehensive, yet, realised this was the only way. Samuel brought up the rear and walked down the steps.

As he reached the bottom he followed Tony, Maureen and Naomi around the corner and towards the trapdoor. He turned on his torch and shone the light ahead. His heart was racing.

When they reached the trapdoor Tony looked at each of them in turn. There was no need for words as he unlocked the padlock.

Samuel helped him lift the trapdoor and shone his torch into the abyss. The light danced off one wall to another. He started his descent using his other hand to guide him down.

Maureen was next to start her descent followed by Naomi, Tony had one last glance around the before he entered the abyss which led to the cavern.

Samuel stepped out into the clearing and saw the cavern entrance. His heart raced faster. He waited for the others to slowly filter out into the clearing.

Tony stepped through and looked at the cavern entrance. He shivered and finally spoke 'any final ideas?'

Maureen gave a weak smile and touched her husband's arm.

Together they entered the cavern.

Charlie McCormack had woken up with a start; he sat up in bed bathed in sweat with last night's nightmare still fresh in his mind. He remembered being in the cavern, cowering in the corner with the shadow slowly gliding towards him. He could hear its voice in his mind. He tried to move but felt frozen to the spot 'feed me your soul,' it had said in his mind. Charlie just kept shaking his head and trying to move 'they will try again,' said the shadow as it inched forward towards them. 'I have protected you,' the voice rang in his head '...shown you more...' Charlie scrambled around trying to escape. The shadow entity slowly drifted forward almost sensing Charlie's fear. 'If you fail me you will die too.' Charlie screamed and woke up.

He moved to the bathroom and looked at his haggard reflection. At the age of 34 he looked much older. He had been gifted with knowledge beyond his understanding. Nothing could go wrong for him, yet, he looked so drawn.

He knew what the shadow wanted; it wanted Mr and Mrs Farley.

He washed and changed and walked through the village towards the Whippletree property.

Samuel and Maureen looked at the pedestal. They felt the tug of the orb, the soul; ignoring the orb they looked for any clues on how to end this without luck.

Maureen and Tony were looking at the pictographs etched into the wall they understood the warning. Do not touch the orb of light.

Yet both knew that they had done so in the past.

The shadow glided silently into the cavern and moved to the side wall. It knew what they planned to do.

Tony felt a shiver run down his spine, glancing he thought he could see a shadow. He slowly stepped towards the wall and reached out.

His hand moved through the air, the shadow glided towards him and entered him before he could utter a word.

Tony smiled, the shadow now controlling him. He stepped away from the wall and moved towards Naomi and Samuel.

Samuel was on his hands and knees feeling around the pedestal in case there was something that could aid them to release the soul.

He stood up slowly and glanced as Tony walked over. 'I have...' he started to say and then Tony slammed him head first into the pedestal. The force of the blow sent Samuel forward, unable to stop himself he collapsed at the side of the pedestal.

Blood dripped from Samuel's forehead onto the floor. Naomi watched in horror, she screamed and ran towards Maureen.

Tony still being controlled by the shadow slowly moved towards them. Maureen glanced at the cavern entrance. She knew it wasn't her husband. Naomi also glanced from Tony to the entrance. She started to run forward and suddenly stopped.

Charlie McCormack had reached the house, he was surprised that the cellar door was open but he made his way down the steps and round to the trapdoor. He had almost laughed when he had found the trapdoor open. He made his way down the steps. He needed no guidance as he descended towards the cavern.

He stood round the corner as Tony slammed Samuel head first into the pedestal. He knew that wasn't Mr Farley. He watched as Naomi the busybody librarian and historian had moved towards the entrance.

Charlie stepped out and blocked her path. 'Charlie,' she said 'you...' Naomi was suddenly flung sideways into the cavern wall; she cracked her head hard against the wall and collapsed to the floor. Charlie knelt down. He felt her neck. Feeling slightly shocked he stood up. Maureen rushed to Naomi. She looked at Charlie who could see the disgust in her eyes.

'Do something,' pleaded Maureen.

Charlie moved towards Tony. The shadow left Tony's body and moved towards Charlie. Charlie took a deep breath as the shadow entered him.

Maureen watched as her husband collapsed to the ground. She closed her eyes briefly 'Sorry Naomi,' she cried. Maureen stood and moved towards her husband.

'Who are you? She screamed.

Charlie laughed. 'The shadow... The guardian of the soul,'

'What do you want with us?' Maureen cried.

Charlie laughed. 'I have everything I need from you both.'

'Why kill Naomi then?' she screamed as tears welled in her eyes.

'She was unnecessary,' he replied.

Tony slowly rubbed his head and moaned. Maureen knelt beside her husband. Tony looked around and gasped when he saw Samuel lying on the ground, he opened his mouth but no words came out. Maureen slowly helped him up. He looked at the stranger in the cavern.

'Who are...?' Tony started to ask.

Charlie looked at Tony and then Maureen 'Touch the soul and join me,' he spat.

Maureen shook her head.

Tony looked around still confused. 'Where is...?'

Maureen sank to her knees crying. 'You have killed them both.'

Tony looked and saw Naomi lifeless against the wall. Sinking to his knees he felt sick. 'Why are you doing this?' he cried.

Charlie still being controlled by the shadow laughed. 'Pitiful, you are so pathetic.'

He walked over to the orb, 'this soul is mine and I feed off its pain and off you,' he pointed his finger at Maureen and Tony.

'I cannot be stopped, I live off fear.'

Charlie's hand brushed near the soul. He could feel the pain and despair.

'TOUCH IT,' he screamed.

The shadow left Charlie who collapsed to the floor; the shadow glided around the orb/soul and vanished inside.

Tony looked at his wife, tears streaming down his face. Maureen kissed him. They looked at Samuel still unmoving by the pedestal and then to Naomi.

The orb/soul started to slowly rise, the light emanating from it changed from bright white to a pale yellow.

Maureen and Tony felt transfixed as the orb rose higher into the air, suddenly two streaks of light shot out of the orb/soul striking Maureen and Tony hard in the chest. The force sent them both crashing to the ground and the shadow reappeared out the orb/soul.

The orb/soul slowly turned back to white and sank back towards the pedestal.

Samuel groaned, he reached up and touched his head. Charlie sat up and looked at Samuel. He scrambled towards him. 'Are you okay Samuel?' he asked compassionately.

Samuel focused and looked at Charlie 'What… what… happened?' he stammered.

Samuel looked around and noticed Maureen and Tony on the floor. He screamed out 'No… No' he moved towards them.

He rolled Maureen over and looked at her. Crying out he fell backwards. Her face had aged; he turned Tony over and found him also aged.

The shadow glided towards Samuel. 'Pitiful man,' it said the words piercing Samuels mind.

'What have you done,' screamed Samuel.

'I took them, I consumed them, and I will take you too,' said the voice deep inside his mind.

Samuel scrambled back pushing himself; he tried to get to his feet. He fell back down and reached the wall. He looked around unable to see the shadow.

Charlie stood by the entrance.

The shadow glided slowly towards Samuel. 'I have taken them all and I will take you.'

Samuel cried out. 'People will find them and questions asked.'

Charlie looked at Samuel he saw the problem. 'I suggest you spare Samuel,' he said. The shadow glided towards Charlie. 'Why?' said the voice inside his mind.

'So you can feed in the future.' Charlie stammered.

The shadow retreated into the darkness of the cavern.

'I will spare you,' the voice entered Samuel's mind 'you will remember and I will preserve them until the time is right.'

'How… how will I know?' cried Samuel.

'I WILL TELL YOU.' The voice bellowed in his head.

Samuel slowly got to his feet and looked at Tony and Maureen. He turned tears forming in his eyes. He saw Naomi against the wall and ran towards her. 'SHE IS DEAD,' the voice screamed inside his mind. 'TAKE HER.'

Charlie helped Samuel carry Naomi out the cavern, once out Samuel fell to his knees and cried. His world was shattered. He had lost his three friends.

Samuel struggled as they took Naomi back up into the cellar. Charlie seemed shocked, scared, his conscious eating away at him.

Samuel lowered the trapdoor and put the padlock in place.

He called for an ambulance and they placed Naomi against the wall, Charlie explained he had found Naomi by the wall to the ambulance man. He knew there would be more questions and he would lie to keep the secret.

Samuel went round the back of the house still in despair. His last wish was for no one else to suffer. He looked at the well and dropped the key inside hoping against hope it would never be found.

Chapter 45

(2011)

An hour had passed with Mary, Tom, Lucas and Claudia discussing the property.
'Even with what I have learnt from my father and grandfather, I cannot see how we can release this soul and deal with the evil too.' Lucas explained.
'You were able to save me,' Mary replied 'how?'
'I was already in my dream state and felt a ripple around me, coldness...' pausing he got out of his chair and fetched a book. 'I can visit many planes which link together yet are apart,' he drew several lines on a piece of paper 'when I sense something I sometimes feel drawn,' he drew a spot on one line and a small stick man on another. 'This enables me to help, channel whatever I need,' he stated as he placed the pen down on the table.
Mary glanced at the clock and looked at Tom, 'surely Marie should be back at the hotel now.'
Tom looked at the clock and agreed. 'Listen,' he said 'come back with us and you can look through the books.'
Lucas nodded and went to fetch his coat. 'We will follow you.'
Mary and Tom left and walked towards their car. Mary rang Marie's mobile but just got the voicemail message. Feeling slightly concerned Mary got in the driver's seat and sped off towards the hotel.
Mary's concerns festered all the way back to the hotel 'we shouldn't have let her go off on her own,' she said her emotions getting the better of her.
'Don't worry,' replied Tom 'she will probably be at the hotel... or her phone could be dead.'
'I know,' she said to Tom, 'I just can't help worrying.'
She drove through the village and turned into the hotels drive.
Mary scanned the car park but Marie's car was not there.
Lucas pulled in less than a minute later and saw the anxious worried look on Mary's face.

Marie sat in the cavern, her hands tied behind her back, her ankles tied together. Charlie was whispering in the corner. Marie just watched, studying him, she could see through his façade now. He wasn't in charge, he was a mere pawn who...
Charlie turned and shuffled towards Marie. 'You do not seem concerned,' he spat. 'You have been here before...' he looked confused slightly as if he was listening to someone else 'yes, but you have escaped twice,' he shuffled closer. 'How have you managed to escape?' He asked curiously.
Marie looked at him 'Go to hell.
'Ha...' he laughed 'I have lived through this nightmare for forty or more years,' he walked past the pedestal and orb 'I have witnessed what happens when people touch the soul... but...' he looked directly at Marie 'It makes me...' he put his hands towards his head 'the voice,' he tapped his hand against his forehead.
Marie looked confused momentarily. 'So... the entity controls or more to the point talks to you.'
Charlie nodded 'yes, yes, yes it does.'
Marie decided to pry some more to get everything straight. 'Touching the orb of light does what exactly?'

'The soul, HA,' he said smartly 'you have no idea, the entity guards it.'

'I know that' retorted Marie 'what happens to the people who have touched the orb?'

Charlie looked around as if looking for something, he scrambled around the cavern.

Great thought Marie, he has lost it.

'Walls have ears and eyes,' he said as he moved around crouched. 'It takes your soul feeds the entity, you lose reality.'

Marie rolled her eyes. 'So the Entity takes over you?'

Charlie shuffled back to Marie and crouched low. 'It feeds off your soul and your fears.' He ran a hand over her face.

He stood up again and moved around 'got to prepare, got to prepare,' he repeated over and over.

Mary fetched the books down and sat in bar/lounge area with Tom, Lucas and Claudia. Lucas was looking through the shamanic journal, whilst Tom, Mary and Claudia looked at the small books from the historian/librarian.

Claudia put the book down. 'Intense, she suffered yet remembered so much, the details.'

Lucas put his book down 'Yes my grandfather and the Hamilton's and someone else were in the cavern.'

'I have a name I have seen before and he is alive,' said Mary excitedly. 'Charlie McCormack according to the historian,' she looked at the others. 'He still lives in the village.'

Tom put his book down. 'Do you think…' he started. Mary nodded.

Claudia looked confused. 'How is he connected?'

Mary smiled 'He was with the Hamilton's when they tried in the first place and failed. Then we have the historian and Samuel and the…' she flicked some pages in her book '… Farley's and they also suffered and have all died, yet…' she raised a hand to emphasise 'Charlie is still alive.'

She reached into a file and removed the letter Samuel had left them.

'Read this,' she urged.

Lucas and Claudia read the note and finally understood. 'So,' said Lucas with a tinge of urgency in his voice 'do you think Marie went back to see him?'

Tom nodded 'I also think we should ALL go.' He emphasised.

Mary was on her feet in seconds. She placed the books in the file and ran into the hall. 'DORIS… DORIS…' she shouted.

Doris wandered out of the dining area. Mary ran towards her. 'Doris place these somewhere safe please.' She placed the file in Doris's hands and ran back towards the doorway.

Doris watched as Tom, and two others left the dining area and ran outside. Shaking her head slightly she placed the file in the safe.

Lucas seemed agitated as he followed Mary and Tom. Claudia could sense it also. 'Do you think the person can be involved in something which is about fifty years old?'

Lucas nodded 'when I go into the other realm time has no relevance,' he replied.

'So this Charlie could be in league with the entity or whatever?'

Lucas nodded and briefly smiled at his wife. 'I think if we manage to separate him from the entity, we can do what wasn't finished.'

Claudia looked at him bemused. 'You're actually bonkers,' she replied.

Mary looked in her rear view mirror noticing that Lucas was still behind them. 'I am fuming,' she said with a tinge of anger in her voice. 'What made her think that going to see the one person who has survived everything was a good idea?'

Tom felt concerned also. 'Maybe we are all wrong?'

'Poppycock,' she replied. 'She has gone to see him.'

She pulled up outside Charlie's cottage but Marie's car was not around.

Mary got out the car perplexed. 'I was so sure she would be here,' she said with urgency in her voice.

Tom walked round the car to his wife as Lucas pulled up behind them. He walked to the door and knocked. He waited but no reply.

Lucas walked down the path and peered in the window. 'Two cups on the table,'

Mary ran down the path and glanced through the window. 'Might have been here and left,' she said hopefully.

Claudia wandered around the side of the house. The hedge was overgrown but she managed to push herself through. She reached the other side and brushed the leaves and marks off her jacket and skirt.

Tom was next to squeeze himself through followed by Mary and Lucas. Mary tried the back door which was locked. She banged hard on the door but still no answer.

Claudia reached the garden shed and looked at the padlock securing the door.

Lucas rubbed his forehead and looked at the shed. 'I do not like the feel of this place,' he said urgently.

Mary looked in his direction. 'He has keys galore in that shed,' she started up the path towards them 'he showed Marie and I the contents.'

Tom looked at his wife. 'Why would he keep keys?'

Mary looked at her husband and then at Lucas, 'to open a door.'

The realisation suddenly dawned on them.

'We need to get to the house.' Mary and Tom said in unison.

They squeezed back through the hedgerow and down the path towards the car. Lucas and Claudia right behind them. 'Wait,' said Claudia as she bent down and picked something up near the gate 'Is this yours?' she held a lipstick in her hands.

Mary looked at it. 'Marie's,' she took the lipstick and headed towards the car 'follow us.' She told Lucas.

Mary drove she knew exactly where her sister was. She felt the anger rising in her blood.

'Charlie was there the first time, he has used and killed several innocent people and he wants us too,' she seethed.

Tom looked anxiously at his wife. 'We still don't know how to stop the entity though?'

'I'll find a way.' She spat the words out.

She saw the house come into view and then Marie's car. Feeling more determined than ever she pulled up behind her sister's car and got out. Tom opened his door and looked at the house. They waited for Lucas to pull up.

Claudia was out the car before Lucas; she walked and stood by Mary. She could see a change in her since the hotel. 'Are you feeling okay?' she asked hesitantly.

'Never better,' Mary replied her voice full of confidence.

Lucas stood next to his wife and looked at the house.

Mary looked at them all in turn. 'Let's go.'

Marie watched Charlie walk around some more; he seemed to just listen to the entity. 'Charlie...' she said 'how about ignoring that...' she tried to think of what to call it 'thing,' she finally added 'and talk to me instead.'

'Ha...' he slowly moved towards Marie 'Why,' he looked at her 'should I listen to you.'

Marie raised her eyebrows. 'Three reasons. One, I have witnessed you being nothing more than a puppet to that thing. Two, what makes you think if Tom and Mary arrive it won't kill you, and finally three, I am sane.'

Charlie smiled and walked off.

'Your Sister will die saving you.' Marie shook her head as the voice penetrated her mind. 'So this is how you control them.' She scoffed.

The shadow slowly glided towards Marie. Marie watched as it edged closer and closer. 'I can control who I want, when I want.' The voice said deep in her mind.

She watched as the shadow moved around the orb and then back to a dark corner.

'So that is it... is it?' she finally said.

Charlie moved towards the shadow/entity. 'It provides for me.'

Charlie listened intently as the shadow/entity talked to him. He smiled at Marie. 'They are here.'

Chapter 46

Mary turned the doorknob and opened the door; she glanced behind her and walked into the grand hall. Tom followed her in; he could feel a chill in the air.

Claudia walked in followed by Lucas. They stood admiring the grandness of the hallway the wooden oak outlay.

Mary closed the door and walked towards the kitchen. She opened two draws removing four torches. 'We will need these when we go down to the cellar.'

Tom reached in his pocket for the cellar key. He inserted it into the lock but found the cellar door unlocked. 'Charlie must have a key.' He said in a low voice.

Turning on his torch he opened the door and Mary stuck the wedge underneath.

Lucas and Claudia looked confused. 'My husband was trapped in the cellar.' Mary stated in a matter-of-fact tone.

Tom looked down into the cellar and turned on his torch, he slowly started down the steps using his hand for guidance as he vanished from view.

Lucas went next and felt the cold damp wall. He closed his eyes and sensed how many people had gone down and suffered. He felt a pang of sadness and then started to walk down the steps.

'I am not sure I want to go down,' Claudia said quietly to Mary.

'I will be right behind you, and the cellar is safe.' Mary replied with a smile.

Claudia felt the cold wall and started her descent into the cellar.

Mary took one last look around the kitchen and started to walk down the steps.

Tom stood at the bottom of the cellar and rubbed his forehead. Lucas joined him, 'Let me help,' he said. He placed his hand on Tom's forehead and gently chanted. Tom felt the pain and anxiety inside lift away. 'Thanks.' Tom replied.

Claudia reached the bottom step. She looked concerned. Lucas put his arm around her to reassure her.

Mary reached the bottom step and looked at them all.

She purposely walked deeper into the cellar. She could hear the footsteps behind her. She finally stopped and looked at the trapdoor. 'You are already waiting for us.' She murmured.

Tom looked at the lifted trapdoor. He stooped down and picked up the padlock. Lucas and Claudia finally caught them both up. 'Watch this,' said Tom. He inserted his key into the padlock. The key changed to a golden hue. Lucas reached across and looked at the key and padlock. 'I have never seen anything like this in my...' he paused momentarily as if a light switch had been turned on.

Mary, Tom and Claudia looked at him 'what is it Lucas?' they asked. Lucas looked at them. 'Just something my grandfather used to say to me,' he paced around mumbling. 'If normal light won't help you see, then golden light will hold the key.'

He looked at them, 'whenever I asked what he meant, he would laugh and say you will understand when the time comes.'

Mary took the padlock and key and placed them in her pocket. 'Let's not disappoint our guest.' She said as she started into the abyss which led to the cavern.

Marie felt a tinge of fear enter her body. Were they really on their way? Was it just Tom and Mary? Or... she looked at Charlie as he sat huddled in the other corner of the room. She needed a distraction. She shuffled slowly backwards so her back was against the cavern wall. She tried to find something to cut the tape that Charlie had used.

She brushed her arms against the wall but it wasn't jagged enough.

Distraction and deception she suddenly thought. 'Charlie, if you do not come over here then I will just have to scream constantly.'

Charlie looked annoyed as he peered at Marie. 'What do you think that will accomplish?'

Marie smiled. It lets my sister and her husband know that it isn't safe here. What if they just leave?' she finally said triumphantly.

'They would never let you suffer.' He retorted.

'I think... if they leave... you will suffer from the thing.' Marie scoffed.

Charlie stood. He hobbled across the room towards Marie. Marie brought her knees closer towards her. 'Listen missy,' he spat 'I have earned the right to survive.'

Marie laughed. 'It will kill you.'

Mary reached the corner and flashed her torch down the final steps. She felt motivated, stronger, more in control. She reached the last step and waited for the others to arrive.

She listened to voices coming from the cavern. One was definitely Marie's, feeling relief she knew she was alive.

Tom reached the bottom step closely followed by Claudia and Lucas.

Lucas closed his eyes and started mumbling.

Mary walked towards the cavern entrance and peered around the corner. She could see Charlie and Marie by the pedestal.

Tom pulled her back 'well?' he mouthed.

Mary nodded letting him know Marie was alive. They moved back towards the steps. 'Stay here,' she whispered to Claudia and Lucas. 'Let us distract them before you enter.'

Lucas and Claudia nodded.

Mary and Tom moved back to the cavern entrance and walked in. 'So is this a private party or can anyone join.' She asked brazenly.

Charlie looked round 'I knew you would both come.'

'You okay Marie?' Mary asked.

Marie nodded 'but the entity or the shadow is in the far corner.' She replied defiantly.

Charlie hobbled towards the corner. The shadow glided out towards Charlie and entered him.

Tom started towards Marie. Unseen hands jerked him back towards the wall. Tom struggled to move.

'Not yet,' said Charlie, his voice was deeper, darker as the shadow spoke through him.

Mary felt the key in her pocket. It reassured her somewhat. 'So you stopped the Shamans trying to release the soul, by using Charlie. You then consumed the Farley's and Samuel,' she said angrily, 'but you want more; the soul is the catalyst for you to feed.'

Charlie nodded. 'Very good, you have done your work.'

Mary smiled and glanced at her struggling husband. 'So you need me willingly to touch the soul.' she said as she walked towards it. Mary walked round the pedestal and looked at the soul.

She knelt down at Marie, 'I love you and always will.'

'What if I refuse?' She finally said as she stood up.

The shadow left Charlie who fell to the floor. It circled the soul and around the room settling by the pedestal. 'I will enter you and force you,' the words entered her mind. 'I control people, I control everything.'

Lucas closed his eyes and started chanting. He sent words of love and kindness towards the soul. Claudia peered around the wall and looked in. She had never seen anything like it before, the orb hanging above a pedestal.

Tom struggled harder trying to get himself released. 'Hey... over here shadow,' he yelled. The shadow glided towards him. 'Leave my wife alone.'

The shadow started to wrap itself around Tom.

Mary rushed forward the key in her hand she watched as the key started to change colour as she neared the shadow. She felt a surge of adrenalin and shoved the key into the shadow as it surrounded Tom. The shadow screamed penetrating all their minds. Holding her hands to her ears she watched.

The shadow left Tom as golden wisps of light started to drift away. The shadow got smaller and smaller as golden light started to attack what was left of the shadow.

As the shadows scream died the golden wisps slowly started to spin around.

The shadow was gone. The golden wisps of light slowly drifted towards the soul.

Tom no longer felt held back as he dropped to the ground; he rushed towards Marie and helped her up. He started to untie the ropes which bound her.

They watched as the wisps of golden light surrounded the soul.

Marie and Tom moved back towards Mary who stood at the far end of the wall. The golden wisps of light started to enter the soul. The soul started changing colour. It had a golden hue.

Lucas walked through into the cavern and towards the soul. He mumbled words and watched as the soul slowly got smaller and smaller. The wisps of light left the soul as it slowly vanished from sight.

Mary walked over to Lucas. 'What happened?' she asked.

Lucas smiled 'It has been released.'

The wisps of light danced around the cavern the pictographs started to vanish. Mary watched as the cavern wall became just a wall.

The wisps of golden light finally fell to the ground. They slowly fell on top of one another revealing the key.

Mary picked the key up as the key faded back to dull lifeless grey.

Mary walked over to Charlie who was starting to stir. 'Are you okay?' She asked.

Charlie opened and closed his eyes several times, he looked around confused. The silence... he looked around the room and saw Marie and Tom. 'Where am I?' He asked.

Mary helped him up and led him out the cavern. 'Do you remember anything?'

Charlie shook his head 'What is going on?' He asked.

'You would never believe us if we told you.' Marie replied as she helped him up towards the steps.

Claudia rushed forward flinging her arms around Lucas. 'You did it,' she said excitedly.

Lucas looked at Mary and Tom. 'We all did it.'

They made their way back up the steps and into the cellar and replaced the trapdoor. Mary noticed that the incantation around the trapdoor had vanished. With padlock still in her pocket she slowly bent down and locked the trapdoor shut.

They made their way up the cellar steps and back into the kitchen.

Epilogue

It had been three months since the shadow had been destroyed, Marie had gone back to work but visited most weekends. She felt closer to her sister than she ever had.
Brian, Barbara and the children were visiting and Mary had dinner to prepare.
Mary walked into the lounge with her cup of coffee and sat down. She glanced at the mantle.
A small glass box had pride of place, inside a small glass holder had the cellar key resting upon it.
Tom walked into the lounge and kissed his wife.
'I have just had confirmation that Doris and George would love to come for dinner.'
Mary laughed. 'They deserve a night off.'
Tom looked at the key. 'Hard to imagine...' he said as he sat by his wife 'that the key to this whole affair was the key.'
Mary kissed him.
KNOCK... KNOCK... KNOCK...
Mary got up and walked to the door. She opened it fully and smiled. 'Two more for dinner,' she said to Tom as she invited Claudia and Lucas into the house.

The End

Printed in Great Britain
by Amazon